Dear Reader,

We're thrilled that some of Harlequin's most famous families are making an encore appearance! With this special Famous Families fifty-book collection, we are proud to offer you the chance to relive the drama, the glamour, the suspense and the romance of four of Harlequin's most beloved families—the Fortunes, the Bravos, the McCabes and the Cavanaughs.

Wedding bells are ringing for the infamous Bravos— even if they don't know it yet! The all-American clan created by *USA TODAY* bestselling author Christine Rimmer is the second family in our special collection. Its members are cowboys and billionaires, lawyers and private investigators. Their exploits take them from the mountains of Wyoming, to a small, close-knit town in California to the glitzy Vegas strip. But whether they're rich or down-to-earth, city or small-town bred, you'll fall in love with each of the Bravos as they take their own compelling journey to a happy ending.

And coming in May, you'll meet Dr. Jackson McCabe as we introduce you to our next special family, the McCabes of Texas, by beloved author Cathy Gillen Thacker.

Happy reading,

The Editors

CHRISTINE RIMMER

came to her profession the long way around. Before settling down to write about the magic of romance, she'd been everything from an actress to a salesclerk to a waitress. Now that she's finally found work that suits her perfectly, she insists she never had a problem keeping a job—she was merely gaining "life experience" for her future as a novelist.

Christine is grateful not only for the joy she finds in writing, but for what waits when the day's work is through: a man she loves, who loves her right back, and the privilege of watching their children grow and change day to day. She lives with her family in Oregon. Visit Christine at www.christinerimmer.com.

FAMOUS FAMILIES

the BRAVOS

USA TODAY bestselling author

CHRISTINE RIMMER

Married by Accident

TORONTO NEW YORK LONDON
AMSTERDAM PARIS SYDNEY HAMBURG
STOCKHOLM ATHENS TOKYO MILAN MADRID
PRAGUE WARSAW BUDAPEST AUCKLAND

For Sandra Dark,
who has made me feel so very welcome in my home.
Thanks, Sandra, for the books and the honey,
the good talks and the Brown Bag Tuesdays.

Recycling programs
for this product may
not exist in your area.

ISBN-13: 978-0-373-36495-4

MARRIED BY ACCIDENT

Copyright © 1999 by Christine Rimmer

www.Harlequin.com

Printed in U.S.A.

FAMOUS FAMILIES

The Fortunes

Cowboy at Midnight by Ann Major
A Baby Changes Everything by Marie Ferrarella
In the Arms of the Law by Peggy Moreland
Lone Star Rancher by Laurie Paige
The Good Doctor by Karen Rose Smith
The Debutante by Elizabeth Bevarly
Keeping Her Safe by Myrna Mackenzie
The Law of Attraction by Kristi Gold
Once a Rebel by Sheri WhiteFeather
Military Man by Marie Ferrarella
Fortune's Legacy by Maureen Child
The Reckoning by Christie Ridgway

The Bravos by Christine Rimmer

The Nine-Month Marriage
Marriage by Necessity
Practically Married
Married by Accident
The Millionaire She Married
The M.D. She Had to Marry
The Marriage Agreement
The Bravo Billionaire
The Marriage Conspiracy
His Executive Sweetheart
Mercury Rising
Scrooge and the Single Girl

Chapter 1

When the pickup truck hit Melinda Bravo in her cute little BMW, she was giving herself a pep talk.

"Relax, breathe deeply," she had said aloud, though there was no one in the car to hear but herself. "You are a few minutes ahead of schedule. You are calm and collected, appropriately dressed and one hundred percent ready to make this presentation. Evelyn Erikson is glamour personified and the designs are gorgeous, perfect for her. She will adore them. You were right to insist that Rudy let you do this one yourself."

Melinda paused in her pep talk as the light in the intersection ahead turned yellow. She glanced to both sides. The adjoining street looked clear. In fact, there were no other cars in sight.

She pressed the accelerator to gain a little more speed, and picked up the pep talk right where she'd left off. "You are going to make a huge sale and Rudy is going to realize just how capable and talented you—"

It happened right then, before she could even finish her sentence. A flash of midnight-blue exploded in her side vision, stunning the words right out of her.

Then came the impact. The sound of it—a thunderous, crackling crunch—seemed to eat up the world. The car went flying sideways, tires squealing in an agony of peeling rubber as they tried to hold the road and failed.

Melinda caught a glimpse of her own stunned face in the rearview mirror, eyes wide, mouth a silly, slack O. She gripped the wheel and waited to die.

A fraction of a second later, the car hit something that stopped it cold. Out of nowhere, a huge pillow came at her. Her face was smothered in softness.

Air bag, she thought in numb shock. It's just the air bag…

Metal groaned.

The air bag went instantly flat, collapsing over the steering wheel in a soft puddle of rubber.

And then there was silence.

Out of that eerie quiet came a tiny pitiful whimper: her own. Melinda sucked in a tight, whistling breath through a windpipe that had somehow become way too small. And then she just stared—past the slack form of the deflated air bag, beyond the dashboard, out the windshield, where the L.A. sun beamed down and the sky was a bright, clear expanse of pure blue.

An accident, she thought stupidly, I've just been in an accident. She dared to turn her head—toward the passenger side window first. She saw that her car had been rammed against the right-hand concrete curb. A big wooden telephone pole loomed about eight inches from the passenger door.

Another weak whimper escaped her. She turned her head

the other way, looked out her own side window and then a bit farther back.

Melinda let out another sound—a cry of pure dismay. A shiny dark blue pickup had taken a nosedive into the rear half of her car. The left end of its front bumper stopped not five inches from her driver's side door.

Melinda blinked, faced front again and looked down at her body. No blood. No bones sticking out of torn flesh. Not even any bruises that she could see yet. With a shaking hand, she grabbed the rearview mirror and angled it so that she could see her face.

She looked just as dazed and disoriented as she felt. But as for injuries, she couldn't see a one. Even her hair remained sleek and perfect—a simple and businesslike French twist, which she'd smoothed into place a few hours before.

Unharmed, she thought numbly, and tried to be grateful for that. But then, in the mirror, she caught a glimpse out the rear window. Her trunk was sprung, and ridiculously bent out of shape.

The lingerie. Oh, no…

She pictured the pretty gold and pink boxes, which she had stacked in there so carefully under Rudy's critical eye. "Please God," she muttered under her breath, "let the lingerie be all right…"

She heard a creaking sound. She let go of the mirror and whipped her head to the left in time to watch the driver's door of the pickup swing open.

A Stetson got out. The hat was connected to a tall cowboy in battered jeans, old boots and a plaid shirt. The cowboy skimmed off the hat. She saw that he had thick brown hair, hair that gleamed in the bright sun. And his kind-looking eyes found her immediately—no great feat since she continued to sit there, staring foolishly back at him, from her ruined car.

The cowboy shut the pickup door. It took him a single step and he was right beside her car. He pulled her door open and leaned toward her. She saw that the kind eyes were hazel. Light hazel. Mostly green, with hints of blue and brown. "You all right, ma'am?"

"I...yes. I think...I'm fine. Not hurt. No injuries at all." She fumbled for her seat belt, found the latch. But her fingers weren't working right. She couldn't get it to give.

The cowboy slid his hat back onto his head. "Here." He reached inside the car.

Melinda felt a flash of warmth, from his body. There was the scent of some aftershave or clean-smelling soap. For a split second, he was actually leaning across her, his hard chest brushing her breasts. Then he retreated back outside the car again, giving her no time at all to stiffen in reaction to his sudden, uninvited closeness.

"There."

She realized he had popped the latch of the seat belt for her. "Thank you," she said, as graciously as she could manage, considering that her brain seemed to have shut down and her tongue felt like a slab of wood in her mouth.

"Happy to oblige." He stepped back a little more and stood behind her door, holding it open all the way—so that she could get out, she realized. Too bad her body felt as numb and dead as the air bag, which had deflated so completely, it was draped over her knees.

A frown creased the tanned skin between the cowboy's straight eyebrows. "Are you *sure* you're all right?"

"Yes. Of course. I am fine. Just... disoriented."

"Shock," he said in a tone of authority. "It's nothing to fool with. We probably oughtta call an ambulance and—"

She put up a hand. "Please. I told you. I'm all right." She didn't have time for any ambulance right now.

He was still frowning. "You don't look all right."

"Well, I am. There is nothing wrong with me. Nothing at all." She shoved at the rubber folds of the air bag and somehow managed to swing her feet to the pavement. Then, for a minute, she just sat there, gathering the strength to stand, watching a minivan and then a convertible rolling by in the free lane a few feet away, the drivers shaking their heads and staring, the way people always do when they drive by an accident.

The cowboy's broad shoulders lifted as he shrugged. "All right. It's your life." He held out his hand. It was big, the knuckles large and the fingers long. It looked very capable. "Come on."

She let him help her to her feet, thinking that his hand was warm and rough and that hers felt safe inside it. She pulled free as soon as she was upright and she took in a long, slow breath. It was okay. Her legs would hold her up.

"Feeling better by the second," she told him, and forced a smile.

"Glad to hear it." He smiled back. He had a square jaw and a cleft in his chin. And that smile of his didn't stop at his mouth. It went all the way to those kind hazel eyes.

For some sick reason, she thought of Christopher. Christopher's jaw was narrow, fine-boned, his forehead high and smooth, belying his forty-plus years. His hair was fine, and as pale as her own. Christopher rationed his smiles very carefully. He certainly wouldn't be giving them out for free to some woman he'd just pulled from a smashed up BMW, some woman who should have looked closer at the intersecting street before speeding through a yellow light.

The cowboy was frowning again. "Feeling dizzy?"

"No. No, not dizzy at all." She looked away from him, toward the pickup. In the cab, on the passenger side, she saw a young woman. The woman smiled—the same kind of smile as the cowboy's, open and generous, all the way to the eyes.

Melinda turned to the cowboy again. "Your passenger. Is *she* all right?"

"Annie's okay." His smile turned to a grin. "And I'm just fine, too, in case you were plannin' to ask."

Melinda didn't smile back this time. It seemed dangerous, somehow, to start smiling too much with this man. "Good," she said firmly. "Then at least no one's been hurt." She looked at the two vehicles again.

The sight did not cheer her. From where she stood, it appeared she wouldn't be driving the BMW again any time soon.

The urge came, very powerfully, to break down and cry. To just go ahead and give in, throw back her head and wail out her misery and frustration at the fabulous blue sky above.

But she didn't. She held it together. She was going to salvage as much of this mess as she could.

"Ma'am," said the cowboy, "why don't I—?"

She cut him off by whirling on her heel and striding around the end of his big pickup, heading for the sprung-open trunk of her car. A station wagon, rolling by slowly so its occupants could gawk, honked at her because she stepped out in front of it. She cast the driver a killing glare and kept on walking until she reached her destination.

She looked down into the open trunk.

Thank God for small favors. It wasn't that bad. The boxes, so tastefully embossed in their lower left corners with the name of Rudy's shop, Forever Eve, had tumbled all over each other. Some of them looked a little less fresh, a bit frayed and bent. But the pink and gold ribbons had held. For the most part, her merchandise seemed to be intact.

"How 'bout I see if I can get my pickup free of your car and out of the road?" It was the cowboy. He had followed her around the pickup and now stood a few feet behind her.

She turned to him. "Fine. Do it."

He ambled back to the other side of the pickup and climbed in. He said something to his passenger, then started the engine and put the thing in reverse. The truck came free easily, though the crunching and groaning of metal was not pleasant to hear. The cowboy backed around and pulled in at the curb on the intersecting street.

Melinda dared to approach her car again. It was a disaster. The rear half looked as if it had taken a direct hit from a huge steel fist. And something was wrong with the rear wheels. They slanted at a bizarre diagonal to the road. She cast a glance at the pickup. The only thing wrong with it was a battered front grill and bumper.

The cowboy strode toward her again and stopped when he reached her side. They stared at her ruined car together for a moment. Then he said, "Whoa. Looks like that rear axle's bent up pretty bad." He took off his hat once more and hit it twice against his lean thigh.

Just like Zach, she thought, feeling a little curl of wistfulness down inside. Zach was her big brother and she loved him, even though she'd never understood him. He ran the family ranch in Wyoming. His lifelong fascination with cows and wide-open spaces had made him almost as big a disappointment to their parents as Melinda was herself.

The cowboy caught her watching him. He smiled again. Melinda recognized the gleam in those nice eyes of his: male appreciation.

The gleam wasn't new to her. She saw it often in men's eyes. All her life, Melinda had been told how beautiful she was. And she'd grown rather tired of fielding unwanted passes over the years. But somehow, this man's admiration didn't bother her at all—as inappropriate as it probably was, considering the sweet-faced girl who waited in his pickup.

Melinda broke the hold of those gleaming eyes and the

cowboy put his hat back on. "I'd say you'll have to call yourself a tow truck."

"Marvelous," she muttered, as the reality of this grim situation struck her anew. She resisted the sudden urge to shout accusations, to demand, What were you thinking of? Why didn't you keep those gorgeous eyes of yours on the road?

But accusations would get her nowhere. She knew the fault belonged as much to her as to him. And he really was being so helpful and, well, just plain *nice* about this.

No, let the insurance companies deal with placing blame. Right now, she needed to call a cab and pray that it showed up in time to get her to Evelyn Erikson's Bel Air mansion within—she glanced at her Rolex—*fifteen minutes?*

She'd never make it. And Evelyn Erikson was as famed for her temper as for her beauty and her talent. The legendary star would not appreciate being kept waiting by a salesperson.

My big opportunity, Melinda thought with equal parts irony and despair.

She really did need this sale. And she'd only gotten a chance at it because she was the one who took the call from Evelyn Erikson's personal assistant. Melinda had turned on the charm during that call. And she'd managed to convince the star's assistant that she should be the one to bring the merchandise to the mansion.

The cowboy was still waiting there. She needed to deal with him and send him and his girlfriend on their way. "I suppose we'd better exchange insurance information." The cowboy was staring at her again, those wonderful eyes soft as velvet with concern—and something was sliding down the side of her face. A tear. God. How pitiful. She dashed the thing away. "You do have insurance?"

"I sure do."

She swiped at another idiotic tear, silently praying that

her mascara wouldn't run. Just what she needed, to show up at Evelyn Erikson's mansion with red eyes and smeared makeup. "I'll get my purse."

The cowboy shook his head. "Hey. Maybe you oughtta take it a little easy here. Sit yourself down, take a few deep—"

"I said, I'll get my purse." She bit off each word crisply and firmly.

The cowboy shook his head again, but he gave her no more arguments. She hustled over to her still-open driver's door, ordering her mind to focus on what to do next.

The cab. Yes. She'd call for it first. Then, while she waited for her ride, she and the cowboy could exchange insurance numbers.

With an impatient shove at the bulky, interfering mass of the collapsed air bag, Melinda leaned across the driver's seat looking for her shoulder bag. Terrific. It had been thrown off the seat during the accident. The contents were strewn all over the passenger side floor.

She let out a tiny groan and leaned farther into the car, stretching across the seat and the console, grabbing the bottom of the purse and giving it a good, strong shake. Everything left inside went tumbling out: her compact and her wallet, her checkbook and her order-form tablet, a little packet of travel tissues, her magnifying mirror, three Bic pens. Everything but the cell phone she needed.

With a grunt, she tossed the purse into the back seat and began fumbling through the mess on the floor.

The phone wasn't there. Muttering under her breath in frustration, she wiggled farther into the car and put her head down, so that she could peer under the passenger seat.

"Ma'am. Are you *sure* you're all right?"

The cowboy. Wonderful. She cast a grim glance back over her shoulder. He stood right outside the door, making a clear effort not to stare at the mortifying amount of thigh her hitched-up skirt revealed.

"I told you. I'm fine. I just-I'm looking for my phone." Melinda lowered her head again and shot one more angry glance under the seat. Then she stuck her hand in there, groping. She came up with a lipstick and a container of Tic-Tacs, but no phone.

And the cowboy still stood a foot or two from her backside, no doubt enjoying the view.

More frazzled by the second, Melinda slithered out of the car and pushed herself up straight. Then she yanked her skirt back down over her thighs, straightened her trim little jacket and smoothed the sides of her neatly pulled-back hair.

The cowboy just stood there, waiting politely for her to pull herself together.

Then she remembered that she was supposed to have been getting the number of her insurance company—which was still on the floor in the car somewhere, along with everything else. She closed her eyes, mentally counted to five, then opened them again. "I'm sorry. I'm just…I really need to call a cab. And my phone…it seems to have disappeared."

"You need a ride," he said. The smile came back, lighting up that open, handsome face. "That's no problem. Annie and I can take you."

She shot a glance at the pickup again, saw the form of the young woman whose name was apparently Annie, the young woman who still sat there so patiently, waiting for the cowboy to drive her wherever they were going before they—literally—ran into Melinda. "You're not serious."

"I sure am."

"No. Really, I couldn't—"

"Wait right here. Let me check with Annie. See how she's holdin' up."

"Holding up?" Melinda parroted foolishly. But the cowboy was already striding toward the truck.

He spoke briefly to the person named Annie then strode right back. "Come on. We'll take you wherever you have to go."

"But that isn't right. Surely you can't—"

"Why not? Just climb on in my truck and let's get a move on."

She shouldn't, she knew it. She'd be taking total advantage of the poor man. And really, what did she know about him? He could be some highway kidnapper for all she could tell.

But no. Not with those eyes. And she couldn't help thinking that if they left right away, they just might make it on time. "I've…got a lot of boxes. They have to go with me."

He gestured at the pickup. "See that camper shell? It's nice and clean under there. Your boxes'll be fine in the back. And your car's out of traffic. It should be safe enough right here for a while."

"I…I don't even know your name."

"Cole Yuma." He stuck out his big rough hand.

Melinda took that hand for the second time. It was just as warm as before. Warm and comforting and strong.

Warning buzzers sounded in her head. Get real, Melinda, she said to herself. Don't go letting some cowboy lure you into false feelings of security. No man is going to solve your problems for you. And you certainly ought to know that by now.

She gave that strong hand a firm shake. "I'm Melinda. Melinda Bravo." Quickly she let go.

"Let's get those boxes," he said.

"Good idea."

Together, they gathered them all up and stowed them safely under the camper shell of the pickup truck. Then Melinda raced back to her own car, hauled her purse from the back seat and shoved as much as she could find of its scattered contents back inside. She yanked the keys from the ignition, shut the door and locked it—an action that struck her as vaguely absurd. It would take a tow truck to steal the poor thing. But it was a valuable car, after all. And you never could tell.

She hustled over to the pickup, where Cole was already inside, with the engine running. The girl, Annie, had pushed open the door for her and scooted across the bench seat toward him, to make room.

Melinda put her hand on the door, to boost herself up—and met Annie's wide, sweet hazel eyes. The girl was heartbreakingly young, eighteen or nineteen at the most. And very, very pregnant. Her left hand, on which she wore a thin wedding band, rested on the huge proud mound of her stomach.

Melinda let go of the door.

Down inside, where the emptiness was, she felt a hurtful tug.

And she remembered what she'd been trying all day to forget. Today, July 8, was her due date. Or it would have been her due date, if her baby hadn't—

"Well, come on, girl," Annie said, cutting into a train of thought best not pursued anyway. "Didn't you say you had to get somewhere in a hurry?"

A rather scary possibility occurred to Melinda. "Dear God. Please don't tell me you were on your way to the hospital."

From behind the wheel, Cole Yuma laughed. It was a warm, deep sound. "All right, Ms. Melinda Bravo. We won't tell you that."

"Cole, don't tease." Annie poked the cowboy in the ribs and smiled wider at Melinda. "I'm not due for three weeks yet. Cole and me, we were just goin' shopping, to pick up a few things—for the baby, you know?"

Melinda cast a doubtful glance at the big Spanish-style

houses and sloping lawns that surrounded them. And Annie laughed. "Well, all right, we were checkin' out the sites, too. Seein' how the movie stars live."

"—And you better come on," Cole said. "We can't get you where you need to go if you're standin' there on the sidewalk."

Melinda hesitated a moment longer, feeling dazed. None of this seemed real. None of it. Not the stunningly mild and gorgeous July day. Not her ruined Beamer, huddled against the curb a few yards away. Not this nice cowboy and the sweet, hugely pregnant child-woman at his side. And certainly not the idea of her jumping in beside them so that they could drive her in their pickup to sell expensive lingerie to a famous movie star.

"Melinda, get in," Cole said, authority edging his voice for the first time, making her think that there was more than Mr. Nice Guy under that Stetson he wore. He added one word, "Now." Those kind eyes brooked no arguments.

Melinda hoisted herself up onto the seat next to Annie and pulled the door shut.

"Left or right?" Cole asked.

"Right."

The cowboy eased the pickup out onto the street and turned in the direction she'd given him. They rolled past her wrecked Beamer.

They were on their way. With a minimum of luck, they might even make it on time.

Chapter 2

A few minutes later, they turned off the wide residential street and onto a long private driveway lined with palm trees. Soon enough, a high stucco wall loomed before them. There was a black iron gate across the road, with *E* and *E*, twin letters in gold, woven into the black.

"Lordy," breathed Annie. "Who lives in there?"

"Evelyn Erikson."

"No. You're kiddin' me. Not the movie star?"

"Yes." Melinda suppressed a smile at the awestruck look in those wide, innocent eyes. "The one and only. I'm here to sell her some beautiful lingerie."

"I can hardly believe it. Evelyn Erikson, *the* Evelyn Erikson." Annie caressed her hard belly and whispered in amazement. "Wonders never do cease." Watching her, Melinda felt again that sad, quick flash of emptiness inside.

Just outside the gate stood a pillared structure that looked a little like a Greek Revival-style gazebo.

"That's the gatehouse," Melinda said. "Just pull up beside the window there."

Cole followed her instructions. When he saw the uniformed guard inside, he rolled down his window so Melinda could speak to him. She stated her name and her business and the guard scribbled something on the printed sheet in front of him. "All right, Ms. Bravo. Once you get inside the gates, just follow the road until you can turn right. Go past the tennis courts and the garages, around to the service entrance in back."

The iron gates swung open. Cole drove through them. They sped up the winding driveway, past emerald expanses of lawn dotted here and there with stone statuary and spurting fountains, with palms and waxy-leaved magnolias and pretty lemon trees. Cole turned right when the road branched, and they rolled by the tennis courts and a long stucco building with twenty-two garage doors ranged down the front of it. Melinda knew there were twenty-two because Annie counted them aloud.

Then Cole swung the wheel to the left as the road turned again. They saw the main house then. It was huge, of white stone that blindingly cast back the early afternoon sun. Tall columns held up the massive gallery that ran across the façade.

"My, oh my," whispered Annie reverently.

Cole drove on, until he could pull to a stop by a door at the back. Even this, the service entrance, seemed to insist on being grand, with its own miniature pillared portico. Nearby, another fountain bubbled and splashed. Statues of a fig-leafed David and an armless Venus flanked the short walk.

Personally Melinda found it all a bit much. She could almost hear her mother's voice now. "Melinda. One never flaunts mere *things*," Elaine Houseman Bravo would say.

Apparently Cole's thoughts echoed her own. "You know,"

he drawled, "I'm gettin' the feeling that we're supposed to be impressed."

"Welcome to L.A.," Melinda drawled right back, meeting his eyes over Annie's head.

Annie puffed out a small, impatient breath. "Well, you two can make fun. But I *am* impressed."

"We noticed." Cole grinned at the young woman beside him. She poked him in the ribs, the way she had back on the street where they'd left Melinda's car.

"Hey," he grumbled playfully. "Watch it with that elbow."

"Then don't be such an old snob."

Melinda watched the teasing, intimate exchange and felt a little like an intruder—and maybe just a tiny bit jealous, as well. But jealous of what exactly, she refused to consider.

She had a big sale to make. The dashboard clock said she was only two minutes late. The situation really might be salvageable, after all. But she had to gather up her boxes and hurry inside.

Right then, a stocky, aggressively plain older woman emerged from the door beneath the miniature portico. She wore a gray maid's dress complete with white apron, duty shoes and frilled cap. Briskly she strode down the walk past the statues and the fountain. She spoke through Cole's window, which was already down. "Ms. Erikson is expecting you. I understand you'll have boxes. Where are they? I'm to help you carry them in."

Cole spoke before Melinda had a chance to reply "They're in the back. Just give us a second." He took off his hat and dropped it on the dashboard, then turned to Annie. "You'll be all right here?"

Melinda realized that he intended to go in with her. She couldn't let him do that. She opened her mouth to protest, but Annie spoke first.

"I'll be just fine." The young woman smiled her charming, guileless smile.

Melinda fumbled in her purse for her business card case and a pen. "Oh, no. You two have been wonderful, but I can handle things from here." She found the case and the pen. She pulled a card free. "You are going to go ahead and do that shopping you were planning." Quickly she scribbled on the back of the card, writing down her home phone number and her address. "I'll get a cab when I'm finished." She dropped the card case and the pen back into her purse, reached around the barrier of Annie's big stomach and handed Cole the card she'd just written on. "Here. Call me. About the accident. We can handle everything then. And thank you so much for the ride. I can't tell you how much I appreciate this."

Cole took the card and tossed it on the dashboard next to his hat. Then he leaned on his door. "Let's get the boxes." He jumped down and headed for the back of the pickup as Melinda tried to protest.

"But I—"

Annie shook her head. "He won't leave you here alone with that mean-looking maid and all those boxes you got. Better just give in and let him help you carry them."

"It truly is not necessary."

"Well, it's the right thing to do and Cole is going to do it. So you just go on now. Evelyn Erikson, the movie star, is waitin' for you."

When Melinda reached the rear of the pickup, the stony-faced maid was already there, her lips thinner than ever and her back ramrod-straight. Cole was stacking boxes onto her outstretched arms, his expression almost as grim as the maid's.

At the sight of his clenched jaw, Melinda heaved a weary sigh. She could see that Annie had been right. He would help her with this, no matter what she said.

Heeding Annie's suggestion, she gave in gracefully and put on a smile. "Here. I'll take some of those."

His clenched jaw relaxed and he smiled in return. He gestured at her shoulder bag. "Better put that thing back here. It'll just be in the way." That made sense. After taking out a pen and the order-form tablet Rudy had provided, she set her purse inside the camper. Cole said, "Here you go." He handed over four boxes and took the rest himself.

They made a little caravan, each laden with a stack of pink and gold offerings. The maid took the lead and Cole brought up the rear as they marched along the walk and beneath the portico. The maid had left the door unlatched. She gave it a push with her toe. It swung open.

They entered some sort of servants' foyer. "Essie!" the maid called. Another, younger maid appeared. If possible, she was even less attractive than the older one, with a long, sad-looking face and no chin at all. She shut the door and took the stack of boxes from the older maid.

Melinda thought to ask for Evelyn Erikson's personal secretary, the one who had called to request this private showing of the newest Forever Eve designs. "I wonder, is David Devereaux here?"

"David will be along," the older maid replied disdainfully. "Come this way." She started walking again.

Now they were a caravan of four. The older maid led them through a restaurant-size kitchen, down two hallways, and up a set of wide back stairs. On the second floor, they walked down three more hallways, which became wider and more opulent as they progressed. Tapestries of gamboling nymphs and leering fauns covered the walls. More statuary watched them through blind stone eyes from niches carved at intervals along their way. The floors were of marble, a never-ending checkerboard of white and black. All the furniture was on a grand scale, intricately carved, much of it ebony veined with gold.

At last they reached their destination: a huge pair of carved black doors. The older maid knocked discreetly. After a moment, the doors swung open.

A third maid confronted them, this one older than the first, and harder on the eyes than either of the other two. Beyond that maid's starched shoulder, Melinda could see a marble foyer. And farther in, some sort of huge sitting room, every wall draped in gold silk, with plush gold carpet covering the floor. It looked like some desert sheikh's tent in there. All the furniture was as soft and sumptuous as the walls, and upholstered in similar gold fabric, but embroidered with glimmering threads of eggshell-blue.

Melinda thought of her mother again. Of this, Elaine Bravo would never approve.

From somewhere in that sultan's tent of a room, the star's celebrated throaty voice demanded, "Well, Tasha. Is that the damn lingerie peddler at last?"

"Yes, Ms. Erikson, she's here," replied the oldest, ugliest maid.

"Get her in here, then."

The first maid chose that moment to make herself scarce. She turned on her duty shoes and hurried back down the checkerboard floor of the hall.

The maid named Tasha stepped back to clear the doorway. She gestured toward where the star waited. "This way."

The youngest maid, Essie, took up the lead, Melinda and Cole following, with Tasha in the rear. They went through the foyer, stopping beyond the gold-draped arch that framed the decadent sitting room.

The star, draped in an eggshell-blue satin wrapper, lay on a long, plush divan. She was petting the largest housecat

Melinda had ever seen, a white Persian with a blue satin bow
around its neck and an evil gleam in its sapphire eyes.

"Xerxes, my darling," Evelyn Erikson said to the cat.
"You'll have to get down now. Mummy has salespeople to
deal with."

The cat actually seemed to understand its mistress. It cast
a baleful glance at the row of box-holders in the doorway and
then jumped to the gold carpet, where it promptly sat on its
big haunches and began licking a long-haired paw.

"That will be all, Tasha," Evelyn Erikson said. The oldest
maid turned and left them.

The star's legendary eyes, which were the exact eggshell-
blue of the wrapper she wore and the tracery of vines and
flowers woven into her divan, made a swift and scathing in-
ventory of the three individuals standing before her. Her gaze
lingered on Cole.

"And who are *you,* may I ask?" The famous eyes now
shone with a distinctly rapacious light.

"Cole Yuma. Ma'am." He looked right at her and he made
the single word *ma'am* into a polite but undeniable rejection.
Melinda wondered with some admiration how he managed
that. When he had called *her* ma'am it had never sounded
anything but solicitous and sweet.

Evelyn Erikson let out what sounded like a regretful sigh.
Her thick, bronze lashes swooped down. When she looked
up again, her gaze moved right over Cole—and straight to
Melinda.

Melinda's meager hope that everything might still work
out reached an abrupt demise as she recognized the look the
star sent her way.

Envy.

Evelyn Erikson was a lush and stunning woman. But she
had to be well into her forties, at least. Melinda was twenty-
eight. Men were always stopping and staring, embarrassing

her, when she walked down the street. And perhaps, Melinda thought bleakly, though her slim skirt and matching jacket were modestly cut, she should have chosen a color other than "power red" for this appointment. In red she felt rather like a matador, waving a crimson cape at a snorting, ground-pawing, about-to-be-raging bull.

In a rustle of blue satin, the star rose from the divan. Melinda stared at her in dread. Her carefully rehearsed presentation, to which even the skeptical Rudy had given high marks, flew right out of her head.

Evelyn Erikson's sculpted nostrils flared. "You are late," she accused icily, turquoise eyes agleam. It was a challenge, Melinda knew. Evelyn Erikson was daring her to point out that it couldn't be more than a few minutes past the appointed time. Melinda held her tongue. From the corner of her eye, she saw a muscle twitch in Cole's jaw. She turned her head and glared right at him thinking, Don't you dare say a single word.

He stared back at her for a suspended moment. She felt hopelessly certain he was going to say something that Evelyn Erikson would not like to hear. But then his shoulders lifted in a nearly imperceptible shrug. She knew then that he would keep quiet.

"All right," said Evelyn Erikson. "Let's have a look." She gave a flick of her wrist toward another gold-draped arch, beyond which Melinda could see a huge round bed raised on a platform, covered with a quilted gold spread and piled with a hundred turquoise-blue satin pillows. "Set it all down over there."

The maid called Essie trotted right over, marched up the platform steps to the bed and set her burden down. Melinda and Cole did the same. As Melinda placed her few boxes on the gold coverlet, she couldn't help but take note of the huge mirror suspended directly above the bed, in the center of the suffocating fan of gold silk draped from the ceiling. An unwelcome vision of the ways Evelyn Erikson might put such a mirror to use popped into her mind. She told herself firmly not to think about that. She also took care not to glance at Cole right then. The last thing she needed was to see in his eyes that he was wondering about the mirror, too.

The star stalked up the steps to the bed. She snapped her fingers. "Essie." The maid turned swiftly and left them.

What is the matter with you? Melinda castigated herself. Do something. *Say* something. Now. She cleared her throat. "I thought first, you might like to take a peek at our Premiere—"

The star snapped her fingers again. "I can open the damn boxes myself. Get out of the way."

Hopelessness and extreme embarrassment washing through her, Melinda stepped back. Cole did, too.

Evelyn Erikson ripped the ribbon off one of the boxes and lifted out a delicate scrap of silk the same topaz color as her shining hair. She held the beautiful piece up and sneered, "A teddy. How ordinary." And she tossed it aside.

The star tore into the second box, and the third and the fourth. "A peignoir, a nightgown, a demi-bra and matching tap pants," she announced in disdain as each piece was held up, found wanting and quickly tossed aside. "No. Boring. Forget it. I hate it."

At one point, as lingerie flew, Melinda tried again to inject a positive note. "That bed jacket really would look terrific with your—"

The star whirled on her. "When I want your opinion, *blondie,* I'll give it to you."

Melinda kept her mouth shut after that. She stood beside a silent Cole, clutching her order pad and her pen, watching lingerie fly, trying not to think of what would happen when she returned to Forever Eve and Rudy learned what a debacle she'd made of this important sale.

As Evelyn Erikson finally came to the last of the boxes, Melinda felt a slight movement beside her. Cole. Her free hand—the one without the order pad—hung between them. He slid his hand around it.

She felt instantly soothed. Which was strange. After all, she really did hardly know him. She shot him a glance. And it seemed she could read volumes in those gentle, kind eyes. *It's not your fault. Everything will be all right...*.

A smile of pure gratitude quivered across Melinda's mouth. And down in her solar plexus, something flared: the burgeoning heat of a growing attraction. An achingly sweet sensation, something she hadn't felt in a very long time.

Then she thought, *Annie.*

Innocent, hugely pregnant young Annie, waiting out in the pickup for Cole to come back to her.

For Melinda to stand here in Evelyn Erikson's oppressive boudoir, with that naughty mirror suspended above the bed, holding hands with Annie's cowboy and thinking that he excited her, was worse than inappropriate—it was downright wrong.

She slid her hand free of Cole's grip and resolutely looked away from him.

The star had finally finished tossing lingerie around. She stood with her hands on her hips, staring down in disgust at the tumble of boxes and discarded undergarments. "Hopeless," she said. "Absolutely impossible."

Melinda couldn't have agreed with her more.

Someone tapped on the outside door. "Tasha! Get that!" shouted the star. The maid, who had evidently been huddled somewhere in the outer room, hurried to the big doors.

A moment later, a tall, tanned hunk in swim trunks, Teva sandals and an unbuttoned Hawaiian-print shirt appeared in the sitting room. He strode to the foot of the steps leading up to the area containing the huge bed.

"So. How are we doing?" the hunk said cheerfully.

The star glowered. "David, get this trash out of here. I don't want any of it." And with that, she swept down the steps, through the sitting room and foyer and out the tall black doors, which she left standing ajar. Her big white cat followed regally after her, its fat, fluffy tail held high.

David watched her go, shaking his head. Then he turned to Melinda and Cole. His straight white teeth flashed as he smiled. "What can I say? So much talent and beauty. And such a hopeless bitch."

Melinda took in a long breath and let it out slowly. "You must be David Devereaux." The star's personal assistant, the one who had called her to set up this catastrophe.

"The one and only." He continued to smile that carefree beach-boy smile. "Melinda, right? From Forever Eve?"

"Yes, I'm afraid so."

David Devereaux looked her up and down. "Wow. I should have checked you out in person first. I would have warned you to send someone else." Melinda didn't really want to know why, but David Devereaux told her anyway. "If there's one thing that sends Evelyn into a frenzy, it's a woman who's more gorgeous than she is."

Beside her, Cole made a low noise in his throat, a sound Melinda read immediately as one of pure disgust. He said, "Come on, Melinda. Let's get all this stuff together and get out of here."

It sounded like a terrific idea. She and Cole moved straight to the bed and began gathering up all the strewn lingerie. Melinda put her unused order pad and her pen into one of the boxes. After a moment, David Devereaux helped them. When the last pair of tap pants had been safely tucked away, they each took a pile of boxes and David led them back through the series of halls to the rear stairs.

The servants in the kitchen watched them silently as they trooped by. At last they emerged from that awful house, trudging down the steps beneath the portico and past the statues that flanked the walk.

"In the back of that pickup?" David asked in the relentlessly cheerful tone that set Melinda's teeth on edge.

"Right," growled Cole. He took up the lead, striding to the rear of the truck. He put his stack of boxes inside, then took Melinda's and David's. Finally he handed Melinda her purse and shut the door, latching it with a firm twist of his capable hand.

"Well," David said. "I guess that's that."

"It sure is," Cole replied in a voice as cold as dry ice.

"You have a nice day." And David Devereaux left them, his Hawaiian-print shirt ruffling slightly in the gentle breeze as he strolled back up the walk to the door.

When he was gone, Cole said quietly, "You shouldn't have given me that look in there. You should have just let me say what was on my mind. It wouldn't have turned out any worse than it did."

Melinda sighed. "Maybe not. But it wasn't your problem, Cole, and I think you know that."

He grunted. "Yeah. I guess that's so." Then he put his hand on her shoulder. The touch felt warm. She could almost imagine his strength flowing into her, bolstering her spirits, which had sunk dangerously low. "You gonna be all right?"

She made herself nod. "I am going to be fine."

He gave her shoulder a squeeze. "Come on. We'll take you home."

"Oh, no. You shouldn't have to—"

He didn't even let her finish protesting. "Melinda." His hand dropped away, leaving her wishing it hadn't—and knowing she had no right at all to wish such a thing. "Get in the truck."

She gave in. She needed a ride. And he insisted on giving her one. Where was the conflict—except in her own mind? "Thanks."

"My pleasure."

They turned together and headed for the passenger side of the cab. When they got there, he pulled the door open for her, a gentleman to the end.

She smiled at Annie, sitting there waiting so patiently, clutching her big stomach. "Cole insists on taking me home."

Annie didn't smile back. Her face looked flushed, her eyes way too wide. Her soft brown hair clung in damp tendrils at her temples. "I, um…" She looked down, and Melinda followed her gaze, to the spreading wet stain on her denim maternity jumper.

Melinda looked lower still. Slightly yellowish liquid trickled slowly along the girl's legs. It was already forming a small puddle on the floor.

"I, uh, was just sittin' here. Admirin' those statues. And then, all of a sudden, something kind of *gave*." Annie said the words in a whisper. She looked every bit as stunned as Melinda felt.

Cole said matter-of-factly, "Looks like your water's broken, Annie. I guess we'll be stoppin' off at the hospital before we can take Melinda home."

Chapter 3

Melinda turned around and gaped at him. "She...it...what?"

He looked as if he handled this kind of challenge every other day. "The amniotic sac has broken."

The amniotic sac. Melinda understood the words. She'd pored over a hundred books on pregnancy and childbirth before she lost her baby, so hungry to fully comprehend the miracle happening inside her. "I...I knew that," she heard herself mutter.

Cole was looking at Annie. "Annie girl, you've seen what can happen when the sac breaks all of a sudden."

Annie nodded. "Cord prolapse."

"Do you feel anything...blocking you up down there? Anything sticking out?"

Annie flushed bright red. "Cole." It was a rebuke. "You make me feel like a heifer."

Cole grinned. "Humans and heifers do have some things in common." He raised an eyebrow. "Well?"

Annie shook her head. "No. It feels...there's nothin' in there. Only pressure, more pressure than before. From the baby, you know?"

"Good," Cole said. "Then you're probably doing just fine. But I think we'd better get along to the hospital anyway." He looked at Melinda, who had stood staring, feeling dumbstruck, through the last exchange. "Hop on in and we'll get a move on."

"I...yes. Certainly. Of course." Melinda jumped up onto the seat next to Annie and Cole shut the door.

Moaning, Annie groped for Melinda's hand, as Cole strode around the front of the pickup and got in himself. "I think..." Annie panted, "Contraction. Oh, Lord..." She squeezed Melinda's hand so hard, it felt as if she'd managed to crack a few bones.

Cole started the engine, backed up smoothly, swung the wheel and pointed them in the right direction. Then he roared off. They flew past the long garage and the tennis courts. He took the turn for the gatehouse at a pretty good clip, swinging Melinda against the passenger door, with Annie leaning hard against her.

"Sorry," he muttered. "I took that too fast." They barreled along.

Annie's hand relaxed around Melinda's, the contraction passing as they approached the iron gates. The guard must have had some way to see them coming. The gates swung wide as they approached them and Cole sped right on through.

When they reached the street, Cole brought the truck to a stop and turned to Annie. He spoke very gently. "Did you get yourself set up at a hospital?"

Annie, who had slumped into the seat with the fading of the contraction, sat a little straighter. She glared at him as if he'd insulted her. "I told you, Cole. I've been taking care of my baby. Jimmy and me—"

Melinda wondered, Who's Jimmy? as Cole cut the young woman off. "Annie. It's no time to get into that." Now his soothing tone held an underpinning of steel. "Just tell me where the hospital is."

Annie sighed and her shoulders drooped again. She moved her hand within Melinda's, lacing their fingers together, getting a firmer grip, as if she intended to hold on for a long time. "It's East L.A. General," she said, then told Cole which way to turn.

Another contraction took Annie about four minutes after the first one. She panted and moaned and mauled Melinda's hand as Cole drove with the single-minded concentration of a Mario Andretti, racing through yellow lights and swinging the pickup out and around obstructing traffic, spinning around corners fast enough to send Melinda and Annie pitching sideways every time.

"Oh, I am so scared," Annie whispered at one point, when Cole had swung a hard right and the girl landed on top of Melinda for about the third time.

Melinda whispered back, "Don't be. It's going to be fine, just fine, you wait and see."

When Cole pulled up to the entrance at the rear of the hospital, Annie wouldn't let go of Melinda's hand. "I'm...I'm all wet. I'm so embarrassed. Don't leave me, Melinda. Don't leave me. Please."

"No. Shh. I won't. I won't leave you. I swear."

Cole caught Melinda's eye. "Maybe you could take her on in. I'll find a place to park. Then I'll find you."

"Sounds good," Melinda replied firmly. She put her arm around Annie. "Come on, now. Let's go." She grabbed her purse from the floorboard and pushed open the door, sliding out and coaxing Annie down after her. The girl huddled against her as they headed for the big glass doors.

Inside, they couldn't seem to get anyone's attention right away. People sat in rows on padded benches, waiting, some of them injured, some of the younger ones crying. And some just sitting there, staring into space, waiting their turn. Melinda found them a free spot on one of the benches and tried to get Annie to let go of her long enough to speak to someone at the admitting desk.

Annie only held tighter to her hand. "No. Just…stay with me. Please." Another contraction seized her. Melinda dropped down beside her as Annie clutched her belly with one hand and Melinda with the other, panting and moaning, as she rode that one out.

When it passed, Annie leaned close. Humid warmth from her laboring body swam in the air around them. Warmth and sweetness, from the amniotic fluid that darkened the skirt of her jumper. Melinda recalled reading somewhere that the fluid would smell sweet.

"You stay here, right here with me," Annie said softly. "Cole will come. In a few minutes. We can wait for him."

"But—"

Annie patted the hand she wouldn't let go of. "Really. Don't worry. He'll take care of everything."

Annie was right about that. Not five minutes later, after the young woman had weathered another grueling contraction, Cole came striding in. Five minutes more, and he had a doctor leading Annie to an examining room. Melinda went with her, still holding her hand, as Cole stayed behind to deal with paperwork and try to contact one of the OB-GYNs from the clinic where Annie had received her prenatal care.

The doctor who examined Annie declared she was seven centimeters dilated and "very nicely" effaced. "You are a healthy young woman in active labor," he said.

"That means my baby will be here soon?"

He smiled down at her. "Yes. That is exactly what it means. We're going to put you in a labor room for a while. We will check on you often. When the time comes, we'll move you for delivery."

Annie held up her hand, the one that still gripped Melinda's. "Can Melinda come with me? I need a friend at a time like this, you know?"

The doctor shared his smile with Melinda, who stood on the other side of Annie. "Yes, of course. Your friend may stay in the labor room with you."

The labor room, on the second floor, had three beds in it, each with its own privacy curtain. A bouquet of plastic flowers sat on a table in the center of one wall. A door on the same wall as the row of beds led to a half bath.

A nurse gave Annie a hospital gown, advised her to make herself comfortable, then left them. Melinda and Annie went into the small bathroom, where Annie undressed and Melinda helped her clean up a little. Then Annie got into the gown and Melinda tied the little ribbons at the back.

They returned to the labor room, where Melinda folded Annie's wet clothes and put them in a plastic drawstring bag, which the nurse had provided. Since the other beds were empty, they didn't bother with the curtain. And Annie didn't feel like lying down all the time anyway.

"I want to walk around. The pressure feels better when I'm standin' up."

So the two of them walked up and down the length of the room, pausing and breathing in unison when the contractions came. When Annie tired of walking, she climbed onto the bed to rest. Melinda would arrange her pillows for her, then take her hand again and stand very close.

"Oh, just look at me," Annie said, as Melinda was propping the pillows to ease her aching back. "In this ugly green thing, with my rear end showin' every time I turn around, grunting and groaning. I do feel like a heifer, I surely do."

"Well, you don't look like one, not at all."

"I guess that's somethin'."

Melinda gave the pillow a final nudge and took Annie's hand again. "Having a baby isn't easy. And you are doing a fabulous job."

"You think so?"

"I do."

"I just…I still keep worryin', you know? The baby's not due for three weeks yet—did I tell you that?"

"You did."

"I just hope nothing's wrong."

"Don't worry. I know a little about this process myself. And—"

"You do? You have kids?"

Melinda wondered what to say next. Annie needed encouragement, not to hear how another woman hadn't made it to term. She settled on the simple, if incomplete, truth. "No, I don't have any children. But I…well, let's just say I've studied the subject a little. If you're thirty-seven weeks along, the baby should be ready enough to be born."

"I know that, but—"

"It's going fine, Annie. You heard what the doctor said."

"You're right. I know you're right." Annie blew out her flushed cheeks with a gusty breath. "I am so grateful you stayed. I don't…really have any friends in L.A."

Melinda gave her hand a good squeeze. "I'm here, for as long as you need me." She said the words with no hesitation, finding that she meant them with all her heart. "And you've got Cole. He's a terrific man."

Annie's sweet, flushed face seemed to light from within as she smiled. "Yeah. He is. Not every girl gets a big brother so wonderful." Melinda must have looked somewhat surprised, because Annie actually giggled. "I knew it. I can see by your face. You thought Cole was my..." Her voice trailed off as she glanced down at their joined hands and at the gold band that circled her ring finger. "This isn't Cole's ring. It's Jimmy's. We got married two months ago, a week after I turned eighteen."

The charming giggle had faded, as if it had never been. And Annie's eyes—so much like Cole's eyes, Melinda realized now—were infinitely sad. "We were having such trouble, Jimmy and me. As soon as we knew about the baby, he started workin' double shifts at that job he had, so we could afford to pay for everything. I worked, too. I had a pretty good waitress job. But then I got too big and the boss let me go. Having a baby isn't cheap, you know?"

Melinda nodded. Annie went on, "Jimmy, he kept on workin'. He worked so hard. But even with all those extra hours, he didn't make all that much. And then, about three weeks ago, his boss said he wouldn't be needin' him anymore. Just like that. Poor Jimmy. He walks into work and finds out he doesn't have a job. It was all...too much for him. He just couldn't deal with it. The baby coming. And me... like this, needin' him to take care of me when he didn't know how he was gonna take care of himself. He just...took off. Two weeks ago."

Melinda swallowed back the sympathetic tears that had suddenly decided to burn the back of her throat. She knew all too well how it felt when love failed to be everything a woman hoped it might.

A tiny sigh escaped Annie. "The good thing, though, is that Cole came. Just yesterday. I opened the door and there he was. He wasn't so happy when he saw my big stomach. But I guess I can live with his disappointment in me, because

I truly don't know what I would have done if he hadn't been here."

Annie moaned again, as another contraction had its way with her. When it was over, she said, "I know you just settled me down here. But can we—?"

"Walk? You know we can."

Melinda helped her off the bed and they resumed their slow pacing, up and down the space at the foot of the beds.

"I guess I've messed up my life good," Annie said as they trudged slowly back and forth. "I've let Cole down. And my poor dad." She smiled—a melancholy smile, with a heart full of longing in it. "I love my dad. But he never could understand about Jimmy. Jimmy comes from a bad family. Those no-account Logans. That's what folks call them, where I come from. But it's not Jimmy's fault that his parents were drinkers. Or that nobody ever kept an eye on him, nobody showed him the benefits of going to school. *Of course* he got in trouble a lot. What else was there for him but trouble, you know? What else did he know? Until me. Until I was sixteen and he danced with me at the Harvest Ball and when he took me in his arms, we both knew what we'd found. Oh, but, Melinda…in the end, I guess I went and brought him as much trouble as everything else in his life."

Annie went on in a soft, forlorn voice, confiding that her dad would never forgive her for running off with Jimmy Logan at the age of seventeen, right at the start of her Senior year. And Melinda listened, said, "Oh?" and "Yes," and "I know what you mean, Annie," whenever Annie seemed to require a sympathetic word.

And Melinda did know what Annie meant. Wasn't she herself a total disappointment to her parents?

Annie might be eighteen and short of funds, fresh from somewhere in America's heartland, while Melinda was a decade older and had spent most of her privileged life in

Manhattan, raised by parents who always had money to spare. But she and this young, naïve girl had more than one thing in common.

Like Annie, Melinda knew what it meant to fail to live up to a parent's expectations. In her whole life, she'd never quite managed to garner her father's approval—or her mother's, for that matter. And like Annie, she had given her heart to a man who hadn't stuck by her when she'd needed him most. Annie knew, Annie understood, the sleepless nights and worry-filled days a woman endured when she carried a baby inside her and faced the daunting prospect of raising that child on her own.

It struck Melinda again, nearly stealing her breath: if she only hadn't miscarried, she might be in labor herself right now. Their babies might have been born on the very same day.

Annie was still confiding her secrets. "Cole's come all the way here, for the second time, to try to get me to come home."

"For the second time?"

Annie nodded. They reached the narrow window, turned and walked back, between the ends of the beds and the table with the plastic flowers on it, toward the door to the hall. "Cole came after me about nine months ago, when I first ran off. I wouldn't leave then. Because of Jimmy. Because Jimmy wouldn't go back to Bluebonnet. That's in Texas, in the Hill Country, which is right smack dab in the middle of the state. Bluebonnet is a little dinky town and it's my home. And Melinda, I…I don't care what Jimmy did. I don't care that he's left me. I still love him so. I will always be his."

Annie stopped then, and stared into the middle distance, yearning and hopelessness clouding her pretty eyes. "But now, since Jimmy's run off from me, I do wish I could just go home, at least. But I can't. Because of my dad. He isn't well. He had a stroke a while back. Cole tells me it's not my fault, but I know Dad wouldn't have had that stroke if not for me, runnin' off like I did, and only bein' seventeen then. And for me to come home now, with a baby and no husband—that would finish him off for sure."

Melinda said gently, "Maybe your father would surprise you. Maybe he would understand." She spoke with more authority than she felt. Her own parents hadn't understood at all when she told them she was going to have her baby anyway, whether Christopher Blayne, who already had a grown son and a daughter, wanted to be a father again or not.

Annie was sighing and shaking her head. Then she gasped. Another contraction. She gripped Melinda's hand tighter, crunching the bones. Melinda breathed with her as the pain ran its course.

"Maybe I'll try lyin' down some more," Annie said when that one passed.

They went to the bed. Melinda helped her up and fussed with the pillows again. A nurse came in carrying a small plastic bucket filled with ice chips. "Sometimes a little ice feels so soothing," she said. Then she examined Melinda, announced that it would be some time yet, and left.

Cole appeared a moment later. Melinda was perched on the bed beside Annie, trying to feed her some ice chips and still hold onto her hand. The sight of him, so tall and strong, so capable and kind, caused a rising feeling inside her—a feeling so lovely, she almost wished it could lead somewhere. She almost wished she could be as naïve as Annie, could see a man and know she loved him and follow him anywhere—to the sun-kissed and dangerous streets of L.A., to some small town in Texas—anywhere her love wanted her to go.

"The doctor from your clinic will be here soon," he told Annie. Then he came and stood across from Melinda. Annie held out her free hand and he took it.

Hours passed. Hours when Annie alternately paced and sat propped among the pillows, sucking on ice chips, as her labor progressed. To Melinda, it seemed as if the world contained only the four of them—Annie, Cole, Melinda and Annie's baby—living through Annie's labor, now and then joined briefly by a nurse or Annie's doctor.

Sometimes they would talk a little, between Annie's increasingly powerful and frequent contractions.

Melinda learned why Cole had been so calm when Annie's water broke. He was a large-animal veterinarian, a man who had attended quite a few births already—of calves, foals and lambs, even a llama or two.

"But never of your own niece or nephew," Annie reminded him.

"That's true," he agreed in that deep, steady voice of his. "And never have I seen a mother as pretty as you, Annie girl." He shared a loving look with his sister, then raised those kind eyes to meet Melinda's, across the bed. "Thanks for staying."

"I'm…glad to be here."

And she was. So very glad. And so grateful. She wouldn't even consider leaving now. Nothing existed but the feel of Annie's hand in hers, the sense that she was part of something powerful and important. That she was helping. That she was *needed*.

The appalling and humiliating incident at Evelyn Erikson's horrible, pretentious mansion seemed a hundred years ago. Five hundred. A thousand. And what had happened there didn't matter at all.

This mattered. Sometimes it seemed to Melinda that she could almost hear the heart of Annie's unborn baby, beating fast and hard as the little one struggled to find its way into the world.

Her own baby's heart had stopped all too soon. But this baby… This baby would live. This baby *had* to live. Melinda just knew that. Live to breathe, to cry, to laugh. To feel the warm, abiding comfort of a mother's loving arms.

During those timeless hours, whenever Melinda glanced across the bed and Annie's distended belly, she met Cole's light hazel eyes. Sometimes he smiled at her, sometimes he just looked back, steady as a rock, so sure. So true.

At last, the time came to move Annie to the delivery room. Annie begged to have both Cole and Melinda come with her. But the nurses said they would only allow one labor coach in delivery. So Cole went, and Melinda waited in the small lounge down the hall.

As she sat, glancing too often from her watch to the big institutional clock on the wall, thumbing through tattered copies of *Woman's Day* and *Ladies Home Journal,* Melinda's real life crowded in on her just a bit. Her car still waited, wrecked on an L.A. street corner. She would have to do something soon about having it towed. And she was supposed to have been back at Forever Eve by three o'clock at least, with her load of rejected lingerie and her excuses for her failure with Evelyn Erikson.

She should probably at least give Rudy a call. He wouldn't be at the shop this late, but she had the number of his cell phone. The short row of phone kiosks reproached her, in a nook not fifteen feet away.

But no, she simply couldn't deal with Rudy right now. He would just have to wait till tomorrow to get his merchandise back—along with the bad news.

It was after midnight when Cole came to find her. She looked up from her magazine and he was striding her way.

She stood, dropping the magazine on the little table at her side. His eyes seemed to have shadows in them, and his face looked so serious.

She thought, Something's happened. Oh God, something went wrong…

And then Cole's fine mouth tipped upward just slightly at the corners. "It's a boy," he said. "Strong and healthy. Six pounds, one ounce."

"And Annie...?"

"She came through just fine."

Chapter 4

It took another hour for the hospital staff to get Annie and the baby settled into a room. Then at last, they let Cole and Melinda in to see them.

Annie sat against the pillows. Someone had thought to brush her hair and pull it back in a low ponytail. Still, it looked lank and without luster, as if the job of giving birth had stolen all its shine. Dark smudges marred the tender skin beneath her eyes. And yet Melinda thought she had never seen anyone half so beautiful as little Annie Logan propped up in her hospital bed with her new baby in her arms.

Annie looked down at her child and then up, to share a tender smile with the brother who'd come all the way from Texas just when she needed him most.

"You feelin' all right, Annie girl?"

"I'm tired and I hurt in places I didn't even know I had. But I am feelin' just fine." She turned her gaze to Melinda. "I did it," she whispered, both awestruck and proud.

"Oh, yes," said Melinda. "You most certainly did."

"Come on over here and see him."

Melinda didn't have to be told twice. She moved around, to the far side, between Annie and the drawn curtain that separated Annie's bed from the other bed in the room.

Annie raised her cradling arms a little, holding the baby up. Melinda saw that tiny, Yoda-like face, the squinty eyes and sweet, squashed nose. He yawned, his tiny puckered rosebud of a mouth stretching wide. And then he sighed.

"I did good, didn't I?"

"Oh, Annie. You did fabulous."

Annie lifted the baby higher. "Here. Hold him."

Melinda's heart felt too big for her chest. "Are you sure…?"

"You bet I am."

Melinda bent a little closer to the bed. Her arms seemed to form a cradle without any conscious command from her mind.

"Careful. There we go…" Annie passed the tiny bundle and Melinda received him. It seemed to her a ritual as old as time and life and love itself—two sets of arms, cradling, a baby passed between.

Melinda could feel such tender warmth, through the soft receiving blanket. And oh, he was so light. A woman could carry him anywhere and never grow tired.

"He's just incredible," she whispered, bringing him closer, against her breasts, lowering her head a little so the sweet milky scent of him could come to her clearly. The tiny red face turned, rooting. Melinda felt the tightening, the yearning to give what a mother gives, what she might be giving now, if only—

"I'm naming him James, after his father," Annie announced. Melinda looked up from the precious bundle in her arms and saw the quick, defiant glance that Annie threw at Cole.

Cole's face had gone hard. Melinda knew his thoughts as if he'd spoken them aloud. He didn't want Annie's baby to have the name of the man who had deserted her.

Melinda willed him to look her way. It might have been coincidence, or it might have been something more, but his eyes did find her. She said, "It's a fine name."

His face seemed to harden even more. Melinda just went on looking at him, refusing to give in, to glance away and leave him to his stubbornness. Finally he was the one who blinked. She watched the hardness go out of him, saw the kindness and gentleness return.

"All right." He let out a resigned breath. "James, then. If that's really what you want."

"It is," Annie said. "And his middle name will be Brady, the same as Dad's middle name. We can call him that. Brady. What do you think?"

Cole nodded. "Brady it is."

Annie closed her eyes, sank back to the pillows. "Good." Her lashes fluttered open again. "Now, hold your new nephew."

Melinda carried the baby to his uncle and passed him over, ignoring the sharp pang of loss as the warm bundle left her arms.

Cole looked down at the baby. "Well, hello there, Brady."

The baby made a tiny, gurgling sound that really did seem like a response. Annie grinned and both Cole and Melinda chuckled.

Then Cole turned to Melinda. "I think maybe we'd better find a phone and call a tow service. See if we can get that car of yours towed tonight."

He was right, of course. Annie was exhausted and it was time to go. Still, her foolish heart kept urging her to stay.

After all they'd been through together since Cole's pickup came flying out of nowhere and collided with her BMW, Melinda felt somehow bound to Annie and Brady—and to Cole, as well.

But her watch told her it was one in the morning—twelve hours since the accident that had thrown them all together. One o'clock. Time to get back to her own life and let these three get back to theirs.

"I can call a cab," she said.

Cole looked weary. "By now, you oughtta know better than to start that stuff again."

"But—"

"Melinda," Annie said. "You know how he is. He will get you where you need to go—whether you want him to or not."

Melinda scrunched up her nose. "Oh, all right. I guess you're determined to rescue me, even if I am fully capable of taking care of myself."

His eyes gleamed at her. "You got it right there." He moved over next to Annie, on the side opposite the curtain, between her bed and the plastic-sided hospital bassinet. Gently he lowered her son into her arms. "I'll be back before noon."

"Call me first," she said. "I'll need a few things. My keys are in my purse and it's—"

"Still in the truck. I know."

"I had a little suitcase all ready, it's in the closet by the—"

"I'll call you. You can tell me then what to bring, not to mention where to find it." He leaned close, brushed a kiss against her hair.

She couldn't suppress a yawn. "Okay. Sounds good." She looked at Melinda fondly. "It's so crazy. Yesterday, I didn't know you. And now I feel like I've finally got a best friend. You'll come again, please? When you can?"

Melinda couldn't have said no if she'd wanted to—which she didn't. "I'll stop by this afternoon sometime. How's that?"

"Great. Oh, Lordy. I never even asked how your appointment turned out."

Cole and Melinda shared a glance, then Melinda said, "It was not a success."

"Oh, I'm so sorry," Annie said. "And on top of that, there's your poor car…"

"Don't be sorry. The day was far from a total loss. I met you and Cole. And Brady got here all safe and sound."

"Yeah." Annie yawned again. "Altogether, it was a slam-bangin' wonderful red-letter day."

Cole left his sister's side to take Melinda's arm. At his touch, a little dart of joyful awareness seemed to zing up through her shoulder and straight to her heart.

I did not feel that, she said to herself.

Cole said, "Good night, Annie."

Annie yawned for the third time. "'Night. Call me."

"I will."

Melinda called Triple-A from the hospital before they left. She gave directions to her car and the voice on the other end of the line assured her that a tow truck would meet her there. Then she and Cole climbed into his pickup and drove through the dark streets to the site of the accident.

The BMW sat, wrecked but otherwise undisturbed, right where Melinda had left it. It took the tow truck a while to arrive. When it finally did, Melinda gave the driver her Triple-A card and he began filling out a form on a clipboard.

Cole said, "Let me take you on home."

It really wasn't necessary. She could go with the tow truck. But Cole suggested, "Maybe we could get something to eat on the way."

She realized she was starving. She hadn't eaten a thing since the bagel and coffee she'd bolted down at breakfast the day before. "All right."

She asked the tow truck driver if he could just leave her car in her driveway. Then she could call her insurance company, get an adjuster out to take a look at it and decide what to do next. The driver said that would be no problem at all.

They found an all-night coffee shop on Sunset. Melinda had decaf, a waffle and two eggs. Cole ordered a chili omelet with toast and bacon, a rib-eye steak on the side, a large milk and two baking powder biscuits.

"Gotta keep my strength up," he said wryly, as the waitress set the huge meal in front of him. He picked up his fork and set to work on the food.

Melinda did the same. The meal was pretty much a silent one. But it was a comfortable silence, the kind that might be shared by two very dear friends.

It was four in the morning when they reached Melinda's three-bedroom house deep in the canyons above Sunset Boulevard. Cole pulled the pickup into the driveway, next to the BMW with its caved-in wheels and sprung trunk.

She turned to him, planning to thank him again and tell him good night.

But somehow, that didn't seem right. Or maybe she simply did not want to let him go yet. Maybe she just wasn't ready to admit that this bizarrely magical night had finally come to an end.

He draped one arm on the steering wheel and looked at her. The dashboard lights shone on his strong jaw, casting a tempting shadow across the cleft in his chin. His eyes seemed to say things she knew she shouldn't let herself hear.

"Do you want to come in?" The question was out before she realized she would ask it. "For a last cup of coffee?" Something neither of them needed in the least.

"Yeah, I'd like that."

He reached for his hat, which he'd set on the seat between

them—and then didn't pick it up after all. They leaned on their doors in unison and got out.

She came around the front of the pickup to join him, aware of the call of some bird she couldn't see a few yards away, singing its lonely song under cover of the final darkness before dawn.

Melinda led the way, up the concrete walk, poignantly conscious of the warmth of the night, of the nearby eucalyptus trees rustling in the soft breeze, their scent pungent and dusty, slightly feral. Of the lonely bird singing.

Her house was one-story, sided in wood stained a deep brown, the roof shingled in dark gray. She'd bought it two months ago, when she'd first come to L.A. in search of a fresh start. She had liked its simplicity, admired the way it blended into the dry, semitropical terrain around it.

The twin porch lanterns, which worked on a timer, cast twin pools of golden light on the front step. On either side of the step, birds of paradise grew, their exotic flowers rising up, crested in orange and purple, above fanning nests of high green leaves.

Melinda unlocked the door.

From behind her, Cole said, "Hey. We're forgetting all your boxes." So she stepped into the tiled entranceway just long enough to punch out the code that turned off the alarm. Then they went back out together, to the rear of the truck. It took them two trips to bring in the boxes, which they stacked neatly inside the front door.

At last, turning on lights as she went, she led him into the giant, airy room that made up the heart of the house. He headed straight to the sliding glass doors that opened onto a high deck and the wooded canyon below. There, he stopped and stared out at the darkness, toward the few lights left on in the houses across the ravine.

Melinda hesitated a moment, her gaze on his broad back,

wondering why he seemed so pensive suddenly, thinking that perhaps she ought to say something.

But nothing came easily to mind. So she turned and went around the long counter bar that separated the kitchen area from the living room. She took coffee beans from the cupboard and poured some in the grinder. The whirring scream when she flicked on the machine seemed terribly loud, especially when measured against the silence of the man in worn jeans and a plaid shirt, standing by her sliding door, so tall and composed, facing away from her.

After a few seconds that stretched out like a century, she turned the thing off and busied herself putting the filter in the basket, tapping in the sweet-smelling grounds, getting water from the cooler in the corner and pouring it into the reservoir.

Cole turned from the glass door as she was setting the pot, all ready to brew, on the warming plate. She watched him come from the corner of her eye. And then he went around the counter, behind her, where she could no longer see him.

He stopped a few feet from her. She could feel his stillness, his gaze on her back, feel it acutely—a sensation both sweet and unsettling at the same time.

She pushed the brew button and faced him, ordering her lips to form a smile. "It'll just be a few minutes."

"Fine."

Behind her, unaccountably loud, she heard the sizzle as the warmer heated. The water began dripping into the basket. "Would you like…I don't know, some toast or something?"

"I think the omelet, the steak and the biscuits I ate should just about hold me."

"Oh. Yes. Well, I'd imagine so." A silly giggle escaped her. He went on regarding her with serious eyes. Finally she couldn't stand it. "*What,* Cole?"

He smiled, but only slightly, a musing lift of one corner of his mouth. "You haven't said much about yourself tonight."

She backed up against the counter—and found she felt cornered there. Still, she managed to speak casually. "What do you want to know?"

He cast a quick glance around, at the pretty kitchen with its hand-painted counter tiles and chef-style appliances, at the big room and the attractive view beyond. "This is a nice house. And that was a nice car my pickup rammed into. It looks like you don't have any money problems."

What was she supposed to say to that? She shrugged. "You're right. I don't."

"You're a rich girl."

She answered too quickly, "I'm comfortably off," and then had to order herself not to wince. That had sounded exactly like something her mother might say.

He wouldn't quit staring at her. "I'm not rich. I guess you've got me beat there."

She found she didn't know what to do with her hands, so she crossed them beneath her breasts. "Cole." Another sharp, foolish laugh bubbled up. She closed her throat over it, pushed it back down. "It is not my intention to *beat* you."

"Well." He was still almost smiling. "Good. Got a special guy?"

"No. No special guy. No guy at all, as a matter of fact."

Now he looked amused. "No guy at *all?*"

"That's what I said."

He moved marginally closer. The counter pressed at her back. She had no easy way to retreat from him.

And she wasn't even sure she wanted to retreat from him.

All at once, she found herself poignantly aware of her own crossed arms. They seemed such an obvious attempt at self-protection.

Protection from what?

She dropped them to her sides—and then felt too vulnerable. Her breasts were only inches from his chest.

She thought of that moment right after the accident, when he had opened her car door and reached across her, to free her from her imprisoning seat belt, of his arm brushing her breasts, of the scent of him—aftershave and soap and man.

Right now, this close to him, she could see the faint early-morning stubble of sprouting beard along his jaw.

Slowly he lifted both hands and showed them to her, palms out. The gesture spoke volumes. *I'm going to touch you now. With these two hands.*

It was the moment when she could shake her head, tell him no, slide to the side and make her escape.

But she didn't.

So he touched her. Oh so tenderly, he cupped her face. Waves of longing lapped through her, rolling out, caressing, sliding back and flowing in again.

She should pull away, she knew she should. But she didn't. Now, his scent had really found her. It had more of the man himself in it and less of aftershave than she remembered. It was a good scent, healthy. Seductive. It mingled with the aroma of the brewing coffee behind her, making her think of lazy mornings, of slow kisses in bed.

"Lord." His voice was a little bit hoarse, and very low. His mouth was close enough that she could feel the stirring of his breath across her lips. "You're so beautiful. It's kind of hard on a man, makes his hands itch to touch you."

The words were sincere. They moved her as a thousand clever compliments never had. She answered honestly in a whisper, staring into those light eyes that were green and blue and a little bit brown all at once. "It's not something I *did,* Cole. It's just—" Her voice broke, so she swallowed, "—how I am."

The other corner of his mouth went up. A real smile, and

such a tender one. "How you are. Comfortably off. And so beautiful it hurts."

She tried to make light of it. "I'm the girl who has everything." It came out brittle, and she wished she hadn't said it. She found herself thinking, Oh, right. I've got everything. Except love and companionship, meaningful work…and a tiny warm bundle to hold in my arms.

"You're a real city girl, huh?" His mouth was so close, whispering to her.

"Mm-hmm," she whispered back. "Born and raised in Manhattan."

A few tendrils of hair had escaped the imprisonment of her oh-so-professional French roll. His fingers found them, where they curled at her nape. He tugged on one, gently, then dropped his hands away and moved back a step.

She wanted to cry out, Wait! You haven't even kissed me yet!

But somehow she managed not to say such a foolish thing.

He braced an arm on the counter, leaned against it again. "Ever had the urge to go country?"

"Never." This was insane. She wished he had kissed her. And felt sad saying never, even though it was the truth.

"Maybe you'd like it, if you gave it a try."

"I have tried it, thank you. My brother runs a ranch. In Northeastern Wyoming, near a small town called Medicine Creek. It's the family ranch. Bravos have owned it for several generations. I used to visit there, once or twice a year, when I was growing up. But only when my Grandfather Ross put his foot down and insisted."

"Only then?"

"That's right."

"Because you didn't want to go?"

"Exactly. And I wasn't the only one. My parents wanted nothing to do with the ranch, either. But Grandpa still had enough clout with them to see that his grandchildren got a taste of what his son had left behind."

"Northeastern Wyoming. I've heard that's beautiful country."

"Maybe so. But what I remember is incessant wind and lots of cows. Coyotes howling at night. A dearth of decent restaurants. And the shopping…" She flicked up a dismissing hand, thinking that she sounded shallow and supercilious, and telling herself she didn't care. "There's only one word for the shopping in Medicine Creek, Wyoming."

"And what's that?"

"Nonexistent."

He suggested softly, "There are other things besides shopping and restaurants."

"Certainly there are. Good museums. Broadway shows. The Christmas tree at Rockefeller Center."

He tipped his head to the side. His eyes held both patience and challenge. "If New York is your home, then what are you doing all the way out here on the edge of the Pacific Ocean?"

Her brittle facade cracked. She could feel it breaking apart. "I'm here to…start over." She shrugged, a gesture she knew to be both inadequate and forlorn. "But I have to admit, it's not working out very well."

He reached for her again. She made no effort to evade him. Alarm and exhilaration tingling through her, she found herself pressed against his hard chest.

"A new start?"

She nodded, staring up at him. His arms felt so good around her. His lean, hard body seemed to pull at hers, as if it had somehow been magnetized specifically to her alone. It was terribly disorienting.

"I'm not…a very successful person," she heard herself say. "Not in any of the ways that really count. And I thought, maybe, if I started over somewhere totally new, I would be able to…" Her breath was coming shallow and fast. She forgot completely what she'd been trying to say.

His mouth hovered above hers. "You're a good woman, Melinda Bravo. I saw you today, I saw how you are. You've got heart and you do what's right."

"Oh, Cole. You don't know me. You don't know me at all. I'm just not—"

Her sentence ended half-said, because right then, his wonderful mouth settled on hers.

Tenderness. The word bloomed like a flower in her mind. He gave such tenderness. Tenderness somehow blended together with a stunning, nerve-tingling heat. With a yearning so lovely, so powerful. So right.

She should have pushed him away.

But she couldn't.

Right then, there was nothing—nothing in the world but the yearning in the way he held her, a yearning that called to her, a yearning she could not help but answer. Every part of her felt…engaged. Her body. Her heart. Her mind. Her very soul.

His lips nuzzled hers, and his tongue sought entrance. She gave it, sighing eagerly, then moaning low. Their tongues met. She sighed again.

Could this really be happening? Surely not. She was nearing thirty. She had loved a man and lived with him. She had thought that she knew all there was to know about kissing.

Oh, but she hadn't. No, not at all. Not kissing like this, not kissing that felt so perfect, so total. So…complete.

Cole kissed her as if the mere taste of her nourished him. And as if they could just stand here until daybreak and beyond, pressed so close together, in this endless searing, intimate caress.

The coffeemaker gave a final sputter. There was silence, except for their shared sighs.

Cole lifted his head, looked down at her, his eyes making promises, his hands stroking her back. "Melinda," he whispered low. On his lips, her name sounded like a vow. Or a prayer. His mouth hovered above hers, ready to kiss her some more.

She thought, No. Wait. This is wrong. To be standing here in my own kitchen, kissing this cowboy I only met hours ago.

Somehow, she found the strength to splay her hands on his chest and stiffen her arms so their lips couldn't meet.

He froze, waiting, for her to speak, for her to tell him what had happened, why she'd suddenly changed her mind.

She stammered, "I…this is a bad idea. We have nothing in common."

"So?"

"So, it couldn't go anywhere."

"Are you sure of that?"

"Oh, Cole. I…I was trying to tell you, I'm at a difficult place in my life now. I need to find…where I'm going, what to *do* with myself. The last thing I need is…" She sought the right word.

He found it before she did. "A man?"

"Right."

He just looked at her.

She rushed on. "I'm sorry, Cole. But it's true. The last thing I need right now is a man."

His eyes searched her face. "You mean that? You're certain?"

She made herself say it. "Yes. Yes, I'm certain."

He sucked in a long breath. Then he dropped his hands to his sides and moved back. "I think it's time for me to go."

No! a foolish voice in the back of her mind cried. No, please don't go!

"I…what about the coffee?"

Those eyes of his didn't waver. "Better leave it at this."

She lowered her head and pressed her lips together, in order to keep from begging him to stay.

He said, "It's been...some night."

She lifted her chin high, spoke firmly. "Yes. It has."

He ran his hand back over the crown of his head, finger-combing his thick brown hair. "Thanks. For being there while my nephew was born. It meant the world to Annie."

"I'll see her tomorrow." The words came too quickly, full of an eagerness she couldn't mask. She found herself adding a bit defensively, "I told her I would."

He granted her another long, searching look. Her heart seemed to shrink inside her chest. She just knew he was going to tell her not to come.

But he didn't. He only said politely, "She'll like that. And I'll get the number of my insurance company to give you then, so you can pass it on to your agent."

"That will be fine."

He was still watching her too closely, a look that pulled on her, a look that made her long once again to beg him to stay.

But she didn't beg him. She only said, "Good night, then." And trailed along behind him to lock the door once he had left.

Chapter 5

Rudy was waiting when Melinda walked in the back door of Forever Eve the next morning.

"Darling. So *glad* you could make it today."

She craned her head around the stack of boxes she'd carried in from the cab with her. "Rudy. Look. I'm really sorry about—"

He waved a long, elegant hand. "We'll talk. But first, where is the rest of my merchandise?"

"Right outside."

"Undamaged?"

"Yes. I promise you."

"Then give it all to Sara and join me in my office, why don't you?"

"Certainly," Melinda replied with a briskness she wished she could feel. Rudy left her there with her tottering pile of boxes. She turned them over to the other salesclerk. Then she went outside to help the cabdriver bring in the rest.

When she paid him, she added a generous tip. "Thank you so much for your help."

"Hey. Anytime." He winked at her. "Always glad to give a pretty girl a hand." He strolled off whistling. Melinda watched as the heavy back door closed behind him. Then, unable to put it off any longer, she went to Rudy's office.

He was waiting behind the drawing board that he used as a desk. "Shut the door, darling."

She did as he told her. He said, "Go on. Sit down." She moved a stack of fabric samples from a folding chair to a table nearby.

He waited until she'd taken the empty seat, then said, "So. Decided to steal an afternoon off?"

She thought of Annie, sitting in Cole's pickup, clutching her big belly, amniotic fluid dripping down her legs. "Something came up. An emergency."

"Oh, I'm sure." Rudy brushed at his silk sleeve. Rudy loved silk. And the color black. Today, he was adorned in a black silk poet's shirt with a black scarf at the neck, a black patent leather belt and a pair of tight-fitting black slacks. He looked a bit like Zorro without the mask—a very fey Zorro, and a very put-upon one, too. "When you didn't show up by five, I called the Erikson mansion myself. It was far from a pleasant experience. The woman is a raving bitch. She screeched at me. Repeatedly." He tossed his head and his tight cap of raven locks bounced saucily. "She said you were rude. And totally incompetent."

Melinda said nothing. What was there to say?

Rudy let out a long sigh. "Of course, I settled her down eventually. She'll see me—and only me—tomorrow at two."

Melinda felt somewhat relieved. "You'll turn her around."

"You're right, I will. No thanks to you." He folded his hands on the drawing board and regarded her reproachfully. "You said you could handle it."

"I thought I could."

"She hated everything?"

"I'm afraid so."

"I told you to take the After Midnight designs, didn't I?"

"But I thought—"

Rudy clucked his tongue. "My darling. Everyone in this town knows about Evelyn Erikson. She's fifty years old and she loves pretty boys. She also wants to be twenty again. The Premiere collection is not to her taste."

Melinda felt like hanging her head, but she didn't. She sat stiffly erect. "Yes. You were right."

"Well, of course I was." He fiddled with his sleeve again, then let out another long breath. "Melinda darling, I am going to see to it that Evelyn Erikson becomes an exclusive Forever Eve account."

"I'm sure that you will."

"Her support could mean a great deal to us here."

"I realize that."

"Good. And I do want you to understand that I believe you have talent. Some of your ideas have been…quite exciting, though your insistence on trying them out has struck me as premature. After all, you've only been working here for—what?"

"Seven weeks."

"When you walked in off the street that first day, I thought to myself, 'Ah, yes. Magnificent. The Forever Eve woman, in the flesh'."

Melinda cleared her throat. "Well. Thank you."

"But it really hasn't worked out, has it?"

Melinda knew that she was about to be fired—and she knew why, too. "You promised Evelyn Erikson that you'd get rid of me, didn't you?"

Rudy looked down at his folded hands, then back up at Melinda with the tiniest of shrugs. "So goes it in Lotusland, my sweet. And you know, you really should have called, when you decided not to wander back here yesterday."

"Yes," Melinda agreed in a soft voice. "I realize that." She felt no urge at all to try to explain herself. What was the point? Staring across the drawing table desk at her boss in his poet's shirt and flowing black scarf, Melinda saw the truth and accepted it. She was never going to make a go of it with Forever Eve. It was Rudy's shop and it would always be run Rudy's way. He might admire her ideas, but he'd always fight using them.

And he would never understand the choices she'd made yesterday. What would he care about the accident and how Cole had helped her? What did a young girl from Texas and the imminent birth of her child mean to Rudy Delavaggio and his exclusive lingerie shop?

The answer was simple. They meant nothing. Nothing at all.

Rudy said, "That's a Prada bag you're carrying. You'll hardly starve before you find something else."

"Rudy?"

"Um?"

"You're right."

"Well, darling, of course I am. Let's just write you up a final check and you can be on your way."

Feeling uncannily good about herself, Melinda walked out of Forever Eve without a job. She called another cab, this time to a car rental place where she got herself some wheels. Then she drove straight to the finest baby boutique in Beverly Hills where she bought a complete layette, everything sky blue and sunny yellow—and a stuffed blue bunny with floppy ears. She also looked over their selection of child safety seats and chose the best one they had.

She made one more stop before heading for East L.A.

General, at a florists', for a bright blue and yellow bouquet. It was adorable, arranged in a miniature baby carriage, with a tiny yellow teddy bear sticking out the top.

At the hospital's front desk, she learned that Annie would be checking out that afternoon.

"So soon?" she asked, surprised.

The clerk looked her up and down. "This isn't the Waldorf."

"Well, I know, but—"

"Her doctor makes the decisions. I'm sure if he says she's ready, then she is."

"Well, yes. That makes sense, I suppose." Melinda had the flowers in one arm and the stuffed bunny in the other. She smiled from between them. "Is it all right if I just—?"

The rather harried-looking clerk actually smiled back. "Go on up. Room 341. But check in at the nurses' station there before you go to the room, just to be sure she's ready for visitors right now."

"I'll do that."

Annie's face lit up when she saw Melinda. "You're early! Ohmigoodness. Flowers. They're so *cute.* And the bunny... Melinda, you didn't have to do that."

"I know. But I wanted to." Melinda thought of the other surprises she'd left in the car. She just couldn't wait to present them. Annie was going to be so pleased.

Cole sat in a chair at the foot of Annie's bed, long legs stretched out in front of him, crossed at the ankles. Melinda gave him a careful smile. "Hello, Cole."

He nodded, pulling out of his relaxed pose and planting his boots firmly on the floor.

Melinda turned from him swiftly. She rushed to the hospital bassinet, feeling breathless and giddy—and just a little bit guilty for some silly reason. "Oh. Where's the baby?"

Annie laughed. "Relax. They didn't steal him. They're just

looking him over one final time. Cole, take these beautiful flowers and Brady's new bunny and put them on that little shelf over there."

Cole rose from the chair. He stepped up to Melinda. She felt his sudden closeness acutely. She also experienced a total reluctance to meet his eyes. She gave him another false smile and stared at the wall just beyond his left shoulder as she passed him the flowers and the floppy-eared toy.

He showed no inclination to linger beside her. As soon as he had the things in his hands, he turned and carried them to the high shelf Annie had indicated, where he set the bunny right next to the flowers. "How's that?"

"Oh, that's just fine. That way I can see them and feel spoiled and special, until they let me out of here."

Melinda frowned. "Which, I understand, will be this afternoon?"

"That's right," Annie said. "And don't go lookin' worried. They say we're ready, both of us, me and Brady."

Cole seemed reluctant to sit again. He stood by his chair. "Listen. I think I'll head on out and see about getting that car seat we talked about."

Melinda had no choice. She had to reveal her little surprise. "That won't be necessary." Both Annie and Cole turned questioning eyes on her. She explained, "Well, there's no need. I mean, I already got you one."

Annie giggled in disbelief. "A *car seat?* You didn't."

"Yes, I did. And I got a few other things, too."

"Oh, Melinda. That's not right. You can't just—"

"Yes, I can." She flicked a defiant glance at the stony-faced Cole. "And I did. So we don't need to talk about it anymore."

There was silence. Melinda could feel Cole's disapproval, coming at her in waves. She did not let herself look at him. She turned pleading eyes on Annie. "Come on. I wanted to. And I can afford it. Believe me, I can."

Annie let out a cry and reached out her arms. "Come down here. Come on."

Melinda bent over the bed. Annie grabbed her close and Melinda grabbed back, breathing in that wonderful baby scent that clung to Annie's skin, thinking that it felt so good, to have a friend's arms around her in affection and gratitude.

"It's okay, then?" she whispered against Annie's soft hair.

"Yes. It's okay. And thank you. Thank you so much…"

"It's nothing. You're welcome." She let go of Annie and straightened again. "I had such fun picking everything out."

The two women beamed at each other until Cole said in a flat voice, "I wrote down the number of my insurance company." He dug in a back pocket and brought out a small square of paper.

"Oh. Yes. Of course." Melinda took the paper, way too aware of the quick brushing of his fingers against hers. "I…I wrote mine down for you, too." She dropped the paper in her purse and fumbled around until she found what she was looking for. "Here you go."

He took it. "Thanks. I hope you've got that car seat stashed somewhere close. We're gonna need it to take the baby home."

"Oh, yes. I left it in my rental car."

"Maybe you'd better show me where it is. I'll bring it up now."

He wanted to get rid of her. She could see it in his eyes. He'd collect the other gifts she'd brought and then send her on her way.

Well, too bad for him. She wasn't leaving until she'd seen Brady. "Thanks, but I'll take care of it myself before I go."

He didn't look pleased, but what could he do? Those big shoulders lifted in an easy shrug. "Suit yourself." Then he spoke to his sister. "I've still got a few other things to pick up, so I think I'll just go on."

He turned for the door, but Annie stopped him before he could make his escape. "Cole?"

He paused in midstride and glanced back at his sister. "Yeah?"

"Is somethin' bothering you?"

"No, not a thing. I'll be back at one to get you out of here."

The worried frown between her brows faded away. "We'll be ready."

His guarded eyes found Melinda. "Goodbye, Melinda." The words were polite. And final.

She waved a hand. "'Bye, Cole." And he left them.

Not two minutes later, a nurse brought the baby back. And of course, Melinda had to hold him. He fussed and rooted for her breast.

"He's hungry," Annie said. "My milk hasn't come down yet and he's been crying a lot the past few hours."

Melinda helped make Annie comfortable so that she could nurse, which soothed the baby even though he wasn't getting much nourishment yet from the process. Annie looked up from the tiny mouth tugging on her breast. "The nurses tried to talk me into letting him have a bottle."

"But you said no, didn't you?"

"You bet. If Brady and I don't practice, we'll never get this right."

Melinda reached out, tenderly touched the small head with its cap of downy fuzz. The soft spot pulsed beneath her palm. "He seems to be catching on quickly."

"Yeah. No moss growin' on this boy, let me tell you…"

The time just seemed to melt away. Brady fell asleep at Annie's breast and she put him in the plastic-sided bassinet. At eleven-thirty, Annie's lunch arrived. She just couldn't eat all of it, so she and Melinda shared.

Annie said she couldn't get over it, how the two of them got along. "Like a pair of old shoes, you know? Comfortable and easy, with no places that rub you wrong. I am so glad you came early—and that you're here right now." Annie pulled a Groucho Marx with her eyebrows. "But fess up now. Are you playin' hooky from work?"

So Melinda ended up admitting that she no longer had a job.

"Oh, Melinda. Is it our fault? Because of yesterday?"

And Melinda had to explain everything. About how the job wasn't right for her anyway. And then all about Rudy and Forever Eve—and even the awful experience with Evelyn Erikson.

Annie flushed bright red when she heard about the mirror over the huge, gold-draped bed. "What a terrible woman," she said with a groan. "I never liked her movies much anyway. And I'm really surprised that Cole didn't give her a big piece of his mind."

The bittersweet memory rose up—Cole's hand finding hers, the seemingly contradictory sensations of comfort and arousal his touch had inspired. "Cole wanted to tell her off," Melinda confessed. "But I gave him a look and he kept his mouth shut."

"You shouldn't have. You should have let him blast her with both barrels."

"No. That wouldn't have been right."

"Sure, it would. She deserved it."

"Well, it's all over with now."

"Is it ever. And you're without a job. Oh, Melinda. What will you do?"

"I'll find something else."

"But will you…be all right, until then? I mean, aren't you a little worried? About money, you know?"

"Annie, the truth is, I've got plenty of that. I have a trust fund. A very large one. And a few investments, too."

"A trust fund? You mean your father's rich?"

"Actually, most of the money comes from my mother's side. She's from a very old, very wealthy Philadelphia family—and you are not to worry about me. I will be just fine." She was proud of how self-assured she sounded. In reality, she hadn't a clue what she would do with herself next.

And Annie sensed that. "I guess, really, you're a lot like me," she said quietly, "trying to figure out where in God's big world to go from here."

Looking into her young friend's innocent eyes, Melinda realized she felt truly understood, perhaps for the first time in her life. "We do have a lot in common, you and I."

Annie nodded. "Maybe that's why we get along so great."

Cole came striding in a moment later. He started to smile—and then he saw Melinda, perched on the chair she'd pulled up close to Annie's bed. "I thought you'd be long gone by now."

"Cole!" Annie cried in reproach. "You make it sound like you wish she'd left."

He had the grace to look chagrined. "Sorry. It just surprised me, to see you here. I thought you'd have to head on back to work."

Annie cast a questioning glance at Melinda, a glance Melinda read as if her friend had spoken aloud: Should I tell him? Melinda looked down, gave a tiny shake of her head. She did not feel, at that moment, like telling Cole Yuma that she no longer had a job.

She said, "No, actually. I don't have to go back to work today." She realized then how she intended to spend her afternoon, so she told him, "I thought I'd just help out, with getting Annie and the baby all settled at home."

Chapter 6

What kind of game did this woman think she was playing here? Cole Yuma asked himself.

Whatever it was, he didn't like it one bit.

A few hours ago, she'd let him kiss her and feel her body all along his and start thinking crazy things that probably never could be. And then she'd sent him off with a bulge in his britches.

So all right. He'd gone back to his motel room and taken a cold shower and told himself that he accepted her rejection. He'd come to L.A. to drag his baby sister back home where she belonged, not to fall for some soft, sweet-smelling city girl who looked like a movie star and openly admitted she didn't know what the hell to do with her life. He'd decided that when he had to see her that afternoon, he'd focus on how good-hearted she'd been to stick by Annie while the baby was being born. He wouldn't let himself think about the way her mouth had opened under his, about the sweetness inside there, about her breasts pressing into his shirt.

He'd reminded himself of the obvious: that he was thirty years old. A mature man. A man who understood that sometimes a woman said yes and sometimes she said no and if it didn't work out, you just let it go.

Before he'd headed for the hospital this morning, he'd made a point to have his insurance number handy, so he could pass it right to her when she showed up. He'd thought she'd pat Annie's hand and coo over Brady a little and then be on her way.

Then, when he'd arrived at the hospital and found out they were letting Annie go home that day, he'd even dared to hope he might get them out of there before the woman arrived. He had that card she'd given him, after all. He could call her if he had to, to deal with the insurance thing.

But no such luck. She'd come early. And showed no inclination to leave right away. So *he* had left, positive she'd have the consideration to be out of there when he returned.

Wrong again. Because here she was, giving him that false, bright smile, telling him she'd be hanging around for the rest of the afternoon. And there was Annie, just lit up like a lightning bug over the idea that her new friend wanted to spend her day hanging all over her and the baby.

That soft mouth that he'd kissed started talking again. "I was thinking that since Brady's new seat is in my car, maybe Annie and the baby could go ahead and ride with me."

Annie beamed in pleasure. "That would be just fine."

It would not be fine, Cole wanted to shout. *It would not be fine at all!* But he knew what an ass he would sound like if he said that. So he didn't say it. He'd been brought up right, raised to behave like a gentleman, no matter what he felt inside. And a damn gentleman he would be.

"I'll check with the nurse, then," he said quietly. "See if they're ready to let you out of here."

Cole made arrangements to have Annie's hospital bill sent to him in Texas. Then he carried Annie's things down and put them in his pickup. That accomplished, he went back up to accompany Annie and the baby down to Melinda's car. Following the hospital's rule, Annie rode in a wheelchair, with Brady in her arms. An orderly pushed the chair. Cole and Melinda trailed along behind. Cole told himself that the way she avoided his eyes was just fine with him. He didn't want to look at her, either.

Once they reached the big ramp that led to the parking area from just beyond the wide front doors, Annie was allowed to walk. The orderly wished them well and wheeled the chair back inside.

Melinda led the way then. Cole tried not to stare at her sweetly swaying bottom as she strode between the rows of cars, her blond head high, the long, tempting muscles of her calves flexing with every step.

Naturally it took him five damn minutes to figure out how to get the car seat hooked up right. Melinda stood behind him, giving him more helpful suggestions than he needed by a long shot, as Annie cooed to the baby, who had started to cry.

"I'll get my truck and come around here, then you can follow me," he said when the thing was finally in place, immovable on the rear seat, facing toward the back.

"Oh, you don't have to do that," Melinda said. "Annie knows the way, don't you?" She looked at Annie, who was still making little croony noises at his yowling nephew.

Annie said, "Yeah. It's all right, Cole. We'll just meet you there."

He felt betrayed—by his own damn sister. And the baby would not shut up. "Fine. However you want it."

Married by Accident

Annie put Brady on her shoulder, rocked side to side and patted his back. "And don't worry if we take a while. I think I might have to nurse him before we can go."

"Can't you do that on the way?"

Brady hiccuped and wailed all the louder. Annie rubbed his back some more. "There, there, honey. It's all right. Mama's here…" Eventually she remembered to answer his question. "Oh, Cole." She shot him a pained look. "What's the point of a car seat if you don't use it?"

He really hated the obvious logic in that. It was something he should have known—would have known, if not for his screaming nephew and the woman who stood just a little off to the side, those full lips of hers smiling indulgently, her silky hair, the color of ripe wheat, blowing gently in the faint breeze.

Those full lips said, "Really, Cole. You go on ahead. We'll be fine."

What else could he do? He turned around and left them there, more relieved than he should have been to get shut of all three of them, for a little while at least.

As soon as Cole was gone, Melinda settled Annie and the baby in the front seat and opened all the windows, so they wouldn't be too hot. Annie unbuttoned her shirt and pushed the cup of her bra down beneath her round, swollen breast. Melinda went around and slid into the driver's seat as Brady latched on like the hungry baby he was. He sighed and let out little snorting noises that made both Melinda and Annie grin.

"I think we're learnin' how to do this," Annie said.

"It looks like it to me."

"I should probably put him on the other side, too," Annie said apologetically after Brady had nursed for several minutes.

Melinda nodded. "Definitely. And there's no hurry." She

thought of Cole as she said that. He'd seemed so impatient when he left them. He probably wouldn't appreciate waiting too long at Annie's for them to show up. But it couldn't be helped. The baby came first. "Just take your time."

Another fifteen minutes had gone by before they had Brady strapped safely into his seat and started on their way. Ten minutes after that, they arrived at Annie's East Hollywood apartment.

"Oh, look," Annie said. "We got lucky. There's a free space right there, just in front of the walk."

Melinda parallel-parked, pulling up and then swinging back against the curb, next to the cracked and broken sidewalk. She glanced out Annie's window and saw what would probably be called a "garden apartment," a pair of long, stucco structures perpendicular to the street. A narrow courtyard ran between, with a concrete walk and little plots of white rock and century plants flanking each front step. At the rear of the walk, a two-story building faced the street.

Annie saw the direction of her gaze. "Movie stars used to stay here, back in the twenties and thirties, can you believe it?"

Melinda couldn't. The place had a very Hollywood, *Day of the Locusts* sort of charm. But it hardly seemed suitable to house the rich and famous.

Annie read her doubtful look. "I'm serious. Clark Gable and Carol Lombard, Jean Harlow…you name it. They stayed in my apartment building when they worked at Paramount. Because they built these apartments as trailers, so the stars could come and rest in them when they were working on the lot. Jimmy told me that." Her voice lost its brightness as she said her husband's name. "He learned it from the manager, Mrs. Lucas." Annie sighed. "Mrs. Lucas really liked Jimmy. He used to help her out sometimes, you know, when she needed a handyman around the place?" She was twisting her wedding ring as she spoke.

Melinda reached across the console and put her hand over Annie's. The twisting stopped beneath her palm. "You miss him. A lot."

"Oh, Melinda. It's like an aching, down inside me. Always there. Sometimes I can ignore it. But then something reminds me of him, and I know it will never, ever really go away—not until he comes back to me."

Melinda might have said, You think that's bad? Wait until it *does* go away, and you're left with only emptiness….

But what possible good could there be in a comment like that? She gave her friend's hand a squeeze. "Come on. Let's go inside."

Cole stuck his head out of the door of the second apartment on the right as Annie led the way up the walk. "I was beginning to wonder if you'd managed to get yourselves into another wreck."

"Nope," Annie said. "Here we are all safe and sound."

Cole's tense face eased as he looked at his sister with her sleeping son cradled in her arms. But then he glanced past her and saw Melinda. The indulgent look vanished. "Where's your car?"

Melinda turned and pointed. "Right there, in front of the building."

"I'll go get the car seat and that other stuff you bought and be right back. Give me your keys." Melinda handed them over. He left the door open for them and went past them, down the walk.

Annie led the way inside. The apartment was a single. The bed took up half the room. The baby's crib and bureau/changing table—both obviously new and inexpensive—consumed a good deal of the remaining space. There was a door on the right, no doubt to the bathroom, and a curtained arch near the bed that must have masked a closet. The tiny kitchen could be reached through an open doorway to the left of the curtained arch. A glance in there showed Melinda a section of counter, a sink—and a small window that looked across a driveway at the side of the building next door.

Cole had already brought Annie's things in from the pickup. Her suitcase sat by the closet curtain. He'd put the floppy-eared bunny in the crib and set the bouquet on a little table by the door.

"It's not much, but it's home," Annie said too brightly.

Is it really? Melinda wanted to ask. Oh, Annie, do you even have a car? L.A. isn't cheap. Cole will have to go back to Texas soon, won't he? And how will you manage here with no husband to provide for you, no family nearby and a new-born to care for?

Annie seemed to hear the hard questions, though Melinda hadn't voiced them. She spoke firmly, tilting her chin bravely upward. "Don't you go worryin'. I'm tougher than I look right now. I still have a little money. Jimmy left me everything we had. And honestly, I do know him. I know him to his soul. He'll come back. And when he does, we'll be here."

Melinda couldn't help herself. She protested, "But yesterday, you told me you really did want to go back to Texas."

"Well, I can't. It would just kill my dad, to see me this way, with a baby and no husband in sight."

"You can't be sure of that."

"I'm sure enough—and here's Cole. I can't wait to really get a look at what else you went and bought for Brady." She put the baby on her shoulder, opened the door and stepped back for Cole to enter. "Just put the car seat over there. And lay everything else on the bed."

His face a grim mask, Cole followed his sister's instructions, pausing only to toss Melinda her car keys. Annie changed Brady's diaper and put him in his crib. Then she *oohed* and *ahhed* over the little shirts and the soft receiving blankets, the tiny booties and rompers that Melinda had found during her shopping spree.

"I suppose I ought to wash all these before I use them," Annie said.

Melinda agreed that was a good idea. New clothing was usually treated with sizing, and that could be irritating to a baby's skin. "I'll just take it all back to my house, why don't I? I'll run them through my washer and—"

Cole interrupted her. "There's a coin laundry in back. I'll wash them there."

"But I really don't mind at all."

"Forget it," he said flatly. "It's no problem to do it here."

"Cole's right," Annie said. "It'll be easy for us to wash them." She grinned. "And if you're lookin' for an excuse to come back and see me, well, you know you don't need one. I want you here anytime you get the urge to drop by."

The invitation pleased Melinda. Immensely. "Good." She did not let herself glance at Cole, who was lurking over by the doorway to the kitchen—with a scowl on his face, she had no doubt. "I have an idea," she said. "Let me take everything back to the coin laundry right now and get it started. Then you'll be able to use them as soon as you need them."

"Oh, Melinda. You don't have to—"

"I want to. You have Dreft, don't you? I think it's the best, for the baby's things."

"You sure seem to know a lot about what's best for a baby," Cole said. It sounded like an accusation.

Both women shot him a what-is-your-problem? glance. He shrugged and went through the open doorway to the kitchen, where he immediately began opening cupboard doors, looking in and shutting them harder than he needed to.

Annie answered Melinda's earlier question as if her brother had never interrupted them. "Of course I have Dreft."

Melinda began gathering up the baby clothes. "Then I'll just go ahead and—"

"Annie." In the kitchen, Cole shoved the refrigerator door shut with his boot. "You need milk and eggs. I'm gonna have to make a trip to the grocery store."

Annie just glared at him. He glared back for a moment, then turned on his heel. He strode right past the two women and went out the door.

Annie started apologizing the minute he was gone. "I'm so sorry. He's not usually like that. You saw how sweet he was yesterday. But he...well, he needs to get back home. Our dad's not well, like I said. And there's also the veterinary hospital to worry about. He's got two other vets who work with him, but they can't cover for him forever. And he's just so *stubborn*. He won't believe me when I tell him I'll be just fine here."

Melinda didn't feel at all sure that Annie would be just fine. Also, she knew very well that there was more to Cole's sudden rudeness than his pressing need to get back to Texas.

Annie hung her head. "He's really on edge. Yesterday, before the accident... Well, the truth is, we were arguin'. About me not coming home with him. Cole probably wasn't paying as much attention to the road as he should have been."

Melinda dropped the pile of baby things and sat on the bed next to her friend. "Oh, Annie. Don't you know you should never tell the other party in an accident that it wasn't their fault?"

Annie shot her a sideways glance. "Of course I know that. I'm not a total rube."

Melinda laughed. "You? A rube? Not on your life."

"But I know I can trust you, Melinda. I know I can tell you anything."

Melinda closed her eyes, thinking how good it felt, to hear Annie say those words. Sometimes she felt as if nobody had ever truly counted on her, *trusted* her in the important ways. "Thank you."

Right then, more than anything she really wanted to tell Annie about what had happened between herself and Cole.

But no. Annie had enough problems. She didn't need to hear about how her friend had kissed her big brother passionately—and then asked him to leave. Besides, she doubted that Cole would appreciate her carrying such tales.

Melinda leaned closer to Annie. The saggy mattress gave even more, and their shoulders touched. "Guess what?" Melinda said. "About the accident?"

"What?"

"I wasn't paying as much attention as I should have been, either."

"You're pullin' my leg."

"No. I was talking to myself. Telling myself how I was going to wow Evelyn Erikson with my carload of gorgeous lingerie."

Annie giggled then. "But instead, you got in a wreck. And Evelyn Erikson was not wowed."

"Right. She was not wowed at all. Isn't it funny how life never turns out the way you planned?"

Annie was looking directly at Melinda now, her expression determined. "Listen. I'll talk to Cole. I'll tell him he can't take his frustration out on you."

"Oh, no," Melinda said too quickly, "Don't do that…"

"But why not?"

She backpedaled—believably, she hoped. "It's…been a tough couple of days. I think it's better if we just let bygones be bygones."

"You're sure?"

"I'm positive." She stood and scooped up the pile of blankets and baby clothes again. "Now, lead me to that box of Dreft. I want to get the laundry started."

* * *

It took an hour and a half to wash the clothes and fold them and put them neatly away in the bureau beneath the changing table. By then, Brady was awake again. Annie fed him and Melinda changed him and then just held him for a while. She and Annie talked, sharing what they knew about a baby's care, laughing together, enjoying each other's company.

Cole had not returned by four-thirty. Melinda wondered aloud what might have held him up. He'd been gone for two full hours. Annie said he'd probably made a stop at his motel.

"His motel?"

"Mm-hmm. There just wasn't much room for him here, since the place is so small, so he's staying at a motel. He'll be back soon enough. And in a better mood than when he left, believe me."

In her heart, Melinda knew what was keeping him. He was waiting. Giving her plenty of time to get lost.

She understood. There was something hard and hungry that crackled in the air between them now. Oh, she should never have kissed him. She'd been wrong to do that. And he was justifiably angry with her for leading him on, then telling him no.

And it really was time that she left. With some regret, she handed Brady to Annie. "I think I'd better be on my way now."

"Come back," Annie said. "Soon."

"I will. I promise." She took a Forever Eve card from her purse, and wrote her own address and phone numbers on the back. "There." She set the card on the little table by the blue-and-yellow bouquet. "You've got all my numbers now, even my cell phone—if I ever find the darn thing. You call me, if there's anything at all I can help with."

"I will. And I'm in the phone book. Under Logan. James Logan. Call me, too. If you need me, I'll be there." Annie let out one of her cute little giggles. "'Course, you might have to wait a while before I show up, since Brady and I will be hopping a bus. But we'll get there if you need us."

"I know you will."

"See you. Soon."

Melinda thought of Cole again, of how she owed it to him to stay out of his way now. But what about Annie? She felt so connected, to Annie—and to her baby. Annie really did need her. And maybe, the truth was, she needed Annie, too.

"Yes," she said. "Soon."

At five o'clock, when Cole pulled into the driveway on the way to the carport behind Annie's apartment, he noticed that Melinda's rental car was gone.

Good, he thought with grim satisfaction. He'd managed to stay away long enough this time. With a little luck, she'd have had her fill of playing Good Samaritan to his sister. She'd go back to peddling sexy underwear to ill-bred Hollywood stars and they wouldn't have to deal with her again.

He parked in the back and carried the bags of groceries inside, making two trips, since he'd picked up quite a bit of food. When he let himself into the apartment, Annie was sitting with Brady in the beat-up wooden rocker near the bed. She didn't say a word to him as he went back and forth, bringing everything in. He could see by the pursed shape of her mouth that she was annoyed with him. Probably for not being nice enough to the spoiled little rich girl she considered her friend.

He was putting it all away when he heard the rocker give a long creak as she got up from it. She came and stood behind him, with the baby on her shoulder.

"I can do that, Cole."

"It's no problem." He put a big box of Quaker Oats in the cupboard, and then a bag of flour and one of sugar, too.

She was looking at all the grocery bags crowded on the little kitchen table. "That's a lot of food. How much was it?"

"Don't worry about it." He put away a box of Ritz crackers and a jar of crunchy peanut butter. Annie had always loved her Ritz and peanut butter.

"But I *do* worry about it. You've paid for everything since you've been here. And I know you told them at the hospital to send you the bill."

He stopped, turned to her fully. "I said not to worry."

She put her hand on the baby's back—rubbing—and kept her voice low, though there was anger in it. "Well, just because you said it doesn't mean I won't do it."

Some devil must have been in him. He heard himself say, "You fight your own brother when he's helping out, but you'll let some stranger spend a bundle on you and all you got to say is Gee thanks."

Her mouth pursed up tight again. "Melinda is no stranger. Somethin' special has happened between her and me."

He let out a disgusted grunt. "Oh, come on. Don't be a fool. You only met her yesterday."

"It doesn't matter when I met her. She's my friend. I know what's in her heart. And she can see inside mine. That's precious and rare, and not foolish at all. And I don't know why you suddenly decided to be mean to her. You seemed to like her real well yesterday."

I *still* like her real well, some idiot's voice in the back of his mind whispered. I like her too damn well. "I've got nothin' against her." It was a lie, but he said it anyway. "I just don't want her buttin' in to your life."

"She's not buttin' in." Annie let out a small cry. "Oh, I don't know what's got into you. Melinda made me promise not to say anything to you. She said to let bygones be bygones, but—"

"Oh, so she was talkin' about me, was she?"

"No, she was not. *I* was the one talkin' about you. I was apologizing. For my rude brother. And she said—"

"I don't need to hear what she said. It doesn't matter."

"It *does* matter."

"Forget about it."

She shifted the baby to her other shoulder, and gave him a look he didn't like at all. "Cole. Did something…happen, between you and her, when you took her home last night?"

He got busy unloading the bags again. "No, nothing happened," he lied some more. "Not a thing."

"Then why were you so rude to her?"

He bent to open the low refrigerator, tossed in a carton of milk and shoved it closed, rising to his full height once again. "Look. I'm sorry, okay? Let's just do what that friend of yours suggested, huh? Let bygones be bygones. Now, put the baby down and then lie down yourself. You look like you're about to fall over. Get some rest. I'll put some supper together and—"

"When she comes to see me again, if you're still here, I want you to treat her right."

He didn't like the sound of that. Not one bit. He was counting on the woman staying away. And when he left, by God, Annie and the baby would be going with him.

"Cole. I mean it. You be nice to my friend."

He picked up a container of cottage cheese, hefted it. "Fine. If she comes around here again, I will be nice. Now will you please go lie down on that bed?"

"You *promise* you'll be nice?"

"Don't push me. I said what I'd do. So go lie down. Now."

When Melinda got back to her house, she took the number Cole had given her out of her purse and dropped it into the trash. The next morning, she called her insurance company.

Right away, the clerk asked for information about the other vehicle.

She baldly lied. "Oh, that. It was a pickup—a black one, I think."

"Did you get the number of the other insurance company?"

"The man gave it to me, but I can't find it now."

"How about a license number?"

"No. Sorry. I forgot to look."

On the other end of the line, she heard the clerk sigh. "All right, Ms. Bravo. I'll get an adjuster out to your address within the hour."

Since the car was new and expensive and the front end was still intact, the adjuster declared it worth fixing. He also warned her that her insurance rates were bound to go up. She smiled at him and said she understood. At noon, she stood in the driveway and watched another tow truck take the car away to be fixed.

She went back inside, ate lunch and read the want ads. She even circled a few that looked vaguely promising.

But she kept thinking about Annie, stuck in her tiny apartment with her baby and no easy means of transportation. For now, Cole could deal with making sure she had the things she needed. But what would happen when Cole left? Annie would need a lot of help then.

And she would have to have a stroller, Melinda thought with a smile. A really good, sturdy one, the kind that could carry the baby, his diaper bag—and a load of groceries, too....

Chapter 7

Melinda managed to hold out two more days, through the weekend, before she visited the courtyard apartment in East Hollywood again. Yes, she did go right out and buy the stroller—and she picked up a battery-run baby swing while she was at it. But she held off taking the new gifts to her friend.

After all, Cole would not appreciate her presence—or her presents. And maybe, if she waited a while, he would return to Texas. She wouldn't have to see him, to feel the tension that vibrated between them, to put up with his coldness—or her own acute awareness of him, which kept her nerves on a thin edge.

On Sunday, she scoured the big Employment section of the *Times.* And on Monday first thing, she made a few calls and arranged some interviews. The weather had turned hot, so she dressed in cool white linen and swept her hair back in a single French braid. At ten-thirty she left the house to go on two of the interviews, which were set up for eleven and one o'clock.

By two, she was back at her house, with one job offer and a "We'll get back to you." Both of the interviewers had been male. And both had spent too much time sending long, suggestive glances at her legs and her breasts. She called and turned down the one offer and hoped the "We'll get back to you," had meant what it usually did: that they wouldn't.

She took off her dress and drew a tepid bath. Then she settled into the tub and lay back, thinking of the jobs she'd had over the years. During the time she'd been in college, earning a virtually useless four-year degree in Humanities, she'd modeled a little, both print and runway. And she'd worked for an art dealer, being decorative, answering phones. During her five years with Christopher, she hadn't really worked at all. He'd called her his "assistant," which meant she typed his poems and essays, carried his papers around whenever he spoke somewhere, and told him constantly how brilliant he was.

She had dared to hope, with Forever Eve, that she might be discovering something she could do well. She'd enjoyed showing other women how to choose just the right "intimate" look for them. And even Rudy had sometimes gone along with her suggestions when it came to floor displays. Plus, he'd had no interest in making passes at his female employees, since he preferred men. That had been a big bonus, as far as Melinda was concerned.

But then along had come Evelyn Erikson. And Forever Eve was out of her professional future for good. She was back to pounding the pavement in the hot July sun, trying to find something reasonably worthwhile to do with her time.

And she was also lying here in this deep, comfortable tub

feeling sorry for herself—when she lived in a nice house, drove an expensive car and would never have to worry where her next meal was coming from.

Unlike Annie.

Melinda rested her head on the tub rim, closed her eyes and pictured Annie's sweet face in her mind. "Come back," Annie had said. "Soon." Melinda wondered how Brady was doing. And the stroller and the baby swing were just waiting, out in the garage, for her to stick them in the back of her rental car and take them where they would get some use.

It *had* been three days since she'd seen them, if she counted today. And maybe Cole would have given up on Annie and headed back to Texas by now.

But, no. Melinda couldn't make herself believe that. Three days, counting today, wouldn't be long enough for a man like him to accept the fact that his sister wasn't going anywhere until her wandering husband came home.

So he was probably still there.

And he wouldn't be glad to see her again.

But Annie would. Annie's eyes would light up and that wide, generous smile would take over her cute heart-shaped face.

And just maybe, Cole would be off somewhere, doing the shopping or running the errands or something. Melinda could hold Brady and give Annie the new and necessary baby equipment she'd bought for her. They could talk and laugh together for a little while.

Melinda climbed from the tub, dried off and put on shorts and a crop top. She reapplied her light makeup and managed to get the collapsed stroller into the trunk. The swing, unassembled and still in its big box, fit in the back seat. She slid in behind the wheel, started up the car and backed from the garage.

* * *

It worked out fine. Annie was thrilled to see her again. And Cole wasn't there.

"Did he go back to Texas, then?" Melinda asked.

Annie giggled. "Don't get your hopes up. He's still hanging around. But he's not here all the time. It gets him too crazy, stuck in one room with just me and the baby. Especially in this heat. So he went out for a while. Probably over to the motel to go for a swim. He said he'd be back by four-thirty or so."

It was almost three-thirty right then. An hour, Melinda thought. I could stay for an hour and with any luck I could be gone before he returns.

Annie tried to say no to the stroller and the swing. But Melinda didn't listen to any of that.

"You need these things and I can afford them. I want you to take them and use them. And when Brady doesn't need them anymore, I want you to pass them on, to another mother like you, who loves her baby with all of her heart and needs a little help to get by. Will you do that for me?"

"Oh, Melinda. How do you do that—make it sound like I'm the one doing a favor for you?"

"Because you are."

And right then, as they stood by the door of the too-hot apartment, with the virtually useless window air conditioner roaring away, Melinda told Annie about the baby she'd lost. "My due date was July 8," she said in a whisper.

"Oh my sweet Lord. The day Brady was born."

"Exactly. And it really does mean a lot to me, to think I can buy these things for your baby, when I never had the chance to buy them for mine. Say you understand."

And of course, Annie did.

Melinda said, "And I would appreciate it if you wouldn't tell anyone else, about my baby." She was thinking of Cole.

Somehow, the idea that he might learn about the child she'd lost bothered her. Way too much.

"Oh, Melinda. Don't you worry. I will never say a word." Annie glanced toward the crib where her sleeping son lay. And then she looked back, met Melinda's eyes.

Melinda saw that Annie knew. Of the emptiness inside her. Of the precious, singular life that never would be. Of the nights she still woke up sometimes, her pillow drenched in tears of loss.

"To lose your baby," Annie whispered, "that must be the hardest thing in the world. It's not something you would want to talk about with just anybody, or to have just anybody know. Because it is your pain, and it is your right to choose who you would share it with. I would never take it on myself to tell another soul."

Right then, Brady woke up. He stirred in the crib and let out a few pleading little cries.

Melinda looked toward the sound. "Oh. Please. May I...?"

"You go on. Hold him. He will like that so much."

So Melinda sat in the rocker with Brady for a while. At first, he lay silent, staring up at her dreamily. But then he began fussing again. Annie fed him. Melinda changed him and put him in his crib.

Annie and Melinda sat together on the bed for a while, talking. Annie admired Melinda's French braid, so Melinda braided Annie's hair in the same style. It felt so lovely, to kneel on the bed with Annie in front of her, the silky strands of Annie's fine hair sliding through her fingers as they talked and laughed and finished each other's sentences. Melinda told Annie a little about Christopher.

"He was a lot older than I am," she said. "He'd already been married. He had...I mean *has* two grown children. When I got pregnant, he wanted me to get rid of the baby. He said he'd reproduced himself twice and that was more than enough. He needed peace and quiet for his work—he's a well-known poet. And having a crying baby around would drive him right up the wall."

"So you left him?"

"Mm-hmm. And then, two months later, I lost the baby anyway."

Annie shook her head. "Well, you're lucky to get shut of a man like that, a man who didn't even want his own child."

Melinda thought of Jimmy Logan.

And of course, Annie knew. "Jimmy's not like that," she said in answer to the words Melinda had never even said. "He's just scared, and he hates himself now, for the way things have worked out. But his fear and the bad feelings he has about himself won't be enough to keep him away forever. Our love is stronger. Just wait and see."

"Oh, Annie. I hope you're right."

"I am right. Like I said, you just wait and see."

The hour passed too quickly. Melinda wanted to stay longer, but she knew it wouldn't be wise. She bent over Brady's crib one more time. He was lying on his stomach, his head turned toward Melinda. His little mouth made sucking motions, even in his sleep.

"He's so beautiful," she whispered.

Annie said, "He's my joy."

Melinda turned from the crib and gave Annie a final hug.

Outside, just as Annie shut the door behind her, Melinda saw Cole coming around the back walk from the carports. He strode right for her. And instead of turning and making for the street, she just stood there, watching him approach. He wore old, frayed cutoffs, rubber sandals and an unbuttoned shirt. His legs were muscular, hairy and tanned—like the slice of bare chest his open shirt revealed.

Something tightened under her breastbone, then went

liquid, sending heat rolling through her. It was ninety-eight degrees in the shade and suddenly it felt like a hundred and ten. His sandals made that *clip, clip, clipping* sound.

She managed to cast a glance back, at Annie's apartment. But all the curtains were drawn and the windows shut tight. No way Annie would look out and come rescue her. She would have to face those accusing hazel eyes alone—not to mention the thoroughly unwelcome sensations those eyes stirred in her.

Clip, clip, clip. And he reached her. "Hello, Melinda."

Her heart beat fast and hard, urging her to flee. But she held her ground. "Hi, Cole."

He actually smiled, a clear attempt at civility. But she could read those eyes. Those eyes did not look civil at all. "Didn't expect to see you again."

"Well. Here I am."

"Right." His gaze flicked over her. She felt like a sneak, for coming here when she knew he'd counted on her to stay away. She also felt naked, hollowed out, humming inside. He asked, "Shouldn't you be at work?"

"My job...ended rather abruptly."

He chuckled. In spite of the heat of the day and the other, stronger heat that seemed to vibrate in the air around them, that chuckle sounded as cold as an endless night at the North Pole. "Abruptly. I'll just bet."

She didn't like that cold laugh—or the hard look in his eyes. She shifted her gaze downward and found herself looking at his chest. A few beads of moisture—sweat, or perhaps water from a recent swim—glistened among the wiry hairs there.

He said her name. "Melinda." The sudden gentleness in his tone made her willing to meet his eyes again. She saw kindness in them, just like that first day. "Look. I'm sorry your job didn't work out."

"Well," she said, trying for briskness and not succeeding too well, "sometimes it happens that way."

"Yeah. Sometimes it does." The words seemed to refer to more than just a job.

She felt breathless. "I'll find something else."

"Right." He stared at her. The heat of the day, the heat between them, it all seemed to press on her. She had to work to draw air.

Up the courtyard, a door opened. An older woman came out and walked toward the back, disappearing around the side of the building.

Cole seemed to shake himself. "Well. Good luck."

"Yes. Yes, thank you. And I…really have to go."

"You have yourself a real nice day—what's left of it, anyway."

"I will. You, too." She ordered her feet to move. Then she kept her eyes forward and her head high as she walked away.

Cole went inside feeling a little softer toward Melinda. He knew she had worked damn hard at that job. And he suspected she'd lost it because of a jealous movie star.

But then he spotted a fancy new stroller and a big box with a picture of a baby swing on the front. He didn't say a word about them, but Annie must have read the disgusted glance he gave them.

"She's my friend and she's helping me. Just get used to it, Cole."

"You wouldn't need her help if you'd come on home—and what did you do to your hair? It looks just like *hers*?"

Annie glared at him.

And they had another big fight. He ended up telling her how he'd called home from the motel. How their dad and Gerda Finster—the retired nurse who had agreed to look after the old man around the clock until Cole's return—weren't getting along. How badly things were backed up at the veterinary hospital, with two vets trying to do the work of three.

Annie cried, "Then go home, for heaven's sake. Go home where you belong."

"Fine. I will. And you and Brady will come home with me."

"I'm not going anywhere!" she shouted, which woke up the baby, who started wailing. She hurried over to the crib.

Cole stood in the middle of that too-small, hot room, watching his little sister comfort her baby, thinking about his sick father and the farmers and ranchers who depended on him when ailing animals needed his care. Fury burned inside him. And a lot of that fury was directed at a tall, long-legged woman with violet eyes and wheat-colored hair who would not let him—or his sister—get on with their lives.

He swore, low and crudely, though swearing was something he'd been brought up never to do—at least not out loud.

Annie said, "Cole Yuma. Hush up with such talk."

So he stomped into the kitchen, yanked a pack of cube steaks out of the dinky refrigerator and set about fixing them something to eat.

Melinda couldn't help herself. She felt so powerfully drawn to Annie and the baby.

She came by the next day. And the day after that and the next day, as well.

It got to be something of a pattern. Melinda would job-hunt in the morning and drop by Annie's in the afternoon. For the most part, Cole made himself scarce when she visited, which suited Melinda and Annie just fine. If she and Cole did happen to meet, Melinda never felt comfortable. She would make her excuses and leave right away. He always seemed way too happy to see her go, though he managed to keep the harsh remarks to a minimum.

When Melinda and Annie were alone, Annie confided that her brother was driving her crazy. He wanted to go home and he wouldn't go without her.

"Seems like we have a fight at least once a day now. Oh, I just do not know what to do about that man."

A voice in the back of Melinda's head—probably the voice of her wiser self—urged her to advise Annie to go home with her brother. But she knew that Annie wouldn't listen. And also, there was the sad little ache that throbbed within her at the thought of Annie going. It was selfish, and she knew it. But she would miss Annie and Brady terribly if they left.

She really could talk to Annie about anything—well, *almost* anything. She had not mentioned—never would mention, actually—the forbidden kiss she'd shared with Cole, or the way her traitorous body responded whenever he was near. But she did tell her all about her childhood in the big, comfortable apartment on the Upper East Side. About the parents she had never been able to please. About her brother, the Wyoming rancher. And her older sister, the only one who'd managed to live up to their parents' expectations. Gwen was married with two children now. She wrote lovely children's stories, which she illustrated herself. The books always sold well and, most important as far as her parents were concerned, they consistently won major literary awards.

Annie said, "Well, you can't go livin' your life to make your parents happy, anyway."

"I know. But—"

"It still hurts, huh? That you can't be what they want you to be? Oh, I know what you mean. I never really knew my mom. She died when I was born. But my dad, well, he never had any big plans for me. He just wanted me to live a good, God-loving happy life—and not to run away with Jimmy Logan without even finishing high school first. I know I have let him down. But all I did was follow my heart."

And where did your heart get you? Melinda thought.

"Oh, don't look like that," Annie said. "It was the right choice that I made, I know it. It's a tough time right now. But tough times are a part of life. And just think, if I hadn't gone with Jimmy, I wouldn't have Brady. And you and me, we never would have met."

Melinda found herself wondering whether her friend was the wisest eighteen-year-old in the world—or just another deluded love-struck fool.

On Friday, the day of Melinda's sixth visit to Annie's apartment, Cole showed up when Melinda had only been there for half an hour.

He walked in with two full bags of groceries in his big arms. "Hello, Melinda," he said with careful politeness.

"Hi, Cole…" She felt the yearning his presence always inspired in her—along with a sharp irritation that he had appeared so early, interrupting the precious too-short time she and Annie could share.

He carried the bags into the kitchen. Melinda could see him in there, putting the food away. He opened the low refrigerator, stuck a carton of eggs inside—and then spotted the two parcels wrapped in white paper on the second shelf. He scooped them up, shoved the door shut and turned to glare at Melinda and Annie.

"What's this?"

Annie made an impatient clucking sound with her tongue. "Now just what does it look like?"

Melinda spoke up, making her tone even and cheerful. "I stopped in at Jurgensen's on the way over. They had some beautiful salmon. And I just could not resist picking out a couple of New York steaks. I thought you might—"

He cut her off by turning, yanking the refrigerator open again and tossing the meat back inside. He slammed the door when he shut it. And then he turned on them, glowering, shooting the dark look first at Annie and then at Melinda. "Beautiful salmon," he growled. "And a couple of New York steaks."

"Cole," Annie warned. "Don't you start in now."

Melinda stood. The companionable mood was ruined anyway. "I think maybe—"

"Right," Cole said. "It's time for you to get out."

Annie gasped. "Cole!"

Melinda remained resolutely civil. "It's all right. I really do have to go." She grabbed her purse from the little table by the door.

"Tomorrow, then?" Annie asked hopefully.

Melinda did not look at the man across the room. She smiled bravely at Annie. "Tomorrow. Of course."

Melinda called herself a coward all the way home. Poor Annie. Left alone to get into another fight with her brother— a fight that probably wouldn't have happened if not for the salmon and the steaks that Melinda had so foolishly decided Annie might enjoy.

Salmon and steak, Melinda thought, her own anger rising. What was the harm in her bringing by a little treat now and then? Cole behaved as if she'd committed some crime.

Oh, yes. Annie was so right. The man should go back to Texas where he belonged. It just wasn't good for Annie— or the baby—the way he sulked and stomped around all the time.

She decided, as she pulled her newly repaired car into her garage, that she just might have to have a little talk with him if he didn't start showing some sense about all this.

Yes, she just might.

But not for a while yet, she told herself quickly, as she started to imagine the ugly things that might be said.

No, not for a while.

Unfortunately for her, Cole Yuma had been thinking along the same lines. And the idea of a confrontation with Melinda didn't scare him one bit.

That night at a little after eight, her doorbell rang. When she went to answer, she found him standing on the front porch.

Chapter 8

"Annie doesn't know I'm here," he said. "I wanted to talk to you. Alone."

Dread tightened her stomach. She had a pretty good idea of the things he might say. And in spite of her brave thoughts that afternoon, she really did not want to hear them.

"Well. Are you going to let me in or not?"

No! she wanted to cry. I'm not letting you in. You just… go away.

But all she said was, "Yes. All right," her voice pathetically thin, as if she'd spoken without remembering to take in air first.

She stepped back. He came inside. She shut the door behind him and gestured toward the main room.

He went where she pointed. As he had once before, he strode straight to the glass doors, where he stood facing away from her, looking out through the growing twilight at the deck and the ravine.

She stared at his broad back, her dread increasing. Her palms were sweating. And her poor heart galloped as if she'd just run a marathon. She rubbed her hands together. "Do you…want a drink? Something cold or—"

He turned, the movement violent in its swiftness. "Let's skip that stuff. I didn't come here for a drink."

She pressed both hands flat against her collarbone, felt their clamminess against the bare skin above her V-necked blouse. "All right then. Why *did* you come?"

He took a step toward her. She dropped her hands to her sides and steeled herself for his approach. It didn't happen. He stopped after that single step and said in a voice that was low, hard and even, "You have got to leave my sister alone."

It was what she'd expected and she had her answer ready. "Annie doesn't want me to leave her alone."

He scowled. "Forget what she wants."

She let out a small sound of distaste. The man had such gall. "If Annie wants me to visit her, then why should I stay away?"

"Because what she *wants* isn't what matters right now. It's what she *needs* that's important. And Annie needs reasons to go home, not a rich new friend who will only make it harder for her to leave L.A."

She was not going to let him make her feel guilty. "That's absurd. I wouldn't try to hold her here."

He glanced away, muttering something harsh under his breath. And then he faced her and tried again, more gently. "Look. Annie likes you. She feels a connection to you. I understand that. You were there, beside her, like a sister, when her baby was born."

"Yes, and I only want to—"

He stopped her with a quick wave of his hand. "Let me finish. Annie's…she's like some lost pup, now that that bastard Jimmy has left her. She's hungry for someone to give her loyalty to. And you, well, you seem to need someone, too. I'm not totally blind, Melinda. I can see the way you two hold on to each other."

A sigh escaped her. "And is that so wrong?"

"No, it isn't. It's not wrong by itself. But if it keeps Annie here, when she needs to go home—"

Suddenly Melinda found she really wanted him to understand. "Cole. Honestly, I agree with you. I think she'd be much better off in that little town in Texas with you and your father. But she won't go. She wants to—"

He ran right over her. "She will go. She'll come with me. If you'll just leave her alone. If you'll stop dropping in all the time, bringing presents she shouldn't be accepting from you, giving her hope that she can make it here when you and I both know damn well she can't."

"She's not staying because of me. She's waiting for her husband. She wants to be here when he comes back."

"Oh, come on. You don't really believe that Jimmy Logan is coming back."

He had her there, and she knew it. She dropped the subject of Jimmy Logan's possible return. "But there's also your father. She is certain he won't be able to deal with—"

"He'll deal with it. He loves her more than his life. All he wants is for her to come home, where she belongs."

"No, I really think she's afraid he'll have another stroke when he—"

"Oh, yeah, she's afraid, all right. Afraid to face him, afraid to come home with a baby and with Logan long gone. She doesn't want to see the disappointment in his eyes. She's ashamed, because Dad was right. He thought Logan wasn't good enough for her—and Logan went and proved his point. But she'll live through her shame and Dad's disappointment."

"But will your *father* live through it?"

"You bet he will. He's not going to have another stroke

because she's home. In fact, he's likely to do better with her around. Annie always could handle him when no one else could. She'll see that he eats right and she'll coddle him. He'll lap it up—if I can only get her to come back where she belongs."

"But she doesn't want to go!"

Cole's lip curled into something that could only be called a snarl. "Don't give me that. Tell the truth. *You* don't want her to go."

Melinda crossed her arms over her breasts protectively— and wished she could argue that what he'd just said wasn't true.

He came toward her then, eating up the distance between them in long strides. "Face it. She's not like you, with your fancy clothes and your foreign car, born in a city, with plenty of money, knowing how to get along." He stopped not more than two feet from her. "Annie's a sweet kid from Bluebonnet—with a kid of her own to raise."

His eyes, which could be so kind, showed only hard determination now. "Leave her alone, Melinda."

But she simply couldn't do that. Couldn't turn and walk away from Annie, who needed her so. "No. I'm her friend."

"If you're her friend, then tell her to come home with me. I've been here for a week and a half. I can't hang around forever. I've got my work and a sick father to worry about back home." His eyes narrowed, grew even harder. "And what about you? You've got your own life. Don't you want to... *do* something with it? Don't you think you ought to be out lookin' for another job?"

That hit a raw nerve. "I am looking for a job, thank you."

"I can't believe you're lookin' very hard, since you show up at Annie's every day in the middle of the afternoon."

He was too close. She longed to fall back a little, regain some distance. But that would show weakness. She couldn't show weakness. She stood taller. "I *am* looking for another job. Not that it's any of your business at all."

He loomed even closer. "Just let it go, Melinda. It was an accident. An *accident* that you even met her. An accident that you ended up at the hospital with us. We've got nothing to do with your life. And you've got nothing to do with us. Just walk away."

She wanted to shout at him. At the same time, she feared she might burst into tears. She stammered, "I...I can't..."

He muttered a curse.

And all at once, she heard herself promising, "Please. I know you're right. She *should* go with you. And I'll...I'll talk to her, how would that be? I'll tell her that I think you're right. She'd be better off to go."

His face did not soften. "Don't talk, act. Stay away."

"No. No, I can't just...disappear, as if she meant nothing to me, as if we weren't friends." She couldn't bear it, being so close to him, couldn't bear all that fury and frustration directed straight at her. She gave up trying to hold her ground and attempted to take a step back, to reclaim a little space for herself.

But he didn't let her. He grabbed her arm, hard. She gasped as his cruel fingers dug into her skin. He started pushing her, shoving her toward the front door. "Fine. You say you'll talk to her, you come with me. We'll go talk to her right now."

"Don't!" She struggled against his greater strength, jerking at her own arm "You can't do this!"

But he held on. "Just come with me. Come with me now."

"Let go of me!" She gave a powerful yank and broke free. The force of her effort sent her reeling. She spun backward, regaining her balance, but barely, as she came up against a side table. The table wobbled, then righted itself, the lamp on top teetering.

"Damn you, Melinda..."

He came at her again.

She raised her right arm, brought it back and slapped him, resoundingly, across the face.

Cole froze. And then he swore again.

Melinda stared at his cheek. The shape of her hand showed clear on the skin, dead white at first, then quickly flushing angry red.

Very slowly, Cole lifted a hand and rubbed where she'd hit him.

Damn, he thought. She can pack quite a punch.

For a grim, suspended moment, they gaped at each other. Then he watched as she closed her eyes. With a small, hopeless moan, she buried her face in her hands.

Cole stared at her bent head. He felt about knee high to an inch worm right then. Never in his life had he touched a woman in rage. Where he came from, a man didn't do things like that.

"Melinda. Please. Look at me."

She dropped her hands, shuddered, drew her shoulders back.

"I'm sorry," he said. "I… Look. I shouldn't have done that, grabbed you like that…" He went on, willing her to understand, hoping she might forgive him when he damn well couldn't forgive himself. "I'm…about at the end of my rope, that's all. Annie won't budge. I hate to leave her here. But I've got to get back home."

She stared at him him, violet eyes wide and brimming with hurt. He wanted to reach for her, pull her close, cradle her against his body until she sighed and relaxed in his arms, until he was certain she understood that he would never, ever do her harm.

But who was he kidding? The minute he had her into his arms, he'd start thinking about other things than easing her fears.

And that was the problem, wasn't it? The problem they weren't talking about? The thing that hummed between them whenever he got near her. The thing he wanted to get over that she wouldn't *let* him get over, since she showed up at Annie's place every damn day.

Yeah, all right. Maybe, in some ways, he was as much of a starry-eyed fool as his baby sister. Maybe, for a long time now, he'd been waiting. For the right woman to come along.

He'd known just how she'd be, sweet and innocent. Needing him to care for her, just as he would need the comfort of her tender arms.

And maybe, the first moment he'd set eyes on Melinda Bravo, sitting there trapped in her own seat belt in her fancy wrecked red car, he'd thought, Well, here she is. And about time, too…

Maybe, if she'd been someone else, just a nice woman he'd run into because he'd been arguing with Annie and taken his eyes off the road for a split second too long—maybe, in that case, he wouldn't have been so eager to give her a ride. Maybe he would have let her go into that movie star's mansion by herself as she'd wanted to. Would have let her call a cab from the hospital. Or go on home with the tow truck driver.

If she'd been someone else, he never in a hundred years would have taken her to that coffee shop in the last hours before dawn. He wouldn't have followed her inside her house. Wouldn't have pulled her close and kissed her.

Wouldn't have made a damn fool of himself hoping for something that never could be.

And he certainly never would have ended up, as he'd been doing for days now, telling himself over and over that Melinda Bravo was everything he *didn't* want in a woman, that she was too beautiful, too rich, too sophisticated. That she hated country life. And she'd sworn off men.

If she'd been someone else who was keeping him from taking Annie home, he never would have lost his temper, never would have grabbed her, never would have ended up standing here feeling like a worm.

"Melinda. I mean it. I am truly sorry. I had no right to grab you."

She pulled herself even straighter and forced a weak smile. "You're right. You shouldn't have grabbed me. And I shouldn't have slapped you."

He watched her shoulders droop again. She looked down at the floor, let out a long, pent-up sounding breath. "I suppose your father *is* really getting worried." Her head came up again. "I suppose he's wondering what's going on, why you haven't come home?" She looked at him so pitifully, as if she wished he would lie and say his dad was just fine.

Well, he couldn't make her wish come true. He shrugged. "Annie made me swear not to say anything to him about Brady. So yeah, he's worried, all right. Worried enough that it scares me, because he *is* a sick man."

Melinda stared at him for a long time. He wished he could see what was going on inside her mind.

Were that possible, he would have felt a little better.

Because the moment had finally come when Melinda was ready to face the uncomfortable truth.

She was ready to admit to herself that she was not hanging onto Annie for Annie's sake.

No, she clung to Annie for other, more self-serving reasons.

She clung to Annie because Annie gave her acceptance and real understanding. Helping Annie and the baby made Melinda feel as if she were doing something worthwhile—when nothing else in her life right then seemed to matter much at all.

Annie said she couldn't go home—for her father's sake.

She swore the sick old man wouldn't be able to bear seeing his beloved daughter with a fatherless baby in her arms.

But Melinda didn't really believe that.

No, Cole was right. It had to be much worse for Annie's father this way, being kept in the dark, left in Texas to wonder when his son would finally come home—and what Cole would have to tell him when he did.

"What time is it?" she asked, then glanced at her watch and answered her own question. "A few minutes after nine."

Cole eyed her warily. "Why?"

"Annie should still be up, right?"

"Right."

"Then I'll follow you to her apartment."

"And do what?"

"I'll say goodbye. To your sister and that beautiful baby of hers. And I'll tell her that I think she's hurting her father a lot more by staying here than she would by going home and facing him. I'll tell her that if she *really* loves her dad, she'd better stop dragging her heels and hurry back to Texas with you."

"Oh!" Annie exclaimed when she opened the door and found her brother and Melinda standing on the walk at the foot of her front step. "What's wrong? What's happened?"

Melinda gulped. "Annie, I really need to talk to you."

Annie's doubtful glance swept from her brother to Melinda and then back to Cole again. She accused, "What have you done now, Cole Yuma?"

"More than I should have and less than I would have." He put his hand at the small of Melinda's back and gave a gentle push. Ignoring the silly thrill his touch sent shivering through her, she moved forward, up the step and into the apartment, with Cole following right behind.

He shut the door when they were inside and turned to Melinda. "Go ahead. Tell her."

Annie backed toward the kitchen. "What is going on? I don't like this one bit."

"Tell her," Cole demanded again.

Melinda shot him a fulminating glance. "I will. Just give me a—"

"Tell me what?" Annie cried. She stared at Melinda, those sweet, soft eyes pleading. "What is he talking about?"

"Annie, I…" Oh, how to say this? There was just no easy way.

And besides, Annie already knew—or at least, she seemed to have a pretty good idea. She glared at her brother. "You've been workin' on her haven't you? Harpin' at her to get her to see things your way."

"Damn it, Annie."

"Do not start cursing, Cole Yuma! Do not curse at me!"

Her cry set the baby off. He started wailing from his crib.

"Oh, see what you've done now," Annie hissed at her brother. She raced over, scooped up her child and stood there, rocking back and forth, whispering, "There, there now. It's all right, my sweet boy. It's okay, it's all right…"

Melinda turned to Cole. "Would you please just leave us alone for a little while?"

He canted his head to the side, clearly distrustful.

"Cole. Will you just go?"

"You'd better not back out on me now."

"I will do what I came here to do. Now please. Go."

He held his ground for a minute more, glancing doubtfully from one pair of accusing feminine eyes to the other. Then he backed up. He reached behind him, pulled the door open and slid out, closing it in his own face without ever turning around.

The baby had fallen silent. Annie said to the door Cole

had just escaped through, "You'd *better* not turn your back on us right now, mister." Then she caught Melinda's eye.

And Melinda couldn't help it. She laughed. Annie glared at her for a moment—and then she was laughing, too.

The baby started crying again. Their shared, slightly mad laughter faded. They looked at each other over the head of the crying child. Annie's chin trembled a little—in hurt for the things she sensed her friend had come to say.

Melinda dropped to the edge of the bed. "Oh, Annie, I—"

The baby cried louder. "Wait. Just a minute. Let me quiet him down."

So Melinda waited as Annie sat in the rocker and opened her blouse. Brady stopped wailing the minute he found his mother's breast. Annie looked down at him, a tender smile on her mouth. Then the smile faded.

She lifted her head. "Go ahead. Say it."

Somehow, Melinda forced the words out. "Annie, I…I just can't keep quiet about this any longer."

Annie grunted. "Not with my brother badgerin' you, you can't. He has some nerve sometimes, he really does. I just cannot believe the way he—"

"Annie, will you just let me say this. Please?"

Annie shifted a little, hefted the bundle at her breast, making them both more comfortable. Then she blew out a breath. "Oh, all right. Shoot."

Melinda stared at her friend. "I…you have to know, it's meant so much to me, to know you. And Brady. It's…well, it's made the loss of my own baby a little easier to live with, to have you to talk to, to see you with Brady, to know that I helped a little, when he was born."

"You helped a *lot*," Annie said in a tight voice. "You made it so I could bear it. And more than just gettin' through Brady's bein' born. You've made it so I can bear the way things are right now. So I can—"

"That's it," Melinda said sadly. "That's just my point."

Annie blinked a tear away. "What? I don't understand."

"Oh, Annie, if I weren't here, if you hadn't met me, if there wasn't this…special friendship between us, you would have been on your way back to Texas by now."

"No." Annie's mouth drew into a tight knot. "I would not. I told you. I *can't* go back. My dad—"

"Your dad will probably be very upset with you," Melinda cut in quietly. "But he will accept you. And he'll accept Brady. You know he will. I can see it in your eyes. You just… hate to face him. You're *afraid* to face him. I understand that."

"No, I—"

"Annie, you are hurting your father more by staying away than you could ever hurt him by letting him see that things haven't worked out the way you wanted them to."

"You don't know my dad."

"I don't have to know your dad. I know you. And that obstinate brother of yours. I know that your father raised two very fine, loving children. To do that, he would have to be a fine man himself."

"It will break his heart."

"Annie. *This.* Your staying here, keeping Cole here, leaving your father to wonder what might have happened to you— *this* is what will break his heart."

Annie held her baby closer. She blinked—and twin tears escaped the dam of her lids to trail down her soft cheeks. "Oh, Melinda…"

Melinda stood. "Go home, Annie. Go home right away. Don't cause your poor father any more pain than he's already suffered, worrying about you, wondering if you're all right." She went to the door. "I…I can't come here anymore, Annie. I just wouldn't be your friend if I did."

Annie choked on a sob. "Cole made you say that. He did, didn't he?"

"No, Annie. He wanted me to say that. But he could never *make* me. I'm saying it because it's the right thing to do. I'm saying it because you have a home, and people who love you. And because you need to be with them now—just as they need to be with you and Brady." She reached for the door.

Annie said, "Wait."

Melinda sighed. "Oh, Annie."

"No wait. Just listen. You're right. I *am* a big coward. I don't want to face my dad. But I will. I will do it."

Melinda nodded. "Good. I'm glad."

"There's an 'if.'"

Melinda frowned. "Excuse me?"

"I'll do it—if you'll come to Bluebonnet with us."

Melinda gaped at her friend. Then she groaned. "Oh, Annie. That's crazy."

"Why? Why is it crazy?"

"Well, I can't just…take off for Texas."

"Why not?"

"Well, because. I—"

"You could. You could do it."

"No, I—"

"You don't have a job right now—and you said yourself you don't have to find one right away. And maybe a visit to Bluebonnet would be good for you. You would like the folks there, I know you would. Maybe a little change might help you, too. You might see your life in a whole new light."

"Oh, Annie. Running off to Texas isn't going to help me."

"You can't be sure unless you try it. And anyway, even if it doesn't do much for you, it would mean everything to me. You're my friend. And I *need* you right now. Just for a while, please? Just for a week or two. Because I *am* a coward and I need a friend beside me, to help me face my father. I need—"

"Annie. Stop. No."

Annie's mouth went tight again. "I mean it. I won't go. I won't go without you. And that's that."

"You're being foolish."

"Maybe so. But unless you come with us, I'm stayin' right here."

Chapter 9

Melinda went home certain that she had done the right thing. Somehow, she got through the weekend that followed, though her mother called on Sunday morning, depressing her further. Elaine and Melinda's father, Austin, had run into Christopher at the home of a mutual friend.

"Just a little dinner party," Elaine said. "Good food, enlightening conversation. Your father and I enjoyed ourselves immensely."

"I'm glad to hear that, Mother."

"Poor Christopher. He looked a bit…at loose ends. Of course, he brought a date. Just a friend, though, he said."

"Mother, could we talk about something other than Christopher, please?"

"I'm almost finished. What I wanted to tell you is, he *asked* about you. And he gave us a copy of his latest book of poems—signed, of course. Melinda. The book is dedicated to you. 'To My Linda, my beautiful one. My only love…' Terribly touching, I have to say. I really do believe he realizes he made a big mistake in letting you go and he can't help but hope that things might still work out between you. And your father and I agree that, if he were willing to make a firm commitment this time—and I do believe that marriage might be in the offing, I sincerely do. If that were the case, don't you think it would be the best thing that could possibly—"

"Mother, it is over between Christopher and me. Please accept that."

"Oh, Melinda. When are you going to stop this foolishness? Yes, you lost a child. And it was a difficult, painful experience, I'm sure. But it's been several months now. You need to put it behind you and reclaim your life."

"That is exactly what I'm trying to do."

Elaine pretended her daughter had not even spoken. "Your relationship with Christopher once meant everything to you."

That was way too true. Once, she had thought that her love for Christopher made her life worthwhile. She had considered herself the woman behind the man, told herself that loving Christopher, *supporting* him in his work made up for her otherwise lackluster performance in the arena called life. Her parents had seemed to think so, too.

Her mother said, "I'm trying to tell you that you could have all that back again."

"I don't *want* it back again. I truly do not."

"You say that because Christopher hurt you deeply and it's difficult to forgive."

"No, I say it because it's true. I do not want Christopher back. It turned out that we—wanted different things out of life. I've accepted that fact. And I wish you would, too."

"But you don't even *know* what you want."

"I know what I *don't* want. And that's Christopher Blayne."

"Well," her mother said. "If that's how you honestly feel…"

"It is."

"Then couldn't you at least return home to live? You could come to us, here in the Hamptons, for the rest of the summer. And then, in the fall, we could find you something in the city, some *meaningful* work you might do. Your father has a colleague in the history department who's looking for someone to—"

"Mother. I'm not coming back to New York."

"Oh, you're beginning to sound just like your brother."

She found herself wondering, What's so bad about that? She asked her mother as much. "Zach knew what he wanted out of life—and he got it. What's wrong with that?"

"I am merely referring to the fact that he never would do what we felt was best for him."

"He made his own choices, Mother. I think that's admirable."

"Well. I suppose one could look at it that way. And, over the years, we have come to accept the choices your brother has made. But yours is a different situation entirely. You haven't run *to* Los Angeles. You've run *away*—from your own disappointments."

"Maybe I have. And I'm not coming back. I'm making a new life and that's all there is to it."

"But what possible satisfaction can you find, all the way out there on the West Coast, selling *lingerie* to movie people, for heaven's sake?"

Melinda considered and rejected the idea of telling her mother that she'd left Forever Eve. Such news would only add fuel to Elaine Bravo's fire. "I'm doing quite well, Mother. And I have no plans to return to New York."

"We think you're foolish."

"Oh. Well, I get that. Loud and clear."

"Sarcasm, Melinda, is the refuge of a defensive heart— and the tool of a small mind."

"I do feel defensive about this, Mother. And I've always known you never considered me particularly bright."

"I *know* you're bright. What has always bothered me is your unwillingness to put your intelligence to good use."

"I'm almost thirty. I think it's time I got to decide for myself how I want to use my own mind."

"Oh, lately, it seems I just cannot get through to you."

"That makes us about even then, wouldn't you say?"

"Why this hostility? Did I ask for this?"

"Mother, I am not moving back to New York. And I'm certainly not ever getting near Christopher Blayne again. As soon as you and Father accept that, you will find that my hostility will greatly diminish. Am I making myself clear?"

"Poignantly so."

"Then could we please talk about something else?"

After that, the tone of the conversation improved somewhat, but Melinda still hung up feeling lower than before—and thinking about Annie. Hoping she'd given in to Cole's demands and agreed to go home. And perhaps understanding a little better Annie's final plea that Melinda come with her, to stand by her, if things got too tough with her father.

After dealing with her mother, Melinda wouldn't have minded a little support from Annie about now.

She actually smiled, thinking of the things Annie might say, if Melinda described the conversation with Elaine. Things like, "It's your life and you gotta live it yourself," and "That man dedicated some *poems* to you? What is the matter with him? He turns his back on his baby, and then he goes out and writes some *poems* and thinks that's gonna make up for what he went and did?"

Oh, yes, a little support from Annie would have been lovely right then.

But she couldn't talk to Annie—and she had accepted that.

Melinda got out the Sunday *Times*, turned to the Employment section, and went to work with her red felt pen.

Then later, since the heat wave had broken and it was a bright and balmy eighty degrees out, she packed up a picnic lunch and drove to Griffith Park, where she walked the nature trails and spread a blanket on the grass beneath an oak tree to enjoy her lunch. It really was a pleasant, if somewhat lonely, afternoon.

She returned to her house about four.

And Cole's pickup was waiting at the curb.

She could see him, sitting there on the step.

She parked in the driveway and got out. Ignoring the leap of her pulse and the witless feeling of lightness the sight of him inspired in her, she marched up the walk to see what was wrong now.

He got up as she came toward him and took off his hat. "I've gotta talk to you."

She led him inside. He tossed his hat on a chair, but seemed too full of impatient energy to have a seat himself.

"I've been yellin' at my sister for two days straight," he said. "And she's been yellin' right back at me. The baby's been screaming."

"She still won't go with you?"

"No. Not unless you come along." He looked down at his boots, and then back up at her. The mute appeal in his eyes struck her like a physical blow.

She backed up a step. "No. Wait a minute. You were the one who wanted me out of her life. You were the one who said—"

"Listen. I know what I said." He looked infinitely weary. "But I've argued with her until we're both sick at heart. And she won't budge. She'll only go home if you go with her. So I am to the point that could be called desperate now. And I am willin' to do anything—*anything*—to get us back where we belong. If there is crow to eat, I'll chew it raw. Just help me out here, Melinda. Help me to get my baby sister back home."

Melinda called her mother that night to explain that she'd made some new friends and was going to Texas to visit them for a week or two.

"*Texas?* Melinda. I don't understand. What about that job of yours?"

"I… Actually, I quit my job."

"Oh, Melinda."

"Mother. Don't worry."

"How can I help it? If you would only—"

"Mother, please. I'm going to Texas and I'll be back in two weeks at the most."

"But *why?* And who are these new *friends* of yours?"

"It's hard to explain. But they are very nice people. I…ran into them by accident and… Oh, I really don't want to go into it now."

"But—"

"I promise, there is nothing for you to be concerned about. I just wanted you to know where I was. I'm taking a little vacation, that's all. To see the Texas Hill Country. It's supposed to be quite beautiful there."

"Nothing to be concerned about? How can you say that?"

There was more in that vein. Melinda bore it as long as she could. Then she gave her mother the address and phone number Cole had provided for the house in Bluebonnet. She asked Elaine to call only in case of emergency and promised to get in touch again as soon as she returned to L.A.

They left for Bluebonnet on Tuesday. Cole drove his pickup, of course. And Melinda drove her BMW.

At first, Melinda had tried to suggest that she might fly—

and that Annie and the baby could fly with her. But Annie said she was nervous about taking Brady on a plane.

"He's not even two weeks old," she said. "When he gets up that high, his ears just might *explode* from the pressure—or something."

"Annie, the cabin of a jet is pressurized. There's nothing to worry about."

"Then how come all those baby books recommend that I wait till he's older?"

"Annie, I know what you're up to. It's just another stall tactic, to put off dealing with your father for a few days."

Annie's face flushed a charming pink. "You're right. I admit it. I am a stone coward, and I hate to face my fate. But Brady and me, we're takin' the highway, like Cole. And it would just mean so much to me if you would ride along, too. Besides, you'll be glad when you get there, to have your car."

"I could rent one."

"You're not listenin'. We are going to have fun. Brady and me will switch off, you know? Ride with Cole sometimes, and then other times with you. And maybe, for a little of the trip, I could drive that cute red car of yours and you could keep me company, and tend to the baby when he fusses."

"Sounds just lovely."

"Oh come on. Don't go actin' like some big-city snob. We'll get to stay at the Holiday Inns and swim in their pools. You know you're gonna have a ball."

"I cannot wait."

"That means yes, doesn't it? You'll take your car."

"Did I ever have a choice?"

"Nope. You never did."

Annie didn't have that much to pack. Cole rented a two-wheeled U-Haul to pull behind his truck. Between the trailer and the bed of the pickup, there was plenty of room for everything.

On Tuesday morning before they left, Annie carried a letter down to Mrs. Lucas, the apartment manager, who lived in back. The letter was for Jimmy.

"This way," Annie explained with a tear in her eye, "when he comes back, he'll know where he has to go next. I truly do hate to make it harder on him. He did swear he'd never go back home. But some things, well, they just can't be helped."

Melinda doubted that Annie's runaway husband would even return to L.A.—and she saw no possibility at all that he'd show up in the small town he despised. But she didn't tell Annie that. Annie had a right to her dreams.

They left at a little before nine in the morning, Melinda in the lead, Annie and the baby riding with her. Cole followed them, ready to pull off the highway behind them whenever the baby made it necessary to stop.

They made surprisingly good time, considering Brady demanded feeding and changing just about every two hours. At seven that night, in Flagstaff, they found a big motor hotel called the Vacation Inn. It had a huge pool. Annie was thrilled. Melinda watched the baby in Annie's room while Annie went for a swim.

She returned a half an hour later and insisted that Melinda enjoy a dip herself. "Oh, Melinda. You're gonna love it. They've even got a waterslide."

Actually a swim did sound like a great idea. Melinda put on a suit and threw a beach wrap over it. Then she grabbed a towel and took the elevator to the first floor.

The pool area was enclosed, with a Plexiglas dome roof. Above the dome, cotton-white clouds drifted across a slowly darkening sky. The smell of chlorine thickened the air and children shouted and laughed as they splashed in the water and rocketed down the high, twisting blue slide.

Cole was there. Melinda spotted him right away, sitting several yards from poolside in a patio chair, next to a round glass-topped table. He saw her, too. And he smiled.

Melinda smiled back, warmth spreading through her, thinking how nice he'd been since she'd agreed to help him get Annie to Bluebonnet. Yes, that unnerving physical attraction remained, keeping her just a tiny bit off balance whenever he was near. But he spoke to her gently now. He let his natural kindness show. She even dared to hope that in his gratitude for her aid with Annie, he'd forgiven her for a kiss full of promises that never should have happened—and the unequivocal rejection that had followed right after.

In the shallow end of the pool, not far from where Melinda stood, a group of kids were playing keep-away with a beach ball. Water splashed high. Melinda laughed and jumped back as the cool drops hit her.

From his patio chair, Cole laughed, too. Then he waved her over.

A sudden ridiculous shyness claimed her. Why, she might have been thirteen again, in the throes of her first mad crush on a certain literary novelist her parents had admired and sponsored. The novelist was a painfully thin fellow, a young genius of twenty-two, with haunted eyes and jaundiced skin. Every time Melinda saw him, she would be stricken with such a torrent of overwhelming unfulfilled longing, that she just couldn't bear it. She would turn and flee. She'd hidden from her own adolescent yearning in coat closets and in bathrooms, under stairwells and in empty lecture rooms. As far as she knew, the young genius had never even realized the desperate passion he'd inspired.

Adolescent. Yes. That was exactly what she felt like around Cole Yuma too much of the time. Full of hungers and longings she could neither understand, nor trust herself to control. Just like the confused and lovesick teenager she'd once been, she only wanted to turn and run.

But adulthood brought with it certain responsibilities. An adult didn't hide in a coat closet to get away from feelings she feared she couldn't handle. An adult pulled her shoulders back and tipped her chin at a confident angle and marched right over to the object of her persistent and thoroughly exasperating infatuation.

An adult said things like, "Annie insisted that I come for a swim."

And got answers like, "Well, the water's great."

An adult tried not to stare at a man's tanned and muscular shoulders, not to allow herself to become fascinated by a pair of strong legs and well-formed masculine feet. An adult set her towel down on the pebbled glass of the patio table and said, "I guess I'd better try it, then."

Of course, right then, an adult realized that in order to swim, she would have to remove her beach wrap, thus revealing her black lace maillot. Which, other than the high French cut at the thigh, was actually quite modest, since it was fully lined.

An adult untied the knot of her sash and felt the beach wrap fall open. An adult coolly dropped the sash on top of her folded towel and let the light fabric slide from her shoulders. She took a minute to turn, and drape the wrap over the back of her chair, to step out of her sandals and set them neatly by the table.

And when an adult glanced up and caught the quick flare of heat in a certain man's eyes, she knew how to pretend she hadn't seen that flare at all.

"Coming in?"

Cole grinned. "You gonna try the slide?"

Melinda shrugged. "Annie told me I'd better."

"She's a tyrant, that sister of mine."

"But a sweet one."

He grunted. "Most of the time." The hard muscles in the thighs she wasn't looking at flexed as he stood. "Come on. Let's hit that slide."

They rode down three times, waiting on line first, slicking the water off their hair and trying not to look too long into each other's eyes.

All three times, Melinda rode down first and Cole followed right after. It really was fun. The slide had four whirling turns and then a long run at the finish, so riders shot like rockets across the water before landing with a huge, loud splash several yards out.

Each time, Melinda would wait after her own ride, safely to the side but still in the water, to watch Cole go twisting down, bathed in swirling water, and come flying off the end. Then they'd climb from the pool together and line up again.

After the third ride, the line had become quite long.

Cole lifted a wet eyebrow at her. "Had enough?"

"I think that will do it."

He went back to the patio table. Melinda swam a few laps in the area beyond the slide, where she wouldn't be hit by anyone shooting off the end. Then she climbed out and joined him.

"It's past eight," he said as she dried off and they both pretended he wasn't watching her do it. "We'd better start thinking about getting something to eat and hitting the sack. Tomorrow, I'd like to get going good and early."

"Fine with me." She tossed the towel on the table and bent to the side to gently wring the water from the ends of her hair.

His gaze lingered, warm and lazy, on her hands, her wet hair, her face, her shoulders. Then he seemed to catch himself. He glanced away, toward the pool. "I saw a pizza place while we were coming in." He looked back at her again, with guarded eyes and a carefully friendly smile. "You like pizza all right? Maybe with sausage and pepperoni?"

"How about a special? Have them throw everything on it?"

"Sure. A special. Why not? But I'm warnin' you. We'll have to watch Annie pick off the green peppers."

"Oh, well if Annie doesn't like a special—"

"Hey. I love my sister, but she can't always have everything just the way she likes it."

Melinda thought of Jimmy Logan. "Come on. Not everything goes Annie's way."

"That's true. She only has absolute power over you and me—and my dad, sad to say. He can't refuse her anything. But in this case, she's gonna have to pick the peppers off. Because I like a special, too." He pushed himself from the chair. "I'll go get dressed, give the pizza place a call and head over there to pick it up. I'd say…forty-five minutes? In Annie's room?"

"I'll be there."

"Oh, yuck," Annie groaned. "You went and got us a special."

Cole laughed. "Melinda begged me."

"I most certainly did not beg," Melinda announced with great dignity. "I…requested one with everything on it."

"And naturally Cole just jumped at the chance."

The three of them sat on the bed around the open pizza box while Brady lay in the soft-sided portable playpen Melinda had bought him the day before.

Annie began working over a couple of the slices, taking off peppers—and mushrooms and onions, too. She stacked the vegetables neatly in the corner of the pizza box.

Cole slanted Melinda a grim look. "Don't watch her. It will

only make you want to lecture her about her manners. And if you do, she'll ignore you. And that'll bug you no end."

Annie wiped her fingers on a napkin, then slapped her brother lightly on the arm. "Oh, you just stop."

Melinda pulled a big slice free, slid a napkin beneath it, took a bite, chewed and swallowed. "Mmm. Wonderful. The peppers are particularly good, don't you think, Cole?"

"Yeah, and the onions…the best."

"Not to mention the mushrooms."

Annie ignored them. She continued carefully picking off the offending ingredients until nothing but sauce, cheese and meat remained.

Once they'd polished off the pizza, they just sat around for a while, finishing the tall iced soft drinks Cole had brought them to go with the meal. Annie had taken a handful of star mints from the big bowl at the hotel's front desk. She offered to share and they each took a few.

"You two better have a mint," Annie taunted. "After all those yucky onions you ate."

"Mmm," Melinda teased back. "Onions. Green peppers. Don't get me started."

So Annie swatted *her* arm and ordered, "You just stop."

Then Cole said, "We're gonna make it to Amarillo tomorrow. That's over six hundred miles. With the way you women have to stop every ten minutes—"

"Cole," Annie chided. "We do not stop that often—but we do have a baby to worry about."

"Exactly. So we'd better leave by six a.m. We'll be lucky to get to Amarillo by six at night—and give ourselves a little wind-down time. Then, on Thursday, we can probably make it home by late afternoon."

"Home," Annie said softly.

"That's right." Cole reached out and ruffled Annie's hair. "Home."

Watching them, Melinda thought of her own big brother, Zach. Over the years, she'd lost touch with him. They still shared phone calls at holidays and such. But those were always brief, rather awkward conversations. She would ask, "How have you been?" And he would answer, "Well, I'm just fine…"

Had there ever been a time when Zach had ruffled her hair? She couldn't recall. Zach was so much like Cole, really. A quiet, steady strength seemed to emanate from him, the same as from Cole.

Cole was looking at her. "Ready to turn in?"

"What? Oh. Yes, I suppose so."

They left Annie's room together and started down the hall. Cole said, "You okay? You got real quiet back there."

They'd reached the door of her room. She stopped, and so did he.

She said, "I was just thinking."

"About what?"

"My brother, Zach."

"The cattle rancher from Wyoming?"

"Mmm-hmm." She had her card key in her hand—but she didn't turn to use it.

"You were missing him?"

"Well, I…yes, I guess I was—which is pretty strange."

"Why?"

She knew she ought to say good night and leave him. But she didn't. She relaxed against the wall beside the door. "Zach and I were never that close. He was ten when I was born. And by the time he was thirteen or so, he'd managed to get our parents to let him live at the ranch in Wyoming full-time. So I never really felt as if I knew him all that well."

"But you wish you did?"

She nodded. "He's…a good man. He's married now, for the second time. They have a baby on the way—and they each have a daughter, from previous marriages. They're very happy, running the ranch together, with the kids and all the ranch hands—oh, and Edna Heller. She lives with them, too." Melinda smiled to herself.

Cole watched her, an answering smile tugging at the corners of his mouth. "Who's Edna Heller?"

"My brother thinks of her as a second mother, and so do my cousins, Nate and Cash. For years, she was the housekeeper at the ranch. But really, she and her husband, Ty, were more like part of the family than employees. Edna is...she's very feminine. Slim and pretty, you know? But she has a will of tempered steel."

"So," Cole said, "you come from country people, after all."

She corrected him pointedly. "No. I come from New York."

"Sounds to me like you come from Wyoming—by way of New York."

She shook her head. "Uh-uh. My brother's a throwback, that's all."

"And happy to be one. You also said that." His expression grew thoughtful. "If you miss your brother, maybe you ought to give him a call."

"I *do* call. Or he'll call me. At birthdays and Christmas, when one of us thinks of it. And I called and sent a gift when he and Tess got married."

"Tess. That's his new wife?"

"Mmm-hmm."

Cole's gaze wandered, from her eyes to her lips and back again. It seemed to Melinda that she could feel the gentle touch of his regard, brushing down her cheek, across her mouth, then up again, slow and sweet and warm.

He braced a hand on the door frame near her head. It felt... comfortable, and exciting at the same time, just to stand there in the hall of that Vacation Inn, letting Cole's gaze caress her as she told him about her family. The scent of him teased her. He smelled of a recent shower, and of star mints, and something enticing and hard to define that was only him.

"Any other brothers?"

She shook her head. "But I do have a sister. She's two years older than I am. Gwen. The perfect one."

"Well now, Melinda." His caressing gaze teased her. "Didn't you know that nobody's perfect."

"Gwen is. She mastered in English Literature at Yale. She has two bright, attractive children and a wonderful husband, which means he has lots of money and the good taste never to talk about it. He runs a large architectural firm. Did I mention that Gwen also writes children's books? Well, she does. The kind of books that kids love to read and adults love to *have* their children read. She even makes her own bread. And grinds her own flour, too—the food value is so much higher that way."

He chuckled. "Gotta make sure those good-lookin' smart kids get their vitamins."

"Exactly."

His laughter faded and his eyes grew serious. "You and that sister got problems, between you?"

"No, not really. I've envied her, wished I could be more like her. But it's pretty hard to hate her, no matter how much I might want to. Because Gwen really *is* perfect. On top of all her other sterling qualities, she happens to be a very nice person."

"Just like her sister." He said the words so softly, raising the hand that wasn't braced on the door frame and brushing her under the chin—just once, so quickly she almost could have told herself he hadn't touched her at all.

But he *had* touched her. The echo of it seemed to spread out through her body in a series of slow, lovely ripples. And he was leaning so close. All she would have to do to feel his lips on hers would be to move her head forward, just an inch, maybe two...

She grasped for the escaping thread of the conversation. 'I...what?"

He seemed to have lost the thread, too. He lifted an eyebrow, made a questioning sound.

"You...oh, I remember. You said I'm nice. Just like my sister."

"Yeah," he agreed after a long, breath-held pause. "That's what I said."

He straightened, dropped his arm from the door frame and moved away a step. Was that regret she saw in his eyes?

Forbidden longing shivered through her. She wished he would come closer again, wished that he would put his face right up to hers, so she could feel his breath across her cheek. So she could move her head slightly and tell herself that it had just happened, somehow—that their lips had met and, well, what could she do, but kiss him? What could *he* do, but wrap his arms around her and pull her close to him? What could *they* do, but stand there in that hallway, kissing each other endlessly, oblivious to everything else in the world but the feel and taste of each other?

Oh, she was like a child with a book of matches, a child who knew fire was dangerous, but still quivered with anticipation as she imagined what it might be like—to flip the cardboard cover back, pull off a red-tipped stick and strike it. To cry out in naughty, forbidden delight as the bright flame exploded into life.

I am a woman who doesn't know where she's going, Melinda thought. *And the last thing I need is to start a fire on the way there.*

Cole was watching her, his eyes guarded now. "You'd better get some sleep," he said. "We're getting out of here early."

And then he turned and walked on to the door of his own room, leaving her to stare after him, wondering what might have happened if he had only stayed—and knowing she had no right to wonder any such thing.

Chapter 10

They did make it to Amarillo the next day. But it was a grueling trip. Brady fussed constantly. He seemed to have had quite enough of sitting in his safety seat. He wanted the comfort and security of his mother's arms. Around noon, they pulled into a truck stop. They switched Annie and Brady to the pickup before they left again.

That lasted about two hours. Then, near Albuquerque, Cole pulled off at a gas station. Melinda followed right behind. As soon as the pickup stopped, Annie jumped out and ran back to lean in Melinda's window.

"Seems like he's cryin' even louder, sittin' right between us…"

So they switched the baby to Melinda's car again and Melinda gave Annie a chance behind the wheel. Melinda sat in back, talking soothingly to the crying child, stroking his fuzzy head to reassure him, trying not to think about how nice it would be just to take him out of his seat and hold him close until he fell asleep.

Annie even said as much at one point. "Don't you just wish we lived back when they didn't have things like safety seats? I guess a lot more kids got killed, but you can bet they were happy and *quiet* when they died."

"Don't even think about it," Melinda advised.

"I know what you mean," Annie agreed. "It is too temptin', too temptin' by half."

Outside, the dry high desert rolled past. And inside, Brady cried. High desert turned to the rolling, drying grasses of the high plains. Brady cried on.

By late afternoon, though, the baby finally seemed to accept his fate. He fell asleep in midwail and Annie and Melinda drove along in silence, so relieved to have peace, they didn't want to ruin it, not even with a little music or some friendly conversation.

Finally, at seven-thirty that night, they reached Amarillo. They found a Holiday Inn by eight and Annie insisted on her swim. It was nearly ten by the time they ordered sandwiches from the coffee shop downstairs.

Cole ate fast and then said he was turning in. With a final warning that they'd better get to bed soon because they would be on the road by six again, he left for his own room.

He didn't ask Melinda to go with him.

She suspected that he felt the same way she did. For the two of them, a short walk down a hallway together was way too fraught with forbidden temptations. Why put themselves in situations where they had to resist?

Down the hall from Melinda and Annie, Cole let himself into his room, shoved the door shut and flopped flat on the bed with his boots on.

He laced his hands behind his head, closed his eyes—and tried not to think about Melinda.

Tried not to picture Melinda. In that black lacy bathing suit of hers, for instance. A suit that revealed way too much leg for a man's peace of mind, but pretty much covered everything else—and somehow, at the same time, seemed like it covered nothing at all.

He tried not to think about how sweet she'd been, to come along to Bluebonnet after all the grief he'd given her, just to make sure that Annie would get herself home where she belonged. About what a sport she was, taking the baby in her car most of the time, listening to him wail from Flagstaff clear to Tucumcari.

He tried not think about how her eyes had softened, going the innocent blue of a Hill Country sky in high summer, when she talked about that brother of hers and how she wished she knew him better.

He tried to remember that Melinda Bravo had money to burn, a snazzy red car and a big house in the canyons above Sunset Boulevard—not to mention a face and a body that could cause a man to forget his own name. He tried to remember that a woman like that didn't need some country vet to make her life complete.

Hadn't she told him so in no uncertain terms?

Cole lifted his head off the pillow and looked down at his boots. Time to get out of them and get under the blanket. With a grunt, he sat up and swung his feet to the floor.

As he undressed, he reminded himself all over again of all the reasons he shouldn't let himself get too near Melinda. At the same time, he couldn't help thinking that she wanted him, too. He'd seen it in her eyes. Felt in that one barn-burner of a kiss they'd shared the night Brady was born.

Maybe she wasn't suited to him in the least. And maybe

he couldn't offer her a damn thing she couldn't buy for herself ten times over.

Besides having less money than she did, he had a handicapped father he was determined to take care of at home, not to mention a little sister with a baby and no husband. He spent his days bumping around on back roads, visiting the ranches around Bluebonnet, caring for sick stock. When he wasn't out in the field, he tended smaller animals at the veterinary hospital a few hundred yards behind his house. Then at night, he went home—and took care of his dad.

How would Melinda Bravo fit in to that kind of life?

He didn't have to ponder deeply to know the answer to that: she wouldn't and wouldn't *want* to.

But he wanted her. And she wanted him.

And sometimes, when he looked at her, he couldn't help asking himself what point there was in temptation anyway, if a man didn't go ahead and give in to it now and then.

Brady was reasonably quiet the next day. He only cried when he was hungry or when his diaper needed changing.

Annie was quiet, too. She stared out the window as they drove down the middle of Texas, past endless miles of barbed wire fence behind which cattle grazed on drying grasses, and by farmlands where tall, winged irrigation pipes kept everything green. Melinda knew that her friend was thinking of her father—longing to see him, at the same time as she dreaded his reaction when he saw Brady and learned that Jimmy had left her.

They stopped at a café along the highway for lunch. Cole teased Annie a little about her long face, trying to lighten her mood. But Annie wouldn't be cheered up. She ate quickly and took Brady back to the car to feed him in private.

Once she'd left, Cole looked across the booth at Melinda and shrugged. "She'll be fine."

"Yes, of course she will." Melinda tried to inject more confidence into the statement than she actually felt right then.

"She and the baby could ride with me for a while," Cole suggested. "Somehow, they've ended up riding with you most of the way."

"I don't mind. It's nice to have someone to talk to."

"I can't believe Annie's done much talkin' today."

"She hasn't. But that's all right, too."

His gaze lingered too long, the way it had the other night, moving slowly from her mouth to her eyes and back again. "My sister's made a mistake or two in her life. But I guess she knows how to pick a friend."

"Well, I...thank you."

"If you want her to switch to the pickup for a while, you just let me know."

"I will."

Cole turned his attention back to his meal. They finished their food in silence, avoiding each other's eyes—partly because they were both a little worried about Annie. And partly for reasons neither of them found it wise to think about too deeply.

In the afternoon, as they neared their destination, Annie did begin to talk a little. She pointed out fields that would have been a sea of bluebonnets a couple of months before.

"Missed 'em this year," she said, and let out a long sigh.

Around them, the land had risen up in rocky outcroppings. Oaks grew thick on the edges of sun-baked fields where the grasses were turning gold and cattle grazed, leaving the slopes of the hills to sheep and goats. Cedars blanketed the higher places in dark evergreen, while in the canyons, the creeks nurtured willows and palmetto palms.

"It's beautiful," Melinda said.

And Annie nodded. "Most beautiful country on God's

green earth. Oh, how I have missed it…" She named the few small towns they drove through, and smiled in delight when they saw a white-tailed doe grazing with two fawns near the road. The doe lifted its graceful head and pricked up its ears, then bounded off into the trees as they drove past. The two fawns followed their mother's lead.

"The Hill Country is the white-tailed deer capital of the world," Annie announced. "You have to keep your eyes peeled. Sometimes they panic and run across the road."

They reached the town of Bluebonnet at a little after two. The sign on the road at the edge of town welcomed visitors and declared the population to be 403. They drove slowly down the curbless central street, predictably called Main, past a tiny bank and a post office, an insurance place, a grocery store—and a red phone booth that had been there so long, there was grass growing right in the open glass-topped door.

As they left the tiny town behind Annie whispered, "Oh, my sweet Lord, we're almost there…"

Five minutes later, Annie said, "Turn in. That drive right there."

Melinda obligingly swung the wheel to the left. They passed a mailbox perched on a wooden pole and a sign that read Bluebonnet Veterinary Hospital. Ahead, at the end of the unpaved driveway, a weathered two-story wood frame house waited beneath the burning ball of the afternoon sun. The house had a broad front porch shadowed by a deep porch roof and a huge pair of gnarled oaks that grew on either side of the yard.

The dirt road forked off to either side of the house, circling around to the back, where Melinda could see a long, tin-roofed structure, probably a barn, or maybe the veterinary hospital. Beyond that, at the edge of a thick grove of trees, a windmill creaked away in the sultry breeze.

There was a good-size, dusty turnaround space in front of

the house, between the giant oaks. "Just pull up right there," Annie said, her voice low and charged with some painful emotion that didn't match her casual words.

Melinda parked where Annie had pointed, next to a cute sky-blue Volkswagen Bug, which had to be twenty years old and looked like new. She turned off the engine just as Cole's pickup slid in alongside them. Right then, a tailless German shepherd with one ear and a pronounced limp lumbered down the steps, followed by a sleek gray cat.

"That's Cole's dog, Sergeant," Annie said. "The cat is a stray we adopted a few years ago. I call her Spunky." Annie turned to Melinda, her mouth stretching wide in an attempt at a smile. "Well. I guess we better go on in."

Before Melinda could reply, they both heard the front door slam.

A stocky gray-haired woman emerged from the shadows of the porch and marched down the steps. She wore a spotless blue polyester uniform and white duty shoes. There was a scowl on her florid face.

"Uh-oh," said Annie. "That's Gerda Finster. She's a practical nurse and a member of our church."

"The one who's been taking care of your father while Cole was gone?"

"Mmm-hmm. And she doesn't look happy."

Cole had already jumped from the pickup. The dog hobbled over to him. He gave it a pat and evidently an order, because it immediately moved a few steps away and sat. The cat wound around Cole's boots once, then strutted away.

Cole and the nurse met in front of the truck.

"Come on," Annie said, pushing her door open, "let's see what's going on."

Melinda wasn't really certain she wanted to know. But she got out anyway, since Annie did. After the air-conditioned comfort of the car, the midday summer heat wrapped around her and pressed in, a suffocating blanket of dust-thick scorched air. Spunky the cat appeared from under Cole's pickup. It walked up to Melinda and meowed at her. So she picked it up and petted it as the nurse announced, "I've been waiting for you to get here, so I could tell you that I have had enough and I quit."

"But Mrs. Finster—"

The woman put up a broad hand. "No. No buts. That man has simply become… impossible. For the sake of the man he once was, I have put up with him until you got here. And that's more than anyone else I know would have done. Yes, he has a cross to bear. And he is not bearing it well, not at all."

The cat in Melinda's arms began to squirm. She let it slink to the ground as the nurse continued her diatribe. "He won't eat the good meals I cook. And just let me try to help him dress or get from his bed to his wheelchair. You should hear the things he calls me. For a man who often has trouble remembering certain words and would never take the name of the Lord in vain in any case, he certainly can think of frightful things to say to a woman who is only trying to do her—"

"Mrs. Finster."

She glared at him. "What?"

"All right. I understand."

"Well, I should hope so." She squinted at him, rather ruefully. "Look, Cole. I'm sorry. It wasn't that bad when I could go home at night. But I just can't—"

"I know. And I don't blame you. He's been a real tyrant since the stroke. And I can see that my being gone has only made the situation worse. You know how he's always been. So strong and capable. He hates his own awkwardness. And he's been worried…about our family problems."

The nurse, who obviously knew at least the bare facts

of the "family problems" Cole had mentioned, cast a quick glance at Annie. "Annie," she said with careful politeness. "It's good to see you again."

Annie nodded and forced a brave smile. "Hi there, Mrs. Finster."

Cole said, "I'm only grateful that you waited to leave until we got here."

The nurse drew herself up. "Well. I truly did want to help. But the last two weeks have reminded me why I retired five years ago. I'm just not young enough anymore to bear up under a difficult patient's constant abuse."

"It's okay. Why don't you go on in and get your things together and—"

"I'm all packed. My suitcase is waiting in the front hall. I've been sitting by the window, watching for you to drive up."

"Is my father—?"

"Don't worry. In spite of what he keeps calling me, I am not a fiend straight out of hell. He's clean and he was fed at noon. I checked on him fifteen minutes ago. He was fine—except for his attitude, of course."

"Good. Do you want me to write you a check now, or—?"

"Whenever you get around to it. Just send it to the house."

"I'll get it out to you tomorrow."

"No hurry." With a crisp nod of her gray head, she turned, marched back up the steps and went inside. She reappeared a few seconds later, carrying a large shoulder bag and a bulky suitcase.

Cole met her halfway up the steps. "Let me help—"

She doled out a quick, no-nonsense smile. "If I can take care of Preston Yuma around the clock for fifteen days, you can be certain I can carry my own suitcase to the car." She held out her hand. "Here's the beeper. I left the receiver for the baby monitor on the coffee table in the living room—not that he will ever lower himself to call a person on it."

Cole took the device and stepped back. "Well, then. Thank you, Mrs. Finster. Thank you again."

"You're welcome. And you know, if he continues to refuse a stay in a rehabilitation center, you really ought to move him to the lower floor. That big door off the front hall to the room you use now is wide enough for his wheelchair. And he'd be able to get to the table for meals by himself that way. He could also sit in the living room now and then. Make him feel a bit more capable, more involved in things, if you know what I mean. And if he'd just practice more on that walker of his—"

"Mrs. Finster. You're right. And believe me. I have tried to convince him to trade rooms with me."

The nurse shook her head. "I imagine you have. And I'm sure you'll keep trying."

"Yes. I will."

"Well. I'll see you in church, then?"

"You bet."

"And you, Annie?"

Annie answered somewhat sheepishly. "Sure, Mrs. Finster."

"It *is* good to see you home."

"Thank you. It's…good to be home."

The nurse flashed another quick smile, one that included Melinda. Annie swiftly introduced the two and the nurse said she hoped to see Melinda at church, too. Then she shifted her suitcase to her other hand, strode down the last step and straight to the gleaming little Bug, where she hauled up the trunk lid and tossed the suitcase in. Dust flew as she backed, turned and sped away down the driveway.

Once the little car had roared off down the road, the beeper in Cole's hand went off. Cole silenced it, then said grimly, "Get the baby. We'd better go in."

The front door opened onto a dim, wood-floored entry hall, with other doors on each wall and a staircase of dark, polished wood leading up to the second floor. Though the house had to be at least fifty years old, someone had shown the good sense to install air conditioning. After the sweltering heat outside, the coolness felt wonderful. Melinda sighed in relief.

Her relief didn't last long, however. Cole had just closed the door behind them when something crashed to the floor directly over their heads.

"Oh!" Annie cried.

Cole muttered an epithet under his breath and started up the stairs. At the same time, Annie whirled on Melinda, her heart-shaped face twisted in fear for her father. "Here. Please…" She pushed the baby into Melinda's arms and took off after Cole.

Upstairs, Cole raced along the landing to the door of his father's room. He flung it back.

Preston Yuma lay on the floor, his feet tangled in the cross-braces of the forged aluminum walker he was supposed to be learning to use.

With a groan, Preston looked up. "Cole." A stream of nonsense syllables followed. His voice was deep and rumbling, as it had always been. But since the stroke, whenever he was under emotional stress, he often had trouble trying to form words.

Cole strode to his father's side and knelt. "Yes, Dad. I'm home." Carefully he disentangled Preston's feet from the toppled walker and put it aside.

"I…heard you," Preston muttered. "Downstairs." He drew in and released three deep breaths. Cole waited, knowing his father was forcing himself to relax, so that the words he longed to say would come to him. Finally he whispered, "Did you…b-b-bring Annie with you?"

Cole gently took his father by the shoulders, supporting him into a sitting position. "She's with me. And she's fine."

Preston's eyes closed. "Thank you, dear Lord."

"Dad?" It was Annie, standing in the doorway. "Dad?"

The craggy face seemed to burn bright, suddenly, from within. Annie rushed over. "Oh, Dad…" Tears streamed down her face. "Oh, what's happened to you?"

"It's all right," Preston said. "It's all right, Annie girl." He reached out his left hand, the one that still worked right, and wrapped it around Cole's arm. "Help me. To my chair."

Between them, Cole and Annie put Preston Yuma back into his motorized chair. And then Annie wrapped her arms around his neck and cried against his shirt. "I'm sorry, Dad. So sorry. I never, ever wanted to hurt you. You have to know that."

And Preston comforted her, patting her with his good hand, whispering tenderly, "It's all right. I had a stroke. It's not your fault. You're home. And that's what matters…"

Cole stood back, letting them have their reunion, feeling better than he'd felt in a long time. Annie was home. She would see that his father took care of himself. And more than that, Preston Yuma would *want* to take care of himself, now he'd seen with his own eyes that his daughter was safe and well. The depression that had stolen his will to improve would begin to lift now, Cole felt certain.

In his side vision, Cole saw movement in the doorway behind him. Melinda. With the baby.

He turned, met her wide violet eyes. Those eyes asked a thousand worried questions at once. So he went to her. He put his arm around her, pulled her and the baby close against his body. It seemed the most natural thing in the world to do.

He looked down into her incredible face and whispered, "It's okay. Everything's going to be okay."

A tentative smile bloomed on her full lips. "Good. I'm so glad."

Then, from across the room, Preston demanded, "Cole. Who's this?"

Annie let go of her father and wiped her wet cheeks with the back of her hand. "Dad. This is Melinda. She's my friend. I met her in L.A. and—"

But the old man lifted his good hand and patted Annie's arm for silence. "Melinda? A pretty name."

Melinda cleared her throat. "Um, thank you. And hello. I'm happy to meet you, Mr. Yuma."

Annie tried to speak again. Preston gave his daughter's arm another pat. "Shh, now." He turned to Melinda once more. "Come closer, Melinda. Let an old man have a look at you."

Melinda stared at the man who looked like Cole thirty years from now, Cole wasted down to sharp bone and burning eyes. She ached for him—and she couldn't stop herself from shooting a quick, questioning glance at Cole, who immediately squeezed her shoulder. "It's all right. Go ahead."

"Yeah," said the old man in his rough, rumbling voice. "I won't bite. Come here to me."

So Melinda left the shelter of Cole's comforting arm. She went and stood before Preston Yuma. He leaned forward a little, studying her. Then the burning eyes shifted to the bundle in her arms. "What do we have here?"

Behind her, Melinda heard Annie gasp. She started to turn to her, but Preston said, "Please. Let me see."

And Annie said nervously, "Yes. Yes, do. Let him see."

So Melinda knelt beside the wheelchair and pulled back the blankets to show the old man his new grandson's face.

"This is Brady," she explained. "He's just two weeks old, yesterday."

The old man sighed. A smile of real pleasure softened the sharp lines of his face.

"Isn't he wonderful?" Melinda whispered. "Isn't he fine?"

And the old man nodded, made a low, affirmative sound. "Looks just like his daddy."

Annie let out another small, shocked cry. And Melinda frowned. She'd been led to believe that the old man could not abide Jimmy Logan. He seemed way too pleased to think his grandson resembled the man.

Then Preston glanced beyond the baby and the woman who held him, to his son, who remained standing in the doorway. "Nine months ago..."

"What, Dad?"

"When you went after Annie that first time. You got up to more than findin' your sister, I see."

Cole stiffened. "I...what?"

A deep, rumbling chuckle escaped the old man. "It's all right, son. The Lord forgives. And what man wouldn't be tempted by such a face as this one."

"Dad..." Cole began cautiously.

The old man spoke gruffly. "No excuses, son. At least I can see that you've p-p-put things right."

Melinda hastened to correct the misconception. "Oh, no, Mr. Yuma. Cole and I—"

The old man interrupted with another wave of his good hand. "No need to explain, Melinda. I can see the truth when it's right before my eyes. Cole is just like I was with his mama. He's been waitin' for that one special woman to come along."

"Oh, no. You don't—"

"Oh, yes. One special woman, the woman the good Lord created just for him. You."

Chapter 11

For an endless moment, nobody spoke. In Melinda's arms, Brady stirred and yawned.

Melinda looked down at the baby, then back up at the old man. "Mr. Yuma. You've mis—"

Annie placed a hand on her shoulder, cutting her off in midword. "Oh, yes," Annie said. "Dad has *missed* us. And we've missed him. But now we're home. Things are gonna be fine. And we better not wear him out too much right now, you know?"

Melinda craned her head back to frown at her friend. "But, Annie…"

"What?" Annie said, managing to make the single word both a demand and a plea.

Melinda looked past Annie, seeking Cole, seeking support for the truth that really had to be told. Unfortunately, though, Cole would not meet her eyes.

And the old man was reaching out. His claw of a hand

brushed her fingers, which were spread on the blanket, to support Brady's slight weight. "Where is your weddin' ring, Melinda?"

"I—"

But the old man was already casting a chiding look at Cole. "Your wife needs a ring, son. Women do set store in tokens of love."

Annie rushed forward. "Dad, you really do need a little rest now." She turned a fiercely cheerful smile on Melinda. "Why don't you and Brady and Cole go on downstairs? I'll just help Dad to get comfortable and then I'll hurry right down."

Melinda gaped at her friend. They needed to tell him. There was no point at all in letting him believe this absurd lie.

"Please," Annie said, desperation edging her tone. "Go on downstairs. I'll be right down. And we'll…take care of everything." She cast an imploring glance at her brother, who remained in the doorway, infuriatingly silent. "Cole?"

The sound of his name seemed to spur him to action. He walked over and extended a hand to Melinda. "Come on. Let Dad get some rest."

Melinda glared up at him. "But—"

"Come on," he said softly. "We can't handle every little thing all at once, now can we?" He bent, put his hand on her shoulder, and guided her up, careful of the baby. Then he led her out the door.

Downstairs, he took her to a living room off the central hall. The room had dark, waist-high wainscoting, several big, upholstered chairs, a sofa and a number of cherry-wood tables. A large rug patterned with vines and roses covered most of the hardwood floor. The gray cat must have come in when they did. It was curled in a ball, sound asleep on one of the chairs.

"Have a seat," Cole said. "I'll be right back." He was already halfway out the door.

"Cole."

He paused in midstep. "Yeah?"

"Where do you think you're going?"

His eyes narrowed at her sarcastic tone, but he answered gently, "Just to your car for that playpen thing you bought and Brady's diaper bag." He left then, quickly—no doubt to avoid hearing the things she longed to start shouting at him.

She sat on the sofa with the baby and waited until he returned. Then she waited some more, fuming silently, as he put the bag down beside her and set up the playpen in the middle of the rug.

"There," he said. "You can lay him down if you want to."

"Oh," she said very sweetly. "Aren't you helpful all of a sudden?"

"Melinda." It was a reproach.

She said what she was thinking then. "You lied to your father. Your sister lied and then you…you just *stood* there."

He strode back to the door he'd come through and shut it—no doubt so his father wouldn't hear what they said to each other. Then he spoke carefully. "It wasn't a lie. Not exactly."

"Not a lie. Hel-looo. To the best of my recollection, you and I are *not* married. And Brady is Annie's son, not yours and mine."

"I mean that *we* didn't lie to him. He was the one who—"

"Don't give me that. Yes, your father jumped to the wrong conclusion—and you and your sister *lied* by not setting him straight."

Cole paced to the empty playpen, looked down into it, and then ran his hand back over his hair. "He looked so *happy*."

"Oh, of course. That's a valid excuse. Your father looked

happy when he totally misconstrued the situation. So you let him believe his assumptions were the truth. You lied. Lovely. Let's tell some more lies. Maybe that poor old man will just leap out of his wheelchair and dance around the room in pure joy."

Cole's mouth pulled down at the corners and he stuck out his square jaw. "Talk like that isn't worthy of you, and you know it."

"Oh, I see. Now we're going to talk about *worthiness,* are we? Then answer me a question. Are *lies* worthy of you?"

He dropped to a chair, put his long legs straight out in front of him and stared at his boots.

She demanded sourly, "Is there something about those boots you haven't noticed before?"

He deigned to look at her then. "Listen. I haven't seen him happy since Annie ran off. And since the stroke, well, he's sunk into a major depression. But now she's back. He's still a stroke victim, but he's got his dearest wish. And he thinks his second big dream has come true, too. That I would find a wife, and give him a grandchild. When I saw his face up there, I just couldn't bring myself to tell him the truth."

His words tugged at her heart. It took all the strength she had to resist them. She spoke flatly, "Well, you've only put off the inevitable—and made a difficult situation worse. As soon as he's rested a while, we're going to have to explain it all."

He pulled his legs in and leaned his elbows on his knees. Now he was looking at the twining rose pattern on the rug between his boots.

"Cole," she said impatiently.

He let out a low groan. "You're right. I know. And we will tell him."

"As soon as he wakes up. Correct?"

"Yeah. Right. As soon as he wakes up." He stood.

She eyed him with suspicion. "Where do you think you're going now?"

"To start unloading the trailer and the—"

"You're staying right here until Annie comes downstairs. I don't like this at all and I want it settled. I want all three of us in agreement as to what we're going to do."

"Melinda, there's a lot to unload. I might as well get—"

"You might as well sit back down and stare at the rug some more, because if you walk out of this room before Annie gets down here, I am going to march right upstairs myself and lay out the hard facts to that old man up there."

His brow creased in an uneasy frown. "It's not your place to do a thing like that."

"Since he's decided to believe that I'm his daughter-in-law and that Brady is my child, I'd say it very much is my place."

"Oh, come on. You couldn't do it anyway—hurt a sick old man like that."

"I couldn't? Walk out that door and find out."

He hovered there for a moment, scowling. Then, muttering something unpleasant, he dropped into the chair once more.

They sat there, waiting. Cole stared broodingly into the middle distance and Melinda talked softly to Brady, who gazed up at her from the cozy nest of his blanket, his little mouth working, sometimes seeming to smile and now and then to frown.

After a few minutes, Melinda glanced over at the door that Cole had shut. "You'd better open that. I have the strangest feeling your sister is going to try to sneak off somewhere. I want to be sure we catch her when she comes down those stairs."

He grunted. "You're real full of suspicions all of a sudden."

"Thoroughly justified suspicions, I think. Open that door."

He just sat there.

"Cole," she said as a warning.

So he dragged himself to his feet and went to the door that led to the hall. Annie was just tiptoeing by as he opened it. She stopped in midstep, her eyes going wide. Melinda thought of the white-tailed doe they had seen on the road, frozen at that final second before she bolted for the shelter of the trees.

Annie's stillness ended abruptly in red-faced animation. "Oh! Cole. I was thinkin' I'd just go on out and start bringin' all the stuff inside. I mean, you'll want to get that trailer turned in as soon as we can—"

"Better come in here first."

"But I—"

"Annie. Come on."

She stared at him for a moment, then blew out her cheeks in a gusty breath. "Oh, all right." She trudged over the threshold and Cole shut the doors behind her.

As if he knew the sound of his mother's voice, Brady let out a questioning cry.

"He's hungry," Annie said.

Melinda rose and gave her the child. Cole turned away as Annie settled into a chair, opened her blouse and put the baby to her breast. "Would you give me a diaper?" Annie asked. Melinda got one from the diaper bag and laid it over Annie's shoulder, covering the pale slope of her breast. Then Annie said to Cole, "You can turn around now."

But Cole didn't turn. Clearly he felt no more eagerness than his sister did to discuss how they would make this impossible situation right.

Melinda still stood near Annie's chair. She could clearly see Annie's left hand, which supported the baby as he nursed.

"Where is your wedding ring?" Melinda demanded.

Annie sucked in a big breath and let it out in a defiant rush. "I took it off."

"Why?"

"Why do you think? I hid it in a drawer in my room, is what I did. I don't want Dad to see it right now."

"And why is that?"

"You are actin' mean and snooty. I'm just not going to talk to you if you are going to act like that."

Melinda rubbed the bridge of her nose between her thumb and forefinger in an effort to diffuse the tension gathered there. She tried to speak more gently. "Annie, there is no point at all in hiding the truth from your father. He's going to have to find out sometime anyway and—"

"Sometime. But not right now."

"It will do no good at all to—"

"Oh, but it will!" Annie burst out with determined zeal. "It *will* do some good. It will give him a chance to get to know Brady a little, it will give him a chance to…settle down and get used to me being here again. To realize—"

"Annie. It's just another way for you to avoid letting him know that things didn't work out for you in Los Angeles."

"He already knows that. I'm back home, aren't I, and Jimmy's nowhere in sight?"

Melinda looked at her friend and shook her head.

Annie pressed on. "What I'm saying is, he can see with his own eyes that things didn't work out. I'm here. And Jimmy isn't. Let him have a little time to deal with that, before we go hittin' him with the rest of the news."

"Annie—"

"No. Listen. All right, it's true. It's gonna be the hardest thing I ever did, to tell my father the rest of the truth. But it's gonna be real hard for *him,* too. And if we…put it off for a few days, let him think what he wants to think, just for a little while, then I honestly believe he'll take it better than he would take it now."

Melinda sank to the chair next to Annie and tried another approach. "Annie, think. Think about how readily your father has accepted the idea that Cole had an affair with me nine months ago, an affair that supposedly produced a baby. Now, virtually out of the blue, Cole appears with what your father decides is a new wife and a son—and your father is thrilled. If he can accept that—"

Annie pressed her lips together. "Uh-uh. It's not the same. Not the same at all. Cole is thirty. He makes a good living—and my father's been after him for quite a while now to settle down. Him showin' up with a family is only exactly what my dad has been waitin' for. While me, I'm barely eighteen. I got no job. I don't even have my high school diploma. And my husband has run off and left me. How can you call it the same, Melinda? It's as different as day is from night."

Cole turned around then. "Annie's right about that."

Melinda sent him a killing look. "*Now* you decide to speak up—to say something that doesn't help at all."

"It's only the truth."

"You'd be better off not to mention the word 'truth' around me for a while, Cole Yuma. I'm beginning to wonder if either you or your sister know the meaning of the word."

"Melinda!" Annie exclaimed in wounded outrage. "How can you say such a thing?" Brady popped off the breast right then and let out a startled cry—in reaction to his mother's agitation, no doubt. Annie straightened her blouse, laid the baby over her shoulder and gently patted his back, glaring at Melinda all the while.

Melinda slumped back in her chair, closed her eyes and pinched the bridge of her nose again. "I can't believe this is happening."

Annie lowered Brady to her lap, smoothed the diaper onto her right shoulder, readjusted her blouse and then put Brady to work on her other breast. That accomplished, she asked briskly, "Cole, how much can Dad get around?"

"He can get himself from his bed to his chair," Cole admitted warily. "He can even bathe himself, using that sprayer hose I installed in the bathtub and sitting on a stool. At this point, he can also stagger a few steps with a walker."

"But he stays in his room most of the time?"

Cole nodded. "You know how he was. Strong as a horse. He doesn't want to see people. Doesn't want them to watch him struggle with the simplest things."

"So he's *hidin'* in his room, really."

"That's right. I've been tryin' to think of ways to lure him out of there. Since he won't move downstairs, I've been thinking of widening the door of his room and getting a stair elevator for him, thinking that would at least give him a chance to get himself downstairs now and then. But I just haven't gotten around to that yet. I'm kind of hoping, now you're here, that he'll try a little harder, practice with the walker, let me get a physical therapist over from Fredericksburg once or twice a week. He's been told repeatedly that if he'll just put himself through the therapy, within a couple of months he could go back to work at the hospital, maybe take over the small animal hours, teach the vet class we give at the high school every year…"

Annie's chin jutted out with determination. "We are gonna get him to put himself through the therapy, Cole."

"I knew you'd say that." Cole looked at his sister with tender gratitude. "We can work it out. If only he'll pull out of his depression and work *with* us."

"I think he will."

"So do I. Now."

"But for a while," Annie went on, too slyly by half, "until you widen his bedroom door and we get that stair elevator, he'd have a heck of a time leavin' his room unless someone carried him out, right?"

"Right."

"And we don't really need a nurse, now that I'll be here in

the daytime. We could care for him ourselves, if we had to, couldn't we?"

"What are you getting at, Annie?"

"Well, if there was just us, if there were no strangers around to ask questions—and if we all agreed to it—then it wouldn't be that hard, just for a few days, to let him think—"

Melinda could not believe what she was hearing. She shot to her feet. "Absolutely not. I will not be a part of this. It is wrong. Wrong and manipulative." She glowered from brother to sister and back again. "I mean it. Both of you. When your father wakes from his nap, we will tell him the truth. Do you understand?"

Annie stared at her, a series of emotions flashing across her flushed face: hurt, anger, resentment—and finally unwilling acceptance. She looked down at her baby and sighed.

Melinda turned to Cole.

And he nodded. "All right. We'll tell him the truth as soon as he's had some rest."

Annie's silent acquiescence wasn't enough for Melinda— not at that point, anyway. "Annie?" she prodded.

"Okay," Annie muttered without looking up. "We'll tell him the truth. When he wakes up."

They spent the next hour and a half unpacking, lugging Annie's and Brady's things up the stairs and stacking the boxes of household goods that Annie didn't need right then in the garage around the side of the house. There were four bedrooms upstairs: the large master suite, Annie's room and a nearly identical one next to it, which Annie earmarked immediately for a nursery. There was also another bedroom, a bright east-facing one that Gerda Finster had used. Annie led Melinda there.

"You can see the sun come up in the morning beyond those oaks out there." Annie pointed out the window, at the trees beyond the windmill. "It's a pretty sight." The bed was covered with a wedding ring quilt. Annie sat down on it, leaned on one hand and traced the shapes of the entwined rings with a forefinger.

Melinda went and dropped down beside her friend. She bounced up and down twice. "Nice, firm mattress. I like that."

Annie looked up. "Oh, Melinda. I'm sorry if I was mean. I'm just...it's like you said. I'm so scared to hurt him. And scared to see his face when he finds out that Brady is really mine."

"He loves you. He'll accept the truth."

"Oh, I do hope you are right." Annie leaned sideways against Melinda's shoulder and Melinda wrapped an arm around her. They sat for a moment, not speaking.

Then Melinda asked, "Where does that lead?" She gestured toward the door on the wall perpendicular to the one that led to the wide stair landing.

"That goes to the master suite," Annie explained. "But don't worry. It has a lock. My dad won't be bothering you— as if he would or even could."

"Of course I'm not worried about that. But why the door in the first place?"

"This was supposed to be the nursery. That way the lady of the house could slip in and out real easy when her baby cried at night."

"Then you and Cole slept here, as babies?"

"Mmm-hmm. But as soon as we got to be two or three, we moved to our own rooms on the other side of the landing. This became the guest room. It's a good size for that. Big enough for a double bed and bureau and a nice, comfortable chair or two." She gestured toward the pale blue wing-back chair over by the window. "I hope it's all right for you. You could have Brady's room if you want. It's a little larger than this one and—"

"Annie. This is lovely. And I do want to see the sun come up over those oaks out there."

"Okay. If you're sure."

"I am."

Annie chuckled to herself. "It's so funny…about rooms. When Cole came back from veterinary school, he had gotten real independent. Wanted to get his own place. But he'd always planned to follow in Dad's footsteps, to work with Dad and someday take over the hospital himself. So Dad said there was no reason for him to move away. That he could have his own place downstairs. You know what they did?"

"What?"

"They rebuilt the old parlor, the two of them. Cole's got a big bed-sitting area and his own bathroom down there now. And Dad swore he wouldn't keep tabs on what time Cole came in at night. That was a big concession for Dad. I think Cole was sowin' a few wild oats. And Dad thinks a man's oats should be sown only within the state of holy matrimony—if you know what I mean."

Melinda let out a chuckle of her own. "I do."

"Oh, I was so hurt. I wanted my big brother back in his room next to mine. I didn't want him downstairs, livin' like a grown-up, comin' and goin' just as he pleased. But I didn't get my way in that. It was a hard lesson in life for me—that sometimes, a gal is not going to get her way."

"You know, I've noticed that you still think you ought to get your way most of time."

Annie widened her eyes. "Who? Me? No…"

They laughed together, then Melinda said more seriously, "Maybe you've underestimated your father. If he can help his son build a place where he can live his own life, then—"

"I know what you're sayin'. But it's different with me. I'm

his daughter. My mom died givin' me life and that has made me all the more precious to him. He says I look like her. It's just harder for him with me than it was with Cole—to let me make my own choices, to have to watch me live with the choices once I've made them."

"Wait and see."

"I guess I don't have a choice about that at all now, do I?"

"Don't start in again."

"Oh, I won't." Annie pulled a sad face. "I have accepted my fate."

The beeper the nurse had given to Cole went off at four-thirty. Annie hurried upstairs to check on her father.

Then she returned to the garage, where Melinda and Cole were stacking the last of her boxed housewares against a side wall.

"He's awake," she announced bleakly. "And he wants to talk to us."

"Good," Melinda said, "since we need to talk to him, too."

The three of them trooped back up to the master suite, where Preston was sitting in his wheelchair a few feet from the bed. A smile of greeting stretched his mouth. "Ah. Here you all are. Come in. Sit down."

But no one moved. The three of them stood there, huddled by the door, each too apprehensive to take a single step.

Preston said, "Well, now. You three sure look nervous. Don't you worry. What I got to say is good." His brows drew together. "Wait a minute. Something's goin' on." He pondered, then demanded, "Where's that Gerda?"

Cole cleared his throat. "Mrs. Finster quit, Dad."

Preston mumbled something, and shook his head. "I oughtta be sorry, I suppose. But I guess I'm not. That is a good, God-fearing woman, Gerda Finster. But she's been a pure..." He paused, clearly searching for a certain word. Then he found it. "T-torment. That's it. She's been a torment to me. Cheerful and bossy. It's a combination I cannot abide."

"Well," Cole said wryly. "She won't be tormentin' you any longer. She's gone."

Preston sighed heavily. "I suppose someday I'll have to apologize to her. Maybe sometime when I see her at church."

"I'm sure she'll appreciate that."

"Humph. I'll just bet she will."

Melinda cast oblique glances at Cole and then at Annie. Neither of them looked as if they knew how to begin. So Melinda spoke up gingerly. "Um. Mr. Yuma, we—"

He grunted. "*Mr. Yuma?* What's that? You might as well get used to callin' me Father, don't you think?"

Father. He wanted her to call him *Father*...

She shot more sideways glances at Cole and his sister. No help there. She sucked in a breath and tried again. "I…that is, we…"

Preston waved her forward. She noticed that he had a small black object clutched in his hand. "Come on. You come on over here. I told you before I don't bite, and I meant it."

She glanced at Cole for the third time. He stared back, looking miserable. So she made herself step forward, leaving the other two by the door. "Mr. Yuma…"

"Father." He corrected her again. "You have to practice it. Get used to it. You'll be sayin' it from now on. Hold out your hand."

He gave the order so suddenly that she responded without thinking. Her hand went out—and he dropped the object he was holding into it.

"I would be honored," he said, "if you would take that."

She stared down at it. It was a velvet jewel case, the kind that a ring would come in. "I don't—"

"Go on. Open it."

She knew what it was, of course. And she didn't want to

open it. But somehow it didn't seem to be an option to refuse. So she lifted the lid—and gazed bleakly down at the old-fashioned engagement diamond and wedding band inside.

"It was…my Anna's." The rumbling voice broke. He said something else, something garbled that she couldn't understand. And then he said, "Sorry. Sometimes I can't make the words…" She looked up, into a pair of old eyes that had suddenly grown moist with tears. A tightness seized the back of her throat. She could feel her own answering tears, rising, blurring her sight.

"Please," Preston said. "I'd be honored if you'd wear them."

Melinda opened her mouth—and then shut it. Oh, how could she do it? How could she tell this sweet, overbearing old man the truth that he so obviously did not want to hear?

Cole moved forward then, and stood to the left of her, as Annie came up and stood on her right. Melinda felt a little stronger, with the two of them on either side, seeming to offer support.

But then neither of them spoke, neither of them got out the words that Melinda herself couldn't find a way to say. All three of them ended up just standing there in a row, staring mutely down at the little velvet box, the twin gold bands and the single diamond twinkling inside.

"Cole," Preston said. "You go on now. You put the rings on the hand of your bride."

Melinda turned her head, met Cole's eyes. She saw him swallow. And then his mouth became a flat, determined line.

He looked at his father. "Dad…"

Melinda realized he was going to do it: tell the truth that she hadn't managed to make herself reveal.

Annie must have known, too. She let out a small cry.

And Melinda couldn't bear it. She grabbed Cole's hand. He

flinched at her abruptness, but didn't pull away, only gaped at her in disbelief as she passed him the ring box.

"Yes, darling," she said softly. "It's only right that you should be the one to put them on me for the first time."

Chapter 12

Cole's eyes changed. The shock left them. They burned as bright as his father's—but with a different kind of light. A hot light. And a dangerous one.

Playing with matches again, Melinda thought numbly. Still, she didn't pull her hand away, only continued to hold it there, until he took it and carefully, tenderly, slipped on the two rings.

"Ah," sighed Preston. "Good."

Melinda gulped. She couldn't stop looking at Cole. And he couldn't look away from her. Heat seemed to arc in the air between them.

"I knew they would fit," the old man said, satisfied.

And then he said more.

Much more. He told them that he thought it was time he moved downstairs. He would take his son's rooms; Cole and Melinda would have his. Cole was the man of the house, now, after all. He had a wife—and a baby who would make good use of the old nursery.

As soon as they got back downstairs, Annie grabbed Melinda and hugged her. "Thank you, thank you…"

Melinda pulled away. "I have to be out of my mind. This is wrong…"

"Oh, Melinda. No. It's right. Very, very right. And it won't be for long. He already seems so much better than what Cole described to me. Did you hear him? Talking about goin' to church. Has he done that since the stroke?" She glanced toward her brother, who stood a few feet away, a distant, unreadable expression on his face. "Cole? Has he?"

"No, he hasn't."

"See? He's happy. Really happy. And that will make him want to work to get stronger."

"But what happens in a few days?" Melinda asked.

"A few days?"

"Yes Annie." Melinda spoke with strained patience. "A few days. You know, when we tell him the truth?"

Annie's eyes slid away. "Well, I think we should wait a week, at least."

"A *week?*" Melinda silently called herself several unpleasant names. She'd demanded the chance to set things right—and then blown it royally. "We can't keep up a fiction like this for a week."

"Yes, we can."

"Annie. We're not in a vacuum here. Even if you can keep your father from figuring out the truth, what are we going to say to other people? Are we going to tell all of Bluebonnet, Texas, that Cole and I are married and we have a baby boy? That will look just wonderful—when I disappear and my baby starts calling *you* 'Mom.'"

"We don't have to tell anybody. We can…keep to ourselves for a week. It won't be that hard—and don't look at me like that. I will tell Dad the truth. I promise you. One week from today. It's gonna work out just fine. Cole can have Dad's bedroom and you can stay in the guest room, just like you are now. And we'll all be upstairs, with Dad down here where he can use the living room—and sit at the table with us at mealtimes."

"And where he's far enough away from Brady's room that he won't notice the details," Cole added flatly, "like who he cries for when he's hungry."

Annie beamed. "Exactly."

Cole was not smiling.

Annie let out a small, impatient groan. "Oh, come on. Look on the bright side. Dad thinkin' you two are married is good in more ways than one. He never would have agreed to change bedrooms with you otherwise."

Cole muttered grudgingly, "Maybe not."

"Maybe not?" Annie huffed. "*Maybe* not?"

"All right. He's agreed to change rooms because he thinks I have a family now—but you still haven't answered Melinda's question."

"What question?" Annie was all innocence.

"What's Dad gonna say when he finds out he's been tricked?"

Annie pursed up her mouth. "I don't know if I like that word, tricked."

"Don't you get righteous here, Annie girl. We all know what we did. Pretendin' we didn't isn't gonna change it. What are you gonna say when he asks you what happened with Jimmy?"

"He's not gonna ask me. He doesn't want to even think about Jimmy, and you know that very well."

"He's still not going to like it when he finally learns the truth."

"Well, all right. So he won't like it. But by the time he *does* find out, he'll be all settled in down here. And he'll have realized that he does not like bein' trapped in his room all the time."

Cole did not look reassured. Melinda knew just how he felt.

"Come on, you two," Annie insisted. "It's all gonna be just fine—and I think we'd better move him right away, before he has a chance to change his mind."

Cole nodded. "All right. That does make sense. I've got to work tomorrow, but I'll make a few calls. See if I can get a couple of men out first thing in the morning—to move my things upstairs and settle Dad in down here. We can see about having those permanent rails installed in the tub. Maybe even put in a ramp by the front steps."

"Good idea." Annie fairly glowed with eagerness. "We'll get him moved down here immediately. That's the best thing."

Melinda reiterated, "One week, Annie. Swear to me. Next Thursday, no matter what, you will tell your father that Brady is yours…and that I'm not his daughter-in-law, after all."

Annie made a show of crossing her heart. "Hope to die. I will do it. A week from today."

A few minutes later, Cole left to drop off the trailer. When he returned, they ate a simple dinner, after which Annie carried a tray upstairs to Preston. Cole began gathering the dirty dishes from the table.

Melinda stood. "I'll do those."

He stopped halfway to the counter, a serving bowl in one hand and his own empty plate in the other. "There's no need."

"Cole, I really don't mind. And I'll bet you have a thousand things you need to check on right about now."

He studied her for a long moment. Something that might have been regret etched his features and darkened his eyes. She felt the rings on her hand, his mother's rings, remembered the dangerous way he had looked at her just before he slipped them on.

Man and wife, she thought. For a week.

But not really, she told herself. Really, it meant nothing, except to Preston Yuma. They would…behave affectionately, when Preston was near. They should be able to handle that.

It wasn't as if they had to share a bed.

Still, by tomorrow, or the next day, Cole would have moved into the room upstairs, the room next to hers, the room with the connecting door….

From the travel playpen, which Annie had set up in the corner before they started dinner, Brady let out a small, gurgling coo.

Cole glanced toward the sound. "This is one harebrained scheme we've got goin' here, isn't it?"

"Yes." She sighed. "I suppose so."

"I'm sorry we got you into this."

She lifted a shoulder, let it drop. "You didn't. Not really. I had my chance to back out and I didn't take it."

"We shouldn't have put you in the position where you *needed* a chance to back out. And I still really don't see how this crazy lie is going to help my dad at all."

"Unfortunately I agree with you about that."

"So why are we doing it?"

They said the word together, sharing a resigned smile: "Annie."

Cole added, "Someday we're gonna have to learn to tell her no."

We. She shouldn't have liked the sound of that so much.

She took the plate and the bowl from him. "Go on. I'm sure you want to get over to that hospital of yours."

"Yeah," he admitted, "I really should go take a look around, find out what disasters need fixing."

"Then do it."

He took his hat off the peg on the wall. Pausing to salute her with it, he turned and went out the back door.

The next morning, two men arrived at nine o'clock, long after Cole and the other two vets who worked with him had driven off in the vans they used to make rounds of the local ranches.

The workmen spent the morning installing rails in the downstairs bathtub and adding a ramp onto the front porch. Cole came back for lunch, gave his approval to the work they'd done and left again at a little after one.

It took them an hour and a half, under Annie's quite capable supervision, to move all the furniture up and down the stairs. Melinda and Annie worked with the vacuum cleaner and a box of dusting rags, making sure both rooms were thoroughly cleaned. Melinda even took a can of cleanser and a scrub brush and attacked the bathrooms until they shone.

Annie teased her, "You're gonna wreck your nails."

Melinda shrugged. "I'll treat myself to a nail wrap when I get back to L.A."

By late afternoon, Preston had been installed in his new quarters and all of Cole's things had been hauled up to the master suite.

Preston didn't join them for dinner that night. Cole warned Annie, "Don't expect too much too soon. He spills things. And he hates that."

"He will eat at the table," Annie said firmly. "Eventually he will."

Neither Cole nor Melinda argued with her. They both hoped she was right.

After dinner, Cole went back over to the hospital. There were a couple of animals he wanted to look in on. He didn't return until nine. Melinda was in her room by then, sitting in the wing chair by the window, filing down her ruined nails and now and then glancing outside, where swift, small shadows darted through the nearly dark sky.

"Bats." It was Cole, standing in the door she'd left open to the landing. The lame one-eared German Shepherd sat panting happily at his feet. "They come out of their hiding places to hunt insects at night."

She set her emery board on the table by her chair. "They have bats in Wyoming, too, you know."

He leaned in the doorway. "Oh, do they?"

She grimaced in distaste. "Once one got caught in my hair. I screamed. The ranch hands all laughed."

"City girl."

"That's right."

She thought that he looked tired. "Long day?"

"Yeah. And another one comin' up tomorrow."

"But tomorrow's Saturday."

"Tell that to all the animals on the ranches around here. We always keep one vet on call for Saturday and one for Sunday—and he generally has plenty to do. I'll take both days this week, to give Oscar and Randy a break."

"Those are the other two vets who work with you?"

"Yep. Oscar Rendquist and Randy Braun." He pulled himself away from the door frame. "Well, better go in and see what my new room looks like."

"It's clean, I can promise you that. But you still have to decide where you want to put the furniture."

"Later," he said wearily. "Right now, as long as I can fall into the bed—"

"It's not *that* bad." She stood. "I'll bet in a half an hour, with another pair of hands to help, you can have everything right where you want it."

He tipped his head and looked at her. "You volunteering?"

"Sure. Why not?"

For a moment, she thought he might refuse her offer. But then he said, "All right. Come on then."

He led the way around the wide landing that surrounded the stairs, with Melinda right behind and the dog in the rear. In the master bedroom, the dog found a comfortable spot near the door, flopped down and put his head on his paws.

Cole and Melinda set to work. They put the bed on the south wall, between the two big windows, and the chairs and small sofa at the end of the room, where another window looked out over the front yard. The bureau fit neatly on the wall right next to the door that led to Melinda's room. And they set Cole's desk up between his twin oak bookcases, not far from the exit to the stair landing.

"Now I just have to figure out what to do with the stereo." The stereo consisted of a number of components in an oak cabinet, two speakers and a glassed-in case with four shelves full of CDs.

Melinda brushed a lock of hair off her cheek and looked around, considering. "Maybe in the sitting area. You could put it at the end of the couch and then—"

"I'll figure it out tomorrow night." He shot her a speculative look. "Maybe you'll help me."

It felt like a challenge somehow—but she was careful to shrug it off. "Maybe I will."

A silence. They both knew there was nothing more to do. She should go back to her own room, and let him get some sleep. He'd be up hours before dawn, long gone in his van before she and Annie went downstairs and started getting breakfast ready for themselves and for Preston.

She heard herself ask, "What have you got in that CD case?"

"Strictly country." The implication was clear: *nothing that would interest a city girl like you.*

She felt a silly urge to counter his preconceived notions of her. "I like country."

"I'll bet."

"I do. Some of it, anyway."

"Like what?"

"Randy Travis. Willie Nelson. They both sound so…sweet. And sincere."

"Sweet." He was teasing her. "Sweet and sincere."

"There's something to be said for those things. Even a girl from New York City knows that."

Something gleamed in his eyes—a lambent flame. "She does?"

"Yes. She does."

He took a step toward her. "You hungry for a little sweetness, Melinda?"

It was more than he should have said. It pushed the already risky conversation over the line, made it way too intimate.

"I…should go," she said nervously. But she stayed right where she was.

About five feet of braided rug now lay between them. Cole eliminated that space in two long strides. He looked down into her eyes, the flame in his calling to her, hollowing her out, igniting memories—of the two of them, in her kitchen the night Brady was born. The scent of coffee brewing. And the scent of him, the heat of him, too close to deny.

"Why did you come in here with me, Melinda?" The words were soft, but they held a clear challenge.

She rushed to defend herself. "I…wanted to help you. To get your room arranged."

He captured her hand—the one with his mother's rings on it. "You've been helpin' a lot around here. Maybe too much…" His fingers caressed her filed-down nails.

Her chest felt tight. Her pulse had accelerated dangerously. "I…I don't mind helping. Honestly."

He released her hand—and lightly cupped her chin. His thumb whispered across her lower lip, which trembled in response. "I remember the way your mouth tastes."

She stared at him, wide-eyed, wondering why she was letting him say these things to her. "Cole, don't—"

He put his thumb across her lips again, silencing her. "Fact is, I'm gettin' tired of pretending I don't want to taste it again. I think maybe you're gettin' tired of pretending yourself." He dropped his hand away. "Am I wrong?"

She should answer him, she knew it. Should say clearly and firmly, *Yes, you are wrong.*

But what was the point of that? It would mean nothing. *Less* than nothing, since it would be a blank lie and he would know it as such.

He spoke so softly, his voice a verbal caress. "The taste of your mouth isn't the only thing. I think about other things I shouldn't. I think about…that door over there. The one between your room and this one. Have you thought about that door, too?" She didn't answer immediately, *couldn't* answer immediately. Her heart rushed the blood through her body in sharp, hard bursts. Desire pooled in the center of her, then spread out, to flow down her thighs, along her arms.…

He asked again, "Have you?"

She nodded, though she shouldn't have. But she couldn't stop herself, couldn't tell the lies she should have told, couldn't turn away.

"Maybe we were both thinkin' about that door just a little, when we went along with this scheme of Annie's. Both thinkin' how easy it would be, to get to each other. How, with me in this room and you in that one, we could do whatever we wanted to do. And nobody else would have to know." His gaze seemed to probe more deeply into hers.

Soft and helplessly, beneath the insistent pounding of her traitorous heart, she heard herself sigh.

He continued, relentless as the roaring in her blood. "You wouldn't want Annie to know, would you? Wouldn't want to tell her that what you felt for her brother was something too strong to deny—but not strong enough to last for a lifetime?"

She closed her eyes, not wanting to look at him, not wanting to have to admit that what he had just said was way too true.

Tenderly he whispered, "I'm not accusin' you, Melinda. Not judgin' you. Don't think I am. I only know what's in your mind because it's in my mind, too. Come on. Come on, look at me." She opened her eyes again.

His eyes were waiting. "Maybe it's what you said that night at your house. Maybe it can't go anywhere. Maybe you've got things you have to figure out about your life. And maybe I've got more here to hold me than I could ever turn my back on. Maybe this is just a campfire, not a home fire. You know?"

She nodded a second time. She did know. She did....

"And maybe, in this time you're here, you'll leave that door open. For me."

He bent his head down. His lips brushed across hers.

She whimpered.

"Say you want me to kiss you. I want to hear you say it. I don't want you to just…give in to it. I want it to be a choice we both know you made."

"Cole, I—"

"Just say it. Or don't say it."

"I…"

"Say it."

And she did. "Yes. Kiss me, Cole. Please."

He raised his hand again, cradled her cheek—and whispered her name on a torn breath.

She could bear the waiting no longer. With a cry, she surged up, slid her arms over his chest and hooked them behind his neck. His mouth met hers, hard, demanding—then softening, melting, as he pulled her against his body and his tongue mated with hers.

Oh, so good, she thought wildly. So good, so right…

His lips moved hungrily on hers, his body burned hers. His arms pressed her close, so close against his heart, which seemed to be pounding every bit as hard and loud as her own. She clutched his shoulders as she kissed him back, thinking disjointedly of matches, of campfires, of sudden and glorious flares of bright heat.

He lifted his head, his eyes seared into hers. And then he slid a hand between them, to cradle her breast. She gasped, tried to capture his lips again.

But he wouldn't let her. With a low moan, he dropped his hand, took her shoulders, stared into her eyes. "Wait. We'd better wait, I think. One more night…"

Confusion made her cry out again. She had felt him, against her, felt his readiness to make love to her. "But…I thought…"

He looked almost angry. His lips were swollen and soft from the kiss. "Listen. You lie in that bed tonight. On the other side of that wall. You lie there and know that I'm over here. Wanting you. You get up in the morning and you live through the day. Just like I will. And then, tomorrow night, if you still want me more than the trouble doin' this will likely cause us, you leave that door unlocked."

She searched his face, then accused softly, "For a sweet, sincere man, you certainly know how to be cruel."

He made a low sound in his throat. "Maybe. But we shouldn't do this. We both know it. I'm just givin' you a real chance to back out before it starts."

How could he say that, *before it starts?* As if it hadn't started weeks ago, as if they both hadn't been fighting it every time they had to be near each other since the day his pickup had broadsided her car.

He seemed to hear the words she hadn't spoken. "Okay. Before it goes any farther, then."

She knew he was right. They shouldn't be doing this.

And maybe, once she'd turned from him, once she'd walked across the landing from this room to her room, once he wasn't so close, once this dangerous, incendiary moment had passed...

Maybe then, she would find the good sense and the will-power to stay on her own side of the door tomorrow night.

His hand strayed, slid down to the middle of her back and pulled her in against him again. She felt his promise, felt her own body answering.

Then, with a low groan, he grasped her shoulders once more and held her away. "Go now. Go."

She turned from him quickly and made for the door, almost tripping over his dog in her hurry to escape.

The next morning, Annie announced that they needed groceries. So Melinda volunteered to do the shopping. She set off for Fredericksburg after breakfast, armed with a map and a long grocery list.

The trip was pleasant and uneventful. She found Fredericksburg charming. She admired the wide Main Street of the old German town, as well as the interesting homes made of native limestone—and tried not to think about Cole, about the night to come.

She pushed her cart down the aisles of a large, well-stocked supermarket, ordering her mind to stay on the task at hand, not to go wandering off into guilty speculation concerning what she *should* do as opposed to what she *wanted* to do. In the pharmacy section, she paused by the shelves of contraceptives.

She thought of the baby she had lost, the baby whose conception had occurred because she hadn't been as careful as she should have been. Something like that could happen again.

A baby. Yes. Though what she and Cole might share wouldn't last, she did long for a child.

But that would be wrong, to use Cole in that way.

She might be a woman who didn't know where she was going. A woman sorely tempted to light dangerous fires. But she wasn't a cheat. And certain lies actually were beneath her.

She took a box from the shelf and tossed it into the cart.

Melinda returned to the house before noon, driving around back to the rear door. She entered the kitchen carrying a grocery bag in each arm—and found Cole sitting at the table just finishing his lunch.

He looked up and saw her.

"Hello, Cole," she said, feeling foolish and tongue-tied, telling herself not to think about what had happened last night—or the choice she would have to make when darkness came. "Um. Where's Annie?" She set the bags on the counter near the sink.

"In Dad's room. I think she's tryin' to talk him into comin' to the table for lunch."

"The baby?"

He indicated the playpen in the corner.

Melinda glanced over. Brady lay on his back, his soft, round cheek turned toward the wall. "Asleep?"

Cole nodded. "Need some help?"

She lowered her voice, so as not to wake the child. "Oh, no. I can manage. You just eat your lunch." She turned and hurried out the door again.

Cole ignored her instructions and followed right behind

her. He stopped a few feet from the open trunk and saw all the full grocery bags inside. "Where's the receipt?"

She just looked at him. She did not want to argue about money right now. She just wanted to get the groceries unloaded. She wanted for him to go back and finish his blasted lunch and return to all the horses and cows that were waiting for him. With him standing here, looking at her, it was virtually impossible to think of anything but that door between their rooms.

He held out his hand. "Come on. The receipt."

She would have given it to him—if she'd had it. "I don't know. It's somewhere in one of the bags, I think." And what would he do now? Start ripping through all the groceries? Thank God she'd had enough sense to ask the clerk to bag the box of contraceptives separately. It was waiting in the glove box, so she could carry it to her room discreetly when no one else was around.

"Melinda," he growled. "You're not payin' for all this."

"Fine. Okay. When I find the receipt, I'll give it to you. You can write me a check. Or put it on your credit card. Pay me in cash. Whatever. But the important thing is, you can *pay,* all right? You can pay." She turned and grabbed two more grocery bags from the trunk.

"Melinda."

She froze.

He was right behind her. She could feel him there. He didn't touch her. She did not move. But every molecule in her body seemed to melt backward, toward him.

He whispered in her left ear. "All right. I'm a little sensitive about money."

She made a small, humphing sound. "Get over it."

"I'm tryin'."

"Try harder."

He chuckled at that. "All right. I will."

She shifted the bags in her arms, communicating with the slight movement that he should step back, give her some much-needed distance.

"Wait."

She stilled again. "What?"

"I was too hard on you last night. I'm sorry."

She gulped, wanting to turn to him, yet not quite daring to move. She looked down, between the bags she held, into the trunk. "It's all right."

"You're not acting like it's all right."

She stared at the top of a box of Ritz crackers, at a bunch of radishes in a plastic bag, at the lid of a jar of applesauce. "Oh, Cole. I don't...this is all so..." She couldn't for the life of her decide what to say next.

He didn't seem to mind. He whispered, "I wanted you to be certain, that's all. I was pushin' kind of hard. And that wasn't right. And right now, I followed you out here, kind of hopin' to...reassure you, I guess."

A quick, wild laugh escaped her. "Well. Growling at me about money is no way to reassure me."

"Yeah," he said. "I guess it's not." She knew he was smiling, a rueful sort of smile, though she still couldn't bring herself to turn and look at him.

She confessed, "I'm just not in the mood to listen to you lecture me. I'm feeling a little on edge today, if you know what I mean."

"Yeah, I guess I do."

She asked, carefully, "Then, do you...think you could step back?"

A beat, then, "Sure."

She heard him move away. But more than that, she *felt* it. Felt it as a slight easing of the insistent call between his body and hers.

She moved to the side. He stepped forward, scooped up

three more of the bags. "Come on. Let's get these groceries in. It's hot out here."

It wasn't, not really. The weather had cooled overnight. There was a nice breeze blowing. She could hear the windmill over by the oak trees, creaking as it turned.

She shifted the bags a little to get a better grip on them and finally allowed herself to meet his gaze. "Cole?"

"Yeah?"

"The door will be open."

He nodded. "I know."

Chapter 13

Preston wouldn't come to the table for lunch, or for the evening meal, either.

"And he won't eat a thing as long as I'm in the room with him," Annie complained when she, Cole and Melinda were seated around the dinner table at six-thirty that night. "In fact, he is bein' a big, mean old bear. He's never been like that with me before. I can just about understand why Mrs. Finster walked out."

Cole said, "Annie, he's been a mean old bear since the stroke. It's called depression. The sight of you and Brady—and my new 'wife'—cheered him up temporarily. But now he's realized he's still stuck in a body that doesn't work the way he wants it to."

"Well, he'd better get over it. I don't like his attitude."

"You said he was practicing with the walker."

"Only when I'm not around. He won't do *anything* to get better when I'm around."

"He's like that with me, too. A man has his pride, Annie."

"Pride." Annie snapped her fingers in disgust. "That's how much I'll give for a man's pride."

Cole reminded her gently, "It's only been a couple of days since we got here."

"I know, but—"

"If this is too tough for you, we could start lookin' for another nurse right now, and probably find one in a day or two."

Annie's face was so easy to read. She knew what that could mean: a chance that the truth would be revealed sooner than she'd agreed to tell it. "No. No, I can handle it."

"You sure?"

She scowled at him. "Yes, I'm sure." She turned to Melinda, who'd been keeping her attention strictly on her meal. "Melinda, I think you should take him his dinner tonight. And then maybe bring the baby in, after he's through."

Reinforce these ridiculous lies, Melinda thought. But she said, "All right. I'll do that."

The old man was sitting by the window when Melinda entered the room with his tray. He greeted her, then said politely, "Just set it on that little table over there." She went over and put the tray down.

He made no move to approach it, but asked very gently, reminding her poignantly of Cole, "Are you settlin' in all right?"

"Just fine."

"Annie tells me you're from New York City." He drawled the words. Absurdly she thought of a picante sauce commercial, where the cowboys read the back of the jar and were outraged to discover that the sauce was made in New York.

"Yes." He was looking at her expectantly. Maybe he wanted some reassurance that she was "qualified" to be the wife of a Hill Country vet. "Actually, I have spent some time in the country. My family owns a ranch. In Wyoming." She carefully didn't mention how much she'd once loathed the isolation there, not to mention the wind, the dust—and the shortage of decent opportunities to shop.

"What part of Wyoming?"

"Northeastern. Not far from the Big Horn Mountains."

"Hmm. I hear it's pretty there. But if you've spent most of your life in New York City, this must be a big change for you."

"Yes. I'll manage, though."

"My son treatin' you right?"

"He is. Yes. Just fine."

He chuckled then. "'Many waters cannot quench love, neither can the floods drown it.'"

She gulped. "Uh. Yes. Yes, that's true."

"It's not only true, it's poetry. From the Good Book."

"The Bible, you mean."

"Song of Solomon," he said proudly. "Chapter eight, verse seven. Maybe I can't eat my dinner without dribblin' my soup down my shirt, but I haven't lost *all* my—" He strained for a word, the way he sometimes did, and finally found it. "—m-marbles, not by a long shot."

"You certainly haven't—and I guess I'd better just go on. Before your food gets cold…"

His heavy gray brows drew together. "You scared of me? You're nervous as a calf in a crowding pen."

"No, of course I'm not scared of you."

"Long as you don't try to get me to do things I'm not ready to do, you and I will get along just fine."

"Mr. Yuma—"

"Uh-uh. Father."

She made herself say it. "Father."

"That wasn't so hard, was it?"

"No. No, of course not." She cleared her throat. "Father. I'm not going to try to force you to do a thing."

"Well. That is a fine piece of news, let me tell you." He sat forward in his chair and studied her intently. Then he grunted. "Go on. It's time I got to work spillin' food on myself. And you come back later. You and Cole. Bring the baby."

"Yes. All right. I will."

Annie went in and collected the dinner tray a half an hour later. When she emerged from her father's room, she told Melinda, "He's askin' for you. Get the baby. And Cole."

Preston wanted to see the baby but refused to hold him. "Just let me look at his fine face. Might not be safe, you know, if I hold him. Only one of these arms does what I tell it to."

So Melinda brought Brady near and the old man admired him again, declaring for the second time how much he looked like Cole. Then he asked about the veterinary hospital.

Cole started describing an operation he'd performed that day, out in the middle of a pasture several miles away. It was something called a D.A. Cole had needed the rancher and two of his grown sons to help hold a cow down while Cole sewed one of her six stomachs back in place after it had floated off to one side.

Melinda stood near the window, listening to Cole, warmed by the humor in his voice as he told the story, and…admiring him. He always stood so tall and proud. And it was clear from the way he talked that he did love his work.

She wondered what that would be like, to have work that she loved, to know people counted on her to do her work and do it well.

Right then, Cole said carefully, "Dad. We'd like to see you over at the hospital again soon."

Preston's craggy face seemed to close in on itself. He turned his head away, toward the window.

Cole didn't give up. "Dad, we really ought to get in that therapist from—"

"Don't," said the old man. "Annie's been at me all day. It's enough, I tell you. It's enough."

"But we only want—"

"Enough!" the old man shouted. A stream of nonsense syllables followed. In Melinda's arms, Brady stirred fitfully in response to the harsh sounds. Cole simply stood there, waiting.

Finally Preston collected himself. He took several slow, deep breaths. Then he whispered that one word again: "Enough…" He hung his head and his right hand, the one that had been affected by the stroke, twitched fitfully.

Brady let out a small, questioning cry. Melinda cuddled him closer, smoothing his blanket around his sweet face and rocking him gently against her breast. "There, there. It's all right…"

She looked up to find Preston watching her.

"I was a strong man once," he said. Cole might not have been there. Right then, it seemed to Melinda that there was only herself. And the old man. And the slight weight of the child in her arms.

"You're still a strong man, Father," she told him, wondering as she spoke where the words had come from. "Stronger than you know, I think. Stronger than your foolish pride will let you admit. Strong enough to stop thinking about what once was and begin to learn how to live with the way things are now."

Preston looked at her for a long time. Then he nodded. "I'll think on that," he said.

Annie was waiting in the kitchen when they left Preston's room. "I heard him shouting. Is he all right?" She held out her arms and Melinda passed Brady to her.

Cole said, "It was just the usual. I mentioned bringing in a therapist, and how I'd like to see him back at the hospital again."

"And he had a fit, right? Oh, Cole. He is impossible."

Cole advised, "Give him time." Melinda slid him a glance and caught him looking at her, a warm look. "I'm starting to think that eventually, he may just come around."

Melinda and Annie walked upstairs together at a little before ten. Brady was already tucked into his crib in the room next to Annie's. Cole had lingered downstairs, watching a comedy show on the television in the living room.

When they reached the landing, Annie put her hand on Melinda's arm. "Do you think Cole is right?"

Sounds from the television drifted up the stairwell. A man talking. Then laughter. How soon would that program be over? Would Cole come upstairs then?

"Melinda?"

Melinda blinked, smiled at her friend. "Hmm?"

"About Dad? Do you think Cole is right? Is he ever going to eat with us, or even come out of his room?"

"Yes. I'm sure he will." She wasn't, not really. But it seemed like the right thing to say.

Annie peered at her doubtfully. "You're just saying that to make me feel better."

Melinda started to argue—then thought better of it. "I'm not a doctor, Annie. Or a fortune teller, either."

"Do you think…maybe we should just go ahead and tell him the truth now? About you and Cole and Brady and me… and everything?"

Melinda could hardly believe her ears. Annie was having second thoughts.

More canned laughter floated up to them from below. A warm shiver pulsed through Melinda. Within an hour, maybe two, the television would be silent. The door between her room and Cole's would open. Cole would be standing on the other side....

"Melinda? Are you listenin' to me?"

"What? Oh. Yes, of course I heard what you said."

"You are actin' kind of strange. What's the matter?"

"Nothing. Nothing at all. And yes, I do think the best thing to do would be to tell your father the truth about everything right away."

Annie made a face. "I knew you would say that."

"Then why did you ask?"

"You are gettin' snippy. Something is wrong. Tell me. Let me help."

"Annie, there's nothing."

"You sure?"

"Positive. Listen, about the bathroom..."

"You go first. Take a long, relaxin' bath, okay? Wash your troubles away."

"Annie, I do not have any troubles." As soon as the words were out, Melinda thought of the job she didn't have. Of her life that lacked focus and real meaning. Of what she and Cole were going to do that night that they shouldn't let themselves do. "Well," she said correcting herself. "I have no more troubles than usual, anyway."

"You know I'm just across the landing, if you want to talk."

"I do know. And thanks."

They said good night. Melinda went to her room, where she found the gray cat, Spunky, asleep on her bed. The cat looked up and yawned at her.

"Don't get too comfortable," she advised. The cat yawned a second time, curled on its side and closed its eyes.

Melinda went to the room's small closet, where she'd hung

up her cobalt-blue silk robe. She took it from the hanger and carried it to the bathroom that she shared with Annie.

She pinned up her hair and undressed as the tub filled. Once in the tub she made herself sit for a long time, soaking, trying her best to relax as the sweet-smelling steam from her favorite bath salts rose all around her. When she finally did emerge, she dried herself briskly, slathered on lotion and spritzed herself with scent. Then she pulled on her robe, belted it firmly with the matching sash and gathered up the clothes she'd left strewn on the floor.

With a stealth she knew was ludicrous, she tiptoed from the bathroom—and couldn't resist a short detour to the top of the stairs. She peered over the balustrade, listening. It sounded quiet down there. No voices. No canned laughter.

She sent a glance across the stairwell, at the closed door of Cole's room. Was he in there right now? Waiting? Wondering why the door she'd promised to leave open remained locked?

She whirled and made for her own room, so flustered she dropped a tennis shoe, scrambled to pick it up, tripped on the trailing hem of her robe—and dropped the other shoe in the process.

"Ridiculous. So silly…" she muttered to herself, as she bent to retrieve the second shoe.

Right then, she heard boots on the stairs. She rose slowly to a standing position, the second shoe dangling from her suddenly nerveless right hand.

Cole appeared in the stairwell—and saw her. They stared at each other.

Melinda clutched her pile of clothing tighter. The first shoe, on top of the load, teetered a little. She nudged it into a more stable position with the hand that was holding the other one. "I, um, dropped my shoe."

His gaze swept over her.

The clinging robe felt way too thin, suddenly—and Melinda was all too aware of her nakedness beneath the silk. "I…had a nice, long bath…"

He didn't smile. He didn't say anything. He just took the two steps left to achieve the landing and then kept coming toward her.

Instinctively she backed toward the open door to her room. He kept pace with her, one long stride for every two of hers.

Still moving backward, she cleared the threshold to her private space. Cole followed, seconds later. He pushed the door shut with the heel of his boot. She heard a snicking sound as the latch caught. He reached behind him. The lock clicked as he turned it.

Her heart had gone crazy. It rushed the blood through her body so fast she felt dizzy.

He asked, softly, "Did you change your mind?"

Her throat felt as if it had something stuck in it. She gave a fierce shake of her head.

He took another long step and he was before her. Very slowly, he reached out, took her clothes and her shoes. She let them go without protest, dropping her arms to her sides as soon as their burden was gone. He tossed the things on the bed. The gray cat still lay there. It raised its head and stared at them.

"I told that cat he couldn't stay," she whispered around the obstruction in her throat.

A half smile pulled at one corner of his mouth. "He's a she. And when she finds a bed she likes, it's pretty near impossible to get her off it."

"Well, this time she's got to go."

"No. Let's just use my room. My bed."

His bed. The realization of what was happening struck her anew. Her knees felt like rubber. Her heart seemed to fill up her chest. She could feel her aroused nipples, pressing against the revealing fabric of her robe, outlined so clearly for him to see.

He took her hand, turned for the connecting door. "Come on."

Before she could think of anything else to say, he'd twisted the lock, opened the door and pulled her into his room. He led her across the floor, which was cool under her bare feet, and then onto the braid rug, to the side of the bed, where he switched on a lamp.

The sudden brightness startled her a little. She blinked.

He soothed her. "It's okay..." His thumb stroked her knuckles.

She remembered the contraceptives she'd bought. "Wait, I..."

His fingers tightened on hers, as if he wouldn't let her go. "Wait for what?"

"Today, when I was in Fredericksburg, I...well, I bought some protection, you know? It's in the drawer, in the stand by my bed."

He tugged sharply on her hand.

With a stunned exhalation of breath, she landed against his chest. She stared up at him. "I...I only wanted to go and get it."

"There's no need. I stopped in at a drugstore myself today."

"You did?"

"Yeah."

"Oh. Well. Then we can use yours."

"That's right." He trailed his hands over the outside of her arms and along her shoulders, rubbing the silk against her skin. His fingers caressed her bare neck, then slid upward, into her still pinned-up hair. He pulled the pins free, dropping them to the little table by the lamp. Her hair fell around her face.

"Beautiful…"His fingers moved through the strands, then fisted gently. He pulled her head back.

She closed her eyes with a hungry sigh as his mouth came down to settle on hers. His tongue sought entry. She gave it, moaning, drinking him in as his hands rubbed her shoulders, pulling her even closer, so their bodies seemed to melt into one striving, needful whole.

He pulled away suddenly. "Wait."

Her eyes popped open. She made a lost, questioning sound.

He put his thumb on her lip, to still her. "It's just the door. I should lock it."

"Oh. Yes. Of course…" She hovered where he left her, unsure and anxious, as he strode across the room and locked the outside door.

Then he came back to her. He reached for her again. She surged toward him eagerly.

They fell across the bed, a tangle of legs and arms, of cobalt silk and rough denim, rawhide boots and bare feet. He pushed the robe away, found her breast. His mouth closed on it, sucking. She bit her lip to keep from crying out too loudly, as she shoved her fingers through his thick brown hair.

Oh, she couldn't get him close enough. But she did try. She pulled his dark head tight against her. The thread of arousal pulsed, a hot cord of need, from her breast down to her womb and back again.

He worked at the knot of her sash. She felt it fall away. He moved back from her, just long enough to take the edges of the blue silk and peel it free. It fell in a midnight pool around her bared body, held in place by her arms, which remained in the sleeves.

He called her beautiful again.

So strange. She had been called that word before. So many times. But it had never seemed anything but a barrier to her, something that set her apart, made her not quite a real person, more an object, a thing to be admired and displayed.

But now, oh now…looking into Cole's eyes, knowing she pleased him, she only felt gladness that it was so, because what he saw when he looked at her went deeper, encompassed her whole self—including the confusions, the doubts, and the pain.

His hands caressed her naked flesh, stroking, tormenting, grasping and hot, learning her secrets, claiming them as his.

Too eager, she thought, both of us. Too eager by half…

She pulled his shirt open, so she could feel his chest against her breasts. And she touched him, through the worn denim of his jeans. He moaned an encouragement into her ear.

So she fumbled with the metal buttons, until she had him free. She stroked him. He moaned again, his hand seeking and finding the female center of her, testing her readiness for him.

He muttered low and urgently, "I can't wait…"

She didn't argue. Why should she? They had waited so long, it seemed to her. She wanted him. Fully. Right then.

He pulled away. She watched him from her bed of silk, as he took the condom from a drawer, unwrapped it, slid it on.

And then he came down on her. She welcomed him with wanton impatience, wrapping her legs around him, clutching him tight, unable to hold back a deep, glorious cry as he filled her.

His mouth found hers. His tongue delved in, imitating the motions their hips made below.

The denim of his jeans abraded, coarse and rough. She hardly felt it; there was so much to feel, after all. She spun in a whirlwind of erotic sensation. The smell of him: dust and clean sweat and a hint of the animals he healed. Her own lotions and bath salts, the rubbing of silk, the scrape of his chest hair, the strength of his arms so hard around her, his breath across her cheek, his hands in her hair…

He lifted up on his elbows and looked down at her. She met his eyes. It seemed to her that they were a circle, joined in a look, in the intimate clasp of her hips cradling his.

He groaned, "Yes." She gave the word back to him as her climax rolled through her, pulsing as it moved, from the center and out. He closed his eyes, tossed his head back and pressed into her so hard and deep she thought he just might have touched her heart.

He groaned again. She cried out once more, this time in sweet, complete release.

Chapter 14

There was stillness.

Cole lowered his head, pressed his brow to hers. "Melinda." A drop of his sweat fell on her temple. He rubbed it up with a stroking motion of his head against hers.

"Cole." She smiled.

With a sigh, he went lax above her, his heavy, strong body pressing her down. She relaxed, too. Her thighs eased their grip on his hips, her arms cradled him gently. And for a time, they just lay there, lazy and loose, utterly content.

He nuzzled her neck. "You smell like a garden. Flowers and dewdrops. Too bad I smell like a vet."

A low, provocative laugh escaped her. "It's very manly, your smell."

"Manly." He grunted.

"That's what I said."

He lifted up on his elbows again. His eyes were so dark,

the pupils enlarged, open and vulnerable. She had no doubt that her eyes looked much the same.

"Come on," he said, "I'll take a shower. You can wash my back."

She felt devilish suddenly. "And what will you do for me?"

"I'll think of something."

"Make it good."

"Ma'am, I will do my very best."

They made love again, in the shower. And then once more in Cole's bed. Long after midnight, they heard a tentative scratching at the door to the landing.

"That's only Sergeant," Cole said. Naked, he rose and went to the door. He let the dog in and then locked up once more. Sergeant limped over near the sitting area and stretched out beside the sofa there.

Cole came back to her. She watched him, delighting in the depth and breadth of his chest and the hard strength in his powerful legs.

He lay down, on his side, next to her. She canted up on an elbow. "What happened to that dog's tail—and his ear and his leg?"

"Couldn't say. One of the local ranchers brought him into the hospital a couple of years ago. Said he'd found him on the road. The injuries were old and long healed even then."

"Isn't there something that can be done for his leg?"

"I broke it again, and reset it. It works better than it used to, but it's still not really right." He stroked her arm idly as he spoke, his hand skimming up and then down again. "Nobody came lookin' for him. And I got kind of used to him. Now we're old friends." He leaned closer, kissed her nose.

She lifted her mouth a little, so he could kiss it, too. He did, quickly and sweetly.

She slid closer with a sigh. "He's devoted to you."

"Yeah. That's one of the best things about animals. What they do pretty much always makes sense. You treat 'em good, and they want to stick around."

She rolled to her back and turned her head toward him. "Meaning people aren't like that?"

"Meaning people are too smart for their own good in some ways. They get hurt and they won't let go of it. They spend the rest of their lives trying to protect themselves from getting hurt again."

She probably shouldn't have, but she asked anyway, "Are you talking about me, Cole?"

He rose enough to lean over her, to trace the line of her jaw with a long, light caress. "Yeah, I guess I am." His finger whispered along the twin curves of her brows, one and then the other. "Someone hurt you. A man, right? He hurt you real bad?"

She closed her eyes. It was just too hard to look at him right then.

"Come on. Look at me."

She did, though it took considerable effort. "Did Annie—?"

"Annie's told me nothin'. I've guessed that you asked her not to." He waited for her to speak. When she didn't, he prompted, "Well. Did I guess right?"

She caught her lip between her teeth and nodded.

He was quiet, looking down at her, waiting, again, for her to say more.

The appeal in those kind eyes undid her. "All right. There was…a man. He was everything my parents had taught me to want. A teacher. A famous poet."

"You're sayin' you were with him because he was what your parents wanted for you?"

"No—yes. Oh, what I mean is, I did want to please them. They thought of me as… frivolous, I guess would be the word. I showed no talent for doing the kind of work they valued. For music. Or painting. Or writing. Things they call 'serious work.'"

"Did this guy have a name?"

"Christopher. And my parents admired him. They even seemed to admire me, when Christopher and I got together."

"You were married to him?"

"No. He didn't want to get married."

"And your parents thought that was okay?" She could tell by his careful tone, by his studiously bland expression, that he thought a woman's parents ought to be more conservative about such things.

She tried to explain. "They wanted me to marry him, they really did. But Christopher was a professor, like my father, a highly respected poet and lecturer, an artist in residence at Columbia University, and a colleague of my father's. To my parents, a long-term live-in relationship with such a fine man was nothing to sneeze at. Besides, my parents believe that artists and poets always make their own rules."

"Sounds real convenient—for artists and poets." He spoke softly, but the words were fragments of iron.

"Cole. Don't be judgmental. Please. Their approval wasn't all of it. I…I truly did love him."

"You still love him?" Now his tone was gruff.

"No. I don't. When I think of him now, I feel…nothing. Nothing at all. I find that pretty sad, actually."

He smiled then, a hard, rather angry smile. "I don't." The cruel smile vanished. "So you didn't marry him—but you lived with him?"

She nodded. "For five years."

"And then?"

She told the worst part quickly, to get it over with. "I got pregnant. He didn't want the baby. I realized I did. Very much. I left him. And then…I lost the child."

Cole's fingers slid across her cheek and into her hair. "Melinda." He kissed her and then he pulled her close, making his big body a cradle for hers. "That man was a fool. He didn't know what he had. But I guess he's got his comeuppance. Because he lost *you*."

She wrapped her arms around him, returning the embrace, his nakedness against hers, not the least bit sexual now. Just comfort offered, comfort taken.

She closed her eyes, put her lips against his ear and whispered, "Maybe you're right. Maybe animals know better than people do how to live. But for a while I thought I knew who I was, knew what I wanted—out of life, from a man. Maybe I wasn't an artist or a writer. Maybe I wasn't even married to Christopher. But I *felt* married. I felt that I…loved him well, that I supported him and stood beside him and helped him with his work. But then I got pregnant. I…changed. And he didn't. Now he's out of my life and I don't want him back. It's as if I'm not the same woman I was once. But who am I? I'm not sure. I can't even trust what I feel…"

Cole said nothing. He just held her. On the floor by the sofa, Sergeant twitched in his sleep and let out a low, chuffing sigh.

Some time later, Cole pulled away enough to seek her lips. Melinda kissed him back.

After that, there seemed to be no more need for sad confessions. For that night at least, they had each other, a bed to hold them, and the heated, insistent rhythms of mutual desire.

"Tuesday is Dad's birthday," Annie said the next morning, when she and Melinda were sitting at the breakfast table eating French toast and strawberries. "He'll be sixty-two."

Melinda forked up a strawberry, bit into it. It was very sweet. She chewed it slowly, feeling dreamy. Images of the night before bloomed, sweet as fresh red strawberries, in her mind.

Cole's face above hers, his body joined to hers below, pressing hard and deliciously, until she couldn't hold back her excited moans.

"Melinda."

"Hmm?"

Annie had her mouth pursed. "What are you thinking about? You didn't hear a word I said."

Melinda sat up a little straighter. "I was thinking that I adore strawberries—and I heard everything you said."

"You did?" It was a challenge.

"Yes."

"Then what?"

"You said that Tuesday is your father's birthday and he'll be sixty-two."

Annie looked somewhat mollified. "Well. Good." She grinned. "And we're gonna bake him his favorite cake."

Melinda speared another strawberry. "We are? What kind of cake is that, may I ask?"

"Red velvet ice cream cake, with butter cream frosting and red sugar sprinkles on top."

Melinda brought the strawberry to her mouth, took it inside and chewed it slowly. "Um. Sounds good."

"You like to bake, don't you? You like to cook. And you're good at it. This French toast is just right."

"Why, thank you." Melinda did enjoy cooking. She'd cooked all the time, during her years with Christopher. She'd planned and played hostess at a large number of successful dinner parties, preparing the gourmet meals herself. She'd found great satisfaction in choosing the menus, in buying her ingredients fresh from the produce and meat markets not far from their loft apartment, and then spending a whole day in the kitchen, making sure everything was just right.

Annie leaned a little closer, across the table. "We're gonna bake that cake, buy some presents and cook us up a feast—and then tell Dad he has to come out of his room for his party."

Melinda knew a wiser thing to do: what Annie had actually gone so far as to suggest last night. Tell Preston the truth about who Brady's real parents were.

Of course, when they did that, everything would change. Nights like last night might not happen again....

"Okay," Annie said. "What's the matter now?"

Melinda wanted to smile and say, *Nothing. Nothing at all.*

But honesty won out over guilty desire. "I was just thinking about what you said last night. That maybe we ought to—"

Annie waved an impatient hand. "I remember what I said. And I did think about it some more."

"And?"

"And I decided the best thing would be to wait until after Dad's birthday."

Melinda set down her fork. "Oh, Annie..."

"Don't get all disgusted. You agreed we'd let him think what he wanted to for a week. And now I'm saying it can be less than a week. It can be Wednesday. The day after his birthday. But I just want to try that, you know? See if we can get him to come to the table to eat his birthday dinner and open his presents."

Before Melinda could respond, the phone rang. Annie stood and went to the wall extension between the window and the cabinets over the sink.

"Hello, Yuma residence. Oh hi, Velma. How *are* you?" She listened. "Yeah. Thanks. I'm just fine. Mmm-hmm. Home to stay..." Her expression turned wistful. "No, Jimmy's...he's not here... Oh, Mrs. Finster mentioned Melinda, huh? Well, she's a friend of mine. From L.A. A real good friend. She's here for a week or two, to visit, you know?" Annie listened some more, then said, "Church? Today?" She gnawed on her lower lip. "Oh, no. I don't think so. Dad's not doin' so well and…" Velma must have trotted out a few arguments to get Annie to change her mind, because Annie fell silent, except for an occasional murmured, "Um-hm," and, "I know, but…" Finally she spoke firmly. "Listen. We'll be there next Sunday, I promise you. How's that?… Okay, real good. Talk to you then."

She hung up. "That was Velma Kitchner. A school friend of mine. She heard I was back home. And will you quit lookin' at me like that? Lands above, you'd think I did murder, I swear."

"Annie, we can't hide in this house forever."

"We are not hidin'. We're just—"

"We're hiding. So that we don't have to lie to anyone else about what is going on here—or tell the truth and take the chance that your father will find out before you finally agree to tell him yourself."

"And I *did* agree to tell him. A whole day earlier than I said at first. So let's stop beating this old, dead horse and get crackin' on planning this party we're gonna throw."

Cole came in at twelve-thirty for lunch. When he walked in the door, Melinda was standing at the counter near the sink, slicing roast beef left over from the night before. He hung his hat on the peg and approached the sink to wash his hands.

Melinda concentrated on her task, carefully shaving the meat, so the slices would be temptingly thin. He slid her a look and a smile as he flipped on the faucet. She smiled, too, but didn't look at him directly. She kept her eyes on her task, feeling dreamy again, a woman with a lovely, guilty secret she was enjoying way too much.

Cole took the bar of soap from the tray on the windowsill and worked up a lather. "What's for lunch?"

"Roast beef sandwich. You can have it hot or cold."

"I'll take it hot."

Hot. He'd take it hot. Her knife paused in midslice. "All right. With gravy?"

"Yeah." He set the soap down again, rinsed his hands and reached for the towel on the bar near her shoulder. He brushed her arm in passing. The contact sent her senses spinning. She almost sliced her finger instead of the roast.

"Careful." There was laughter in his voice.

"I'm *trying* to be."

"Cole. There you are." They both spun around. Annie was standing in the door from the front hall. Her big eyes narrowed a little as she darted a glance from Cole to Melinda and then back to Cole again. For a split second, she almost looked sly. Melinda felt certain she knew everything—each last caress and passionate sigh that had been shared in the darkness the night before.

But then a big, guileless smile took over her face. "We've been waitin' for you to come in. To tell you about the party we're gonna throw for Dad's birthday Tuesday. Now listen, we're gonna bake a red velvet cake and buy some presents and do it up real nice. And you're gonna have to take a few hours off tomorrow, to watch the baby and keep an eye on Dad, so Melinda and I can drive into Fredericksburg and buy all the things we're gonna need. The gift shops don't open till ten, so I figure you can go on to work like you always do, then come back about nine, so we can leave."

Cole hung the towel back on the bar. He looked supremely casual, but Melinda noticed how careful he was not to glance her way—and possibly betray their secret with a look, as they had almost done a moment before. "A party, huh?" He went over to the table and pulled out his chair.

"Yeah. And we're gonna try our best to get Dad to come out of his room for it. What do you think?"

"I think you shouldn't get your hopes up." Annie's face fell. But then Cole added, "On the other hand, there's no harm in trying, now is there?"

"Nope," Annie declared, beaming now. "No harm at all."

As soon as all the males of the household had been fed, Annie and Melinda set to work planning Preston's birthday party. They sat at the table with a stack of cookbooks. Melinda wrote the shopping list. "So," she said when they'd pretty much decided on the menu, "we'll have fried chicken and mashed potatoes, a molded raspberry salad and sourdough rolls."

"And broccoli with cheese sauce. Dad loves that."

"But what about his poor arteries? Shouldn't we be thinking a little bit about them?"

"It's only one meal, Melinda. One meal is not going to do him in."

"If you say so…"

"I do."

Melinda shrugged and bent over her shopping list again. She began writing down the ingredients they didn't have on hand.

"Melinda?" Annie's voice sounded odd, tentative.

Melinda glanced up and arched a questioning brow.

"I…"

"What?"

"Well, Melinda…I saw. I…I know."

The cryptic words told Melinda everything, but still, she hoped she might be wrong. "Excuse me?"

"Oh, Melinda." Annie's lower lip quivered. "I'm jealous, a little. I know…what it's like. So beautiful and perfect. It's like there's no one else in the world, but you and him. Like whenever he is near, he's all you can see."

"Annie…"

Annie let out a long, dejected breath. "All right. I can see it in your face. You're not gonna talk about it."

"Annie, it's…complicated."

"Oh, Melinda. I don't think so. I think it's just love. Just love, that's all. And I guess I'd be about the happiest sister in the world, if you ended up really married to my big brother, after all."

"Look. Don't get your hopes up, okay?"

Annie laughed then, a laugh with sadness in the depths of it. "Askin' me not to get my hopes up is like askin' the wind not to blow." She tipped up her chin. "But I will…mind my own business about it, if that's what you want. You and Cole can work things out in your own way. I won't even mention it to him."

"I'd appreciate that."

"Okay. But I won't stop hopin'."

"Oh, Annie—"

"You can't make me stop hopin', Melinda. And I think you know that. But I promise you, I will keep my big mouth shut."

Melinda must have looked doubtful, because Annie laughed again. "I know, I know. You'll believe it when you see it. And you *will* see it. I will keep out of it. Cross my heart, hope to die."

At ten-thirty that night, Cole stood in his room alone, looking out the front window at the wide, rounded shadows of the oaks that grew on either side of the walk. He had showered, turning the water up hard and hot, then switching it all at once to cold, thinking maybe he could freeze out the longing within him.

It didn't work, so he'd pulled on a pair of jeans and come back out here, to the room where his father had slept with his mother.

He couldn't see the moon from where he stood. But through the branches of the trees, the stars twinkled at him, thick and bright, seeming close enough that he could reach out through the tree branches and grab a handful of them, then open his fist and watch them glitter in his open palm.

She was waiting.

He could feel her—beyond the door at the other end of the shadowed room behind him.

Need dragged at him.

He resisted.

A pointless resistance, for certain. Because he would give in. But he was just enough his father's son to hesitate before he went and did a thing he didn't believe was right.

He ran a hand back through his still-damp hair, swore under his breath—and wished he were younger. A few years back, he could have simply done what he wanted to do. A few years back, it wouldn't have felt as if he were betraying who he was.

When he was younger, in his early twenties, his sexuality had been his one rebellion against the straight and narrow path Preston Yuma had set for him. He'd sought out easygoing, pretty women then. And he'd thoroughly explored the pleasures of the flesh.

But that period of his life hadn't lasted long. He'd discovered that he actually believed the things his father had taught him. That there had to be more than a soft, curvy body and a willing smile. There should be likeness of mind. Mutual respect. And a vow that bound them, for better or for worse.

About four years back, he'd stopped going out at night to honky-tonks and roadside bars. He'd started waiting.

It hadn't been any picnic. His body still wanted the easy pleasure it had known.

But he had held out. For the right woman.

The right woman, who'd turned out to be a whole lot more than he'd imagined.

The right woman, who pretended to be his wife for his sister's sake, who left her door open at night so that he could slip through it.

The right woman, who was good and tenderhearted and too rich and beautiful by half. The right woman, who had run into the wrong guy first.

The right woman, who would be gone from his life in a week or so.

He heard the scratch of a questioning paw against the door to the landing. He turned to let Sergeant in.

The dog sat when Cole opened the door, waiting as he always did, for a clear invitation.

"Come on, then," Cole said. And the dog rose, bumped at his hand. Cole gave him a pat, ruffled the fur at his collar. "Go on, now. Lie down."

Cole closed the door and turned the lock.

The other door beckoned.

He moved toward it, relentlessly drawn.

The gray cat that Annie called Spunky lay curled in a ball in the center of the bed.

Melinda was sitting in the chair by the window that faced the backyard. She'd left the light off, but the curtains were wide open. No oak trees screened the starlight. It filled the room, so all the shadows seemed to give off a silvery glow.

She wore that blue robe that clung to every sweet, tender curve, and she looked out at the dark shape of the old wind-mill, which circled slowly against the night sky.

She heard him, turned her head sharply, saw him standing

there—and swept to her feet in a rustle of silk. He caught a flash of smooth thigh as the robe settled around her.

Her full mouth quivered a little. She murmured his name on a breath.

It was enough to bring him to her. He crossed the floor in three long strides. Her hair shimmered at him, pale as moonbeams. Her eyes glittered. He lifted both hands, hooked the sides of the robe above her breasts and pulled it wide. Then, a low, hungry moan escaping him, he lowered his head and took one hard, tempting nipple into his mouth. It tasted good. He swirled his tongue around it, nipped it with his teeth.

She moaned. Her slender arms pulled him closer, the blue silk sliding against his cheek. He grabbed the sash of the robe and pulled on it. It gave in a long, easy glide. He dropped it to the floor at their feet, pushed the robe off her shoulders, heard it collapse around her ankles with a sound like a sigh.

She pressed herself into him, her breasts pushing soft and full against his chest. The woman he had waited for, heaven in his arms—his for this night, at least…

The wing chair was right behind her, in front of the star-lit window. He took her by her sleek hips, pushed her down into the chair, going down with her, kneeling at her feet.

He looked up at her, waiting, until she fully looked at him. And then he let his gaze travel down, along the star-washed length of her, over the full, perfect breasts and the tiny waist and the hips that flared just enough to be womanly. She had her long, incredible legs pressed together. The curls where her thighs joined shimmered, pale as moonglow in the dim light.

She said his name again, a pleading, hungry sound. He put his hands on her smooth knees, hooking his thumbs inside. She knew what he wanted. To see her. All of her.

She didn't refuse him. With only slight reluctance she surrendered to the gentle pressure of his hands. He looked.

And then brushed his hand in a slow sweep along the satiny flesh of her inner thigh. She gasped when he touched her. He parted the star-silvered curls, slipped a finger into the silky heat and wetness that told him she was his.

For this night. And the night after. And maybe, if he was lucky, a night or two more after that.

He shifted forward, moving between her open legs, to taste her.

She cried out as his mouth found her. He drank from her, holding her soft thighs apart with determined hands, tasting the secret inner wetness, circling the erect nub of her sex, feeling it swell even more as he pressed his open mouth to it and stroked it with his tongue.

All resistance banished, she moaned and writhed, pressing that sweetness against him. He slid his hands around her, to cup her hips and bring her closer still.

It happened then. He felt the pulsing, the series of tiny tender explosions against his insistent tongue.

"Cole, Cole…" Her hands held his head as he drank her completion, her body quivering tightly, going rigid—and then falling limp with a heavy sigh.

He didn't leave her immediately, but kept his mouth on her, feeling the last tremors as they slowed to an occasional lingering pulse.

Finally he lifted his head enough to rest on her belly. She combed her fingers through his hair.

"I thought, maybe, you would stay away tonight." Her voice found him through the darkness, soft, dreamy—a little bit sad.

He turned his head and kissed her, right below her navel. "I couldn't."

"I'm glad."

He smiled to himself against her belly, thinking that she could no more deny this thing between them than he could.

He found some satisfaction knowing that. It wasn't enough, but it was better than nothing.

Her fingers went still in his hair. He waited for her to speak. When she didn't, he commanded quietly, "Say it, whatever it is."

She did. "Annie says she's telling Preston the truth, on Wednesday, after his birthday."

He made a disbelieving sound. "Right."

"She *has* to tell him by Thursday. If she doesn't, she knows that I will." Her stomach rose and slowly fell as she sighed. "Wednesday *or* Thursday, neither one is that far away."

He sat up then, took her hands, looked into her night-shadowed violet eyes. "How long will you stay?"

She pulled one hand free of his grip. His mother's diamond winked at him. Then she touched his face, laying her palm against his cheek. "I'll go as soon as she tells him."

"She'll want you to stay. She'll say she needs you."

Her thumb brushed his lips. "I've done what I could. She's come home where she belongs. I should have left the day we got here."

"But you didn't."

"No."

"So let's leave what you *should* have done out of this." Keeping hold of her right hand, he rocked back on his heels and stood.

Her fingers stiffened in his. Looking down, he could see anxiousness in her eyes. "Cole? Annie...she knows. About us."

His gut tightened. He didn't need his little sister poking her nose in this, not at all. And for a number of reasons, not the least of which was the sense of responsibility he felt toward Annie.

Cole had prided himself, in recent years, anyway, on the good example he set for Annie of how a man ought to behave.

Annie might have run off with Jimmy Logan, ended up with a baby and no husband, but at least Cole had been able to tell himself that Annie hadn't learned such behavior at home.

He demanded, "How does she know?"

"She guessed. She saw us together, at lunchtime, when you were washing your hands and I was—"

"Nothing happened at lunchtime."

"She saw the way we looked at each other."

He relaxed a little. "Then she doesn't *know*—not how far it's gone, anyway. Unless you told her?"

"I didn't tell her anything. She only thinks that we're...in love."

Love. He wished she hadn't said that word. It reminded him too starkly of all they wouldn't share.

He hauled her to her feet, hooked a hand around her neck and brought her close enough that her soft body touched his all the way down. Desire coursed through him. "She doesn't know—" he pressed his hand to the small of her back, to make his meaning clear "—about this?"

She gasped, put her hands on his chest, resisting the pull between them as she tried to frame her answer. "She might have guessed. I couldn't say. But she promised to stay out of it, to let us work it out on our own."

It could have been worse. He gentled his hold on her, stroked her back, caressed her shoulder. "Are you gonna lock that door tomorrow night?"

"No," she admitted in a small, shamed voice.

"And as long as it's open, I will walk through it. Soon enough, Annie will tell my father what he deserves to know. And you'll leave. Right?"

She nodded.

"So it's all settled. We know exactly what we've got—and pretty much how long we'll have it."

"Yes. Yes, that's true."

"Annie will mind her own business."

"She said that she would."

"Then leave it alone."

"But—"

"Melinda. Leave it alone. Let's make the most of the time we have." He slid his hand down, pressed the small of her back again, bringing her hips up and in, nestling himself between them.

She let out a tiny sound of submission. Those soft hands stopped holding him away. They slid up his chest. She moaned as he covered her sweet mouth with his.

Chapter 15

Melinda and Annie went shopping the next morning. Cole told them they could have three hours and no more. "I want to be back at work by noon. Got it? Noon, at the latest."

They promised him that they wouldn't let him down.

The drive to Fredericksburg took forty-five minutes. When they got there, they raced around the big supermarket, grabbing what they needed off the shelves. Once the food was bought, they hurried up and down Main Street, scouring the charming variety of shops and choosing gifts quickly—two nice shirts and pair of tooled boots with a belt to match, as well as a few novelty items that Annie said were just for fun.

They were back in the car and on their way home by eleven. They reached Bluebonnet's Main Street at twenty to twelve.

They drove by the red phone booth and the tiny post office with its regulation flagpole and rather droopy-looking flag. A few people wandered up and down the street. They waved as

Melinda drove past. In the open space next to the post office, a small group of children played with a big green ball.

At the Bluebonnet Grocery, two old men shared a bench on the wide front porch. Behind the men hung a chalkboard with what appeared to be the day's bargains scrawled on it: Broccoli 69 cents a bunch. Fresh Peaches 79/lb. Near the steps that led down to the street, a black dog snoozed in the shade of the overhang.

"Pull over," Annie commanded just as they were about to pass the store. "Pull in right there. Now."

Melinda pressed the brake automatically, then tried to protest. "But Annie, we have to—"

"This'll only take a minute."

Shaking her head, Melinda parked a few feet from where the black dog lay.

Annie snapped open her seat belt. "Come on."

"Annie, we've got ice cream in the back and it's almost twelve. Brady's probably starving and we promised Cole that—"

"The longer you sit here and argue with me, the softer that ice cream will get."

Grumbling under her breath, Melinda got out of the car.

Annie urged, "Come here. Come on."

Melinda went around the front of the car and grudgingly took Annie's extended hand.

"Annie Yuma, that you?" One of the old men on the porch canted forward and squinted their way.

"Yes, Mr. Tolly. How are you?"

"Good as I'm likely to get. You home to stay?"

"Yes, sir. I am."

"Who's your friend with the fancy car?"

"This is Melinda. She's here for a visit."

"Your friend got a last name?"

Annie's eyes shifted away. Melinda spoke up. "Bravo. I'm Melinda Bravo."

"Well, welcome to Bluebonnet, Melinda Bravo." The old man waved at her. "You're a pretty one. We like pretty women around here."

She pasted on a smile and waved in return. Mr. Tolly spoke to Annie, then. "You tell Preston that we are waitin' to see him around town again."

"Yes, Mr. Tolly. I'll tell him. I will."

The old man sat back, nodding sagely. Then he and the other man put their grizzled heads together and began talking in low voices.

Annie whirled on Melinda and whispered hotly, "You shouldn't have said your last name. If my dad hears—"

"How's he going to hear before Wednesday? He never even comes out of his room."

Annie pulled a disgusted face. "There's no sense taking chances."

"Well, it's too late now, isn't it? And we really do have to get back to the house."

Across the street, two women emerged from the post office. Annie smiled and waved at them.

"How you doin', Annie?" one of the women called.

"Fine, Mrs. Hendricks. Just fine." Annie hauled on Melinda's hand. "Come on."

"Annie, I told you. We have got to—"

"Quit arguin'. Come on." Towing Melinda along behind, Annie marched along the hard-packed dirt that served as a sidewalk between the grocery store and the next building over. Three steps went up the side of that building. Annie dragged Melinda up the steps, then stopped before the empty window to the right of the door.

"Well?" Annie released Melinda's hand and gestured expansively. "What do you think?"

Melinda shrugged. "Of what?"

"Oh, you are just impossible." She flung a hand out toward the window. "Read the sign."

Melinda read aloud. "Store For Rent. So?"

"Look inside."

"Annie."

"Go on. Go on, look."

So Melinda pressed her face against the dusty glass. She saw bare floors and a checkout counter, a couple of glass-fronted display cases, a few random straight chairs—nothing at all to get excited about. She brushed the grime off her nose and declared, "It's an empty shop. So what?"

"Melinda. Think. You could rent it."

"For what?"

"You could…have your own store. You could sell clothes, nice ones, reasonably priced. And gifts. So that folks like us wouldn't have to go all the way to Fredericksburg just to buy a birthday present. And…you could even have one of those little coffee bar things, like they have in L.A. With ice cream and sodas for the summer, and hot things when the weather cools. It could be—"

"Annie. I've worked in one shop in my life. An exclusive lingerie boutique in Beverly Hills. What would I know about running a store in a town like this?"

"You could learn as you go. And you've got good taste. You've got real style."

"Do you really think style is what is needed in Bluebonnet?"

"Well, I certainly do. Don't look at me like that. I'm *serious.* The ladies of Bluebonnet are like everybody else. Don't you go sellin' them short. They could use a little glamour, too, you know."

Melinda closed her eyes and silently counted to ten.

"Annie. Remember what you told me yesterday? That you'd stay out of my business? That you wouldn't interfere?"

Annie's mouth went into the pinched position. "I am not interferin'. I am suggestin', that's all."

"Well, okay. You've *suggested*. Now, we'd better get home."

"I just thought—"

"Annie. Stop."

Annie folded her arms across her middle and scowled down at her shoes. But when she glanced up, she was grinning. "You'll think about it. I know you will. And I won't say another word. Ideas are like seeds, you know? You plant them. Then you just have to wait, give them a chance to grow."

"Annie, it is five minutes till noon."

"Well, come on then." Annie headed for the car. "*I'm* ready to go."

That afternoon, they wrapped the presents in bright paper and pressed the ice cream into a cake layer pan to freeze into shape overnight.

"Tomorrow, after breakfast, we'll bake the cake," Annie said. "And in the afternoon, we'll put it together and spread the frosting on. We'll cook a meal to die for, you know?" She went and picked up Brady, from his portable playpen. He gurgled at her. She said, almost as if she were addressing the baby, "And then you will go in and tell my father—"

"Wait a minute."

"Hmm?" Annie laid her son gently on her shoulder—and more or less batted her eyes at Melinda.

"*Who* will tell your father?"

"Well now, Melinda." Annie patted Brady's back. "He really does *like* you. Whenever he speaks of you, his eyes get a light in them. And you're not like me, someone always pushin' him to get better. It'll take him off guard, if you do it."

"Your father doesn't strike me as a man who will enjoy being taken off guard."

"Who cares if he enjoys it? We have to do what's necessary to get him out of that room. And what's necessary is for *you* to ask him."

Melinda tried to look uncompromising.

Apparently it didn't work. "You will, won't you...*please?*"

"Oh, Annie..."

"It will work. I just know it. If you're the one that does it." Brady let out another happy little gurgle. "See?" Annie said, "Brady agrees with me."

"You simply will not give up when you want something, will you?"

"Then you'll do it?"

Someday, Melinda told herself, she would tell Annie no and mean it.

"Melinda? Melinda, please..."

"Oh, all right. I suppose so."

"You are the *best* friend. The best friend a gal ever had!"

Cole came back in at six. He was quiet all through dinner and he didn't eat much.

Annie remarked on his lack of appetite.

He said, "A case of swamp fever, over at the Linton place. I had to put the animal down."

"Oh, Cole. I am so sorry." Annie put her hand over his.

He looked down at his plate. "I guess I won't finish this."

"That's fine. You go on."

He rose from the table and left them.

Once he was gone, Annie said, "He'll be okay. He just needs a little time alone."

Melinda asked, "What's swamp fever?"

"Horses get it—not real often, thank the Lord. It's infectious anemia. Spread by mosquitoes and flies. There isn't any cure for it. And once a horse has it, you have two choices. You can isolate him or put him down. Isolation's almost impossible on a working ranch. So usually, when they get it, that just has to be the end." Annie pushed her own plate away. "A horse takes a lot of training, you know? A lot of love. There's always someone hurtin' bad, when a horse has to be put down."

Melinda went to Cole that night. Still dressed in the flowered skirt and T-shirt she'd pulled on that morning, she opened the door between their rooms and saw him sitting on the sofa, by the window. The stereo was playing softly, a tune Melinda didn't recognize, but something country, a ballad about lost love.

She went to him, sat down beside him. He gave her a smile.

She said, "Annie explained to me…about swamp fever."

He put his arm around her, pulled her near. She leaned her head on his shoulder, felt for his hand.

He twined his fingers with hers. "Homer Linton's got a daughter. She's fifteen. She owned the horse. A sweet little red mare."

"The girl was there, is that what you're saying, when you put the horse to sleep?"

"I couldn't order her not to be there. She had the right." He sat back from Melinda a little, looked at her deeply, then pulled her head down onto his shoulder again. "It's a part of the job, that's what I tell myself."

"But it doesn't help much, huh?"

"No, not much."

She said, "If you want to talk about it a little, I'm willing to listen."

"You sure?" He did sound hopeful.

"Yes. Tell me. I'm listening."

So he described the deep hole that had waited, bulldozed before he got there, in the middle of a pasture. He said that the rancher's daughter had spoken to the mare so softly, telling her tender things, unwilling to let go.

"Finally her father had to order her to take the horse to the ditch or he would do it. She led the mare over, then wouldn't stand clear. Her father had to pull her away."

"You had to...do it right then?"

She felt his nod against her hair. "The horse was startin' to get agitated, with her owner carryin' on, strugglin' in her father's arms. I moved up and gave the injection fast, before the mare even saw the needle. Thirty cc's, that's what it takes. The girl cried out, a long, deep, awful wailing sound. The mare staggered. Within seconds, she fell. I gave her a shove and she dropped into the ditch." Melinda felt his lips then, pressing lightly at her temple. "It had to be done. Or more horses would die."

"But that doesn't make it any easier."

"No. No easier. No easier at all."

She turned her head, seeking his mouth. They kissed, a quick and reassuring contact, his lips to hers.

Then she stood and pulled him up with her. She led him to the bed, pushed him down and pulled off his boots for him, then his socks. She unbuttoned his shirt, removed it. And then she had him stand again, so that she could dispense with his jeans and the white briefs he wore.

When he was naked, she took off her own clothes and laid them on top of his, over a chair. They slid beneath the covers together. He pulled her close, with her back to him, his body wrapped around hers.

He smoothed her hair and brushed his lips against her ear.

"I could get too used to this." His voice was very low, more breath than sound.

She turned to him then, kissed him, felt desire bloom. She was the one who reached for the drawer, removed the small pouch, opened it and slid the condom in place.

They made love lying on their sides, facing each other, not closing their eyes.

By four the next afternoon, the red velvet cake, filled with vanilla bean ice cream and topped with butter-rich frosting and sparkling red sugar, waited in the freezer for the party that night. Every present had been wrapped. The molded raspberry salad was ready to serve and Annie had hung crepe paper spirals from the brass chandelier over the dining-room table, draping the strips outward in festive loops, then tacking them at the edges of the ceiling.

"You'd better go in and ask him now," she told Melinda. "Then we'll fry up that chicken. Cole promised he'd be back at six."

Melinda hesitated.

"Melinda, are you gonna back out on me?"

Melinda wished that she could. But she had said she would do it. "No. I'm going. I am."

Melinda knocked softly on the closed door. She heard a thump on the other side, then a muffled voice commanded gruffly, "Come in."

He was sitting in his wheelchair, the metal walker just a foot away, the open side toward him. The chair hummed as he turned it her way. His face looked slightly flushed and his still-thick gray hair had fallen over his forehead. He brushed it back with a quick swipe of his good left hand. She realized he must have been practicing with the walker, and hid a smile at his efforts to pretend that he hadn't been.

"Well. Melinda. Hello." He did look happy to see her—for

a moment anyway. Then his eyes narrowed with suspicion. "You look nervous, daughter. What has Annie got you up to?"

Her mouth felt suddenly way too dry. She swallowed. "I… um. Happy Birthday. Father."

He grunted. "I'm right. She's got you up to something."

Melinda had planned to make small talk for a few minutes at least, to build up to the big question gradually. But looking into those guarded eyes, she knew that small talk wouldn't get her anywhere at all.

She attempted to edge up on the invitation. "Annie and I went shopping yesterday."

"I know that. Cole came in to check on me about ten— when he should have been out workin'. I asked him what was goin' on. And he said you two had taken off for Fredericksburg. I told him it was pure foolishness, leavin' him here in the middle of the workday to deal with a cryin' baby and a sick old man while you two went out and had yourselves some fun."

She remained resolutely cheerful. "You know, Father. I don't believe you're as sick—or as *old* as you seem to want us to think you are."

"Humph. So you went shopping. What's that got to do with anything I need to know?"

"Well, we bought you a few presents and all the necessary ingredients to fix your favorite foods—you know, the ones you're not supposed to have?"

He harrumphed some more. "Get to the point."

"We baked your favorite cake. There are crepe paper streamers all over the dining room ceiling and—"

"No."

She dragged in a breath, released it with care—and spoke with great patience. "I haven't even told you what I'm after yet."

"You've told me. I know what you all are up to now. And

I'm not goin' along with it." He actually stuck out his lower lip, like some overgrown child.

Frustration bubbled inside her. She tried to ignore it, to stay pleasant and firm. "Father. Please. Come out and sit at the table for your birthday party."

"No. It's not my idea of a celebration, to look a f-fool in front of my family."

"You will not look like a fool."

He made a harsh, impatient noise. "Little you know."

"Come to your birthday party."

"No."

"Please?"

"No."

She wanted to give up then. She truly did. But she could not face the prospect of going back to the kitchen and telling Annie she might as well take all the crepe paper down. Blowing out another weary breath, she marched over to the bed and dropped to the edge of it.

The chair hummed again, as Preston gave it a quarter-turn in her direction. She didn't look at him. She stared at the walker.

"Don't you keep at me now," he growled. "I've told you. I'm not ready to—"

She cut him off. "You were practicing with that walker, weren't you? Before I came in?"

He snorted and huffed. "So what if I was?"

"You can probably get around this room with that walker if you want to."

"St-st-stagger's more like it."

"But you *can* do it."

"Yeah. That's right. I can."

"Just like you can feed yourself. Maybe not gracefully yet. But you get the job done."

"What are you getting at?"

"You could come to the table and eat the dinner we're going to cook. It's not an impossible thing we're asking of you."

"I'm not doin' it. And that's that."

"You will break Annie's heart if you don't come."

"That's a pure exaggeration, and we both know it, too."

"It is not. Your family needs you. They need to see you improving. They need you to come out of this room and *be* with them again."

He turned his head, looked at her obliquely. "Aren't you part of this family, too?"

She coughed. "Of course I am. We. All right? *We* need to give you this party. We need to have you at the table with us. If you spill cheese sauce on yourself, and fumble with your presents, we're not going to care."

"*I'll* care."

"Well, get over it. You've been in your room long enough, *Father.* It's time you poked your head out, time you started learning to let people see you as you are now. Time you got on with your life—and let *us* get on with ours." The words had more meaning than she'd meant to give them. She thought of Cole, last night, whispering in her ear.

I could get too used to this....

So could she, she realized. Oh, so could she. Every day this deception continued, it got harder to imagine what her life would be when it ended.

"Melinda?" Worry had crept into the gruff voice. "Melinda. Daughter. Are you all right?"

She swiped at the foolish tear that had dared to dribble down her cheek. "I am just fine. And you are coming to your birthday party."

He gave her a long, hard stare, then growled, "I warned you about tryin' to make me do things I don't want to do."

"I don't care about your warnings. If you want to treat me as harshly as you treat Annie, as cruelly as you treated that poor Mrs. Finster, that's fine."

"There is nothin' poor about Gerda Finster. That woman is a pistol and she can hold her own. So can Annie."

"Oh, all the more reason you should torture them then, right?"

"I don't go torturin' women."

"You are coming to your birthday party."

His right hand was twitching. He put his left hand over it, rubbed it a little and the twitching stopped. He tipped his head sideways, slid her a look. "That would be red velvet ice cream cake you baked?"

"That's exactly what it would be."

"And that cheese sauce you mentioned, would it have broccoli under it?"

"It would."

"Fried chicken? Mashed potatoes?"

"Molded raspberry salad, too. But you'll never get any— unless you come to the table."

He groused, "You make Gerda Finster look like an a-a-amateur."

Relief swept through her, followed swiftly by a deep sadness. Tomorrow. Annie had promised to tell Preston the truth then. Tomorrow, the truth would come out. And Melinda would be getting on with her life. She spoke briskly. "So. You'll come?"

"Don't make that sound like a question. You know blessed well I never had a choice."

It was a lovely little party.

Brady lay in his playpen in the corner of the room, gurgling and cooing contentedly, waving his plump arms and stubby feet at the mobile of stars and moons that Melinda had found in Fredericksburg the day before and hooked to the rim of the playpen that morning. Annie had been careful to see that he was well fed before they went and told Preston it was time to emerge from his room.

Preston took the place of honor at the head of the big cherry-wood table. He said a simple grace before they shared the meal.

"Our Father, we pray that we may have patience with our own failings—and that those we love will have patience with us. We thank you for bringin' our Annie on home to us. And for giving us a new daughter and a fine, strong grandson as well. Bless this food to our bodies' use and ourselves to thy service. For Jesus' sake. Amen."

As the Amens echoed down the table, Melinda opened her eyes. Cole was smiling at her from the other side of the centerpiece of candles and crape myrtle blooms that she and Annie had created. It was a good moment, a moment that somehow made the lie of their pretend marriage seem like the deepest, most basic of truths.

They began to pass the food. Preston ate slowly, masking his awkwardness by taking great care with each bite. Yes, he spilled a drop or two of cheese sauce onto his shirt and dribbled water down his chin. Once, he looked up and caught Melinda's eye as he was surreptitiously dabbing his shirtfront with the corner of his napkin.

"I warned you," he grumbled.

She fluttered her eyelashes at him. "I'm sure I haven't the faintest idea what you're talking about."

He grunted—a sound that actually resembled a chuckle. Then he picked up a chicken leg and bit into it.

After the meal, they cleared the table and gave Preston his presents. He opened them slowly, by necessity, but no one minded. It seemed quite appropriate that he should savor his gifts. He admired the shirts and the boots and the belt, declaring that each of them was just what he needed. And he even let out a rusty laugh at the small statuette of a cowboy and a kicking donkey that Annie had found in a novelty shop.

At last, it was time for the cake. Melinda brought the plates and coffee cups to the table as Annie put the candles on; they had settled on twenty-four, because that was how many there were in the box.

Annie held the cake high. "What do you think?"

"I think it looks terrific." Melinda grabbed the cake knife and the glass of warm water that would make cutting easier. "And we'd better get it to the table before we burn the house down."

They entered the dining room singing, and Cole's voice joined with theirs. Annie carried the cake right to Preston and set it down before him. The light from the candles cast his craggy face in warm, sharp relief. The birthday song ended.

"Make your wish, and make it quick," Annie instructed. "The wax will start drippin' and mess up the frosting."

"You think I got the wind to blow out all these candles?"

"If you don't, I will help you."

Preston looked up at his daughter, a tender smile softening the gaunt hollows of his face. "I guess I know that, Annie girl."

She bent and kissed his forehead. "Go on. Hurry. Blow."

"I think I'll need more help than you alone can give me."

Annie signaled energetically to Cole and Melinda. "Come on. Stand close."

They gathered in a knot around Preston's wheelchair. "Okay, now, ready?" They all four sucked in air. "Blow."

The twenty-four candle flames flickered, rose up, sheered flat to the side—and then went out.

They all applauded, even Preston, who managed the feat by holding his weak hand still and slapping the good one against it. From his playpen, Brady let out a sound that resembled a happy laugh.

And the doorbell rang.

Annie gasped. Melinda sucked in more air, which smelled sharply of candle smoke. Cole glanced across the table, through the arch to the living room and the door that stood open onto the front hall.

"Well?" said Preston.

Nobody moved. They were all thinking that this could be it. What would they say to whoever had come calling, when Preston proudly introduced his new daughter-in-law and his grandson, Cole's child?

Preston spoke again, with some humor. "I do believe there's someone at the door."

The bell rang again.

"Yeah." Preston nodded. "That's what that bell means. Someone at the door."

Cole started to move. Annie, standing next to him reached out and grabbed his arm. "No. Wait…"

Preston's lined forehead crumpled down into a frown. "Annie? What's the matter?"

"I just…well, this is *our* party. We don't need anyone interruptin' us right now."

Preston's frown deepened. "It could be something important. Someone with a dyin' animal or—"

"Oh, I'm sure it's nothing like that. I'm sure it's just—"

Preston didn't let her finish. "It is not our way to ignore a knock at the door. You know that, Annie." He looked at his son. "Go see who it is. We have a fine cake to share."

Cole looked down at Annie's hand, which still clutched his arm. With a small, unhappy moan, she released him.

He started to walk around Preston's chair—and stopped when they all heard the creak of the front door. Whoever it was had decided not to wait to be invited in.

"Who's there?" Preston called.

They heard the door close. Footsteps echoed on the wooden floor. And then a young man appeared in the living room doorway. He wore battered jeans and a frayed dark-colored T-shirt. Even from across the room, Melinda could see that his boots were down at the heels. His hair and eyes were midnight black.

Annie let out a sharp cry. "Jimmy! Oh, Jimmy... You've come home!"

Chapter 16

Annie flew across the room, chanting her husband's name like a one-word prayer as she ran. She fell against him, throwing her arms around his neck. His face contorted as her body touched his. Melinda saw fierce joy, and guilt and something else—something desperate and needful.

He said her name only once. "Annie." That word had everything in it, all the emotions the world could hold, including a deep, abiding love.

Annie went on praying his name. "Jimmy, Jimmy, Jimmy..."

His strong, tanned arms banded around her. His head went down as hers came up.

Melinda glanced away. It seemed too personal a thing to witness, the heated kiss of reunion the two shared then.

Perhaps she shouldn't have, but she turned to Cole—and found his eyes waiting. As she looked at him, a thousand disparate images flashed and tumbled through her mind. She saw the dark beauty of their forbidden nights together. She remembered his face across the bed as Annie labored bearing Brady, recalled his cruelty during the weeks in L.A.—and his kindness ever since. It was all there—all that they had been to each other in a brief span of weeks.

And more than just the two of them.

His father was in that look, as well. His father, here at the table, joining the family again at last. And Annie, here at home where she belonged, though both of them had doubted she would ever come.

And Jimmy Logan. In Cole's eyes, she saw acceptance of the younger man. Cole must have understood the look on Jimmy's face, too.

Right then, across the room, Jimmy spoke again. He said two words. "The baby?" He held his wife by the upper arms and stared down at her with fearsome intensity.

Before she could answer him, Brady cried—a small, fitful sound, as if to say, "I'm over here…"

Jimmy's dark head lifted, his black eyes sought and found the playpen in the corner.

"He's fine," Annie whispered. "He is just fine."

Jimmy had already stepped around her. In four long strides he reached the playpen. Annie followed right after. They stood together, looking down at their son.

"You should hate me," Jimmy said softly to his wife.

"Never," she replied without pause. Then she pushed the mobile to the side and bent to pick up the child. She held him out shyly. Carefully Jimmy took him.

The baby looked up solemnly into his father's eyes.

Annie took Jimmy's arm. "Did you…get the letter I left with Mrs. Lucas?"

Jimmy nodded, not glancing up.

"Then you know we call him Brady."

"Brady," Jimmy repeated.

That was when Preston spoke. "Is anyone going to have the c-c-courtesy to tell me what is going on around here?"

A terrible silence followed. Annie clung to her husband's arm. Jimmy did look up then. He frowned at Preston, obviously in the dark.

Finally Preston growled, "Well?"

And Cole gave him his answer. "Annie and Jimmy are married. And Brady is their baby, not mine and Melinda's."

Preston said nothing for a moment. He looked at his cake, with the blown-out candles still stuck in the butter cream frosting. At last, he let out a pent-up breath. "Well," he said. "Happy birthday to me."

Cole tried to explain further. "Dad, we—"

But Preston waved a silencing hand. He turned to Jimmy. "Come over here, young man."

Jimmy Logan stiffened. He held his son tighter, drawing back from the command in the older man's voice. But Annie gently took the baby from him, looking into his eyes as she did.

Jimmy stepped forward.

Preston said, "You took my Annie away too young."

Jimmy started to speak.

Preston waved him to silence. "You took my Annie away too young. And then you... what?"

Jimmy flinched, then drew himself tall. "I...I walked out on her in L.A. She had my baby alone."

"No, I wasn't alone!" Annie cried then. "Cole and Melinda—"

Preston cut her off. "Let the man speak for himself, Annie. You never have learned to keep silent when you should."

Annie pressed her lips together and looked down at her son.

Jimmy said it again. "I left her. She had my baby alone."

Preston studied the younger man. "I have hated you, did you know that?"

Jimmy's Adam's apple bounced up and then down as he swallowed. "I know it."

"But…" Preston's right arm twitched. He rubbed it thoughtfully until it stilled. Then he continued, "I am learnin'. Even an old man can learn. I am learnin' a truth I should have already known. That hate is a killin' thing." A pained smile twisted across his lips. "It almost got me. But not quite."

He rubbed his right arm some more. The baby cooed. Preston went on, "The good Lord teaches us that we cannot relive the past. I will ask you two questions. Are you ready to be a father to my grandson now? And a husband to my daughter?"

"I reckon I am." Annie stepped forward then and stood close to Jimmy. He put his arm around her, encompassing both her and their child. "Though I can't see any reason why you should believe me. I've come back with nothin'."

Preston looked at his daughter, and then back at the son-in-law he'd just discovered he had. "Without my hate to blind me, I can see now that you have love. Love is always a start. You might have to take help, you might have to s-s-swallow your pride. It has a bitter taste, pride, but a man can learn to push it down and get on with things. Do you think you can do that?"

Jimmy's Adam's apple bounced again. "I can. I will."

"Are you through runnin'?"

"I am."

Preston nodded. "So be it. Have you had your supper?"

Jimmy blinked at that question. It was probably too mundane by half, considering the tough ones he'd just had to answer. He muttered, "I ate."

"Good enough. Melinda, get another one of those little plates." He glanced from her to Cole. "Well, come on. Let's have some of my birthday cake."

Annie brought the baby to the table. Jimmy took the empty chair next to hers and Cole returned to his seat. Melinda pulled the candles from the cake, sliced it and passed it around.

Right then, she remembered the coffee. Excusing herself, she went into the kitchen and came back with the pot. She served a cup to everyone but Annie, who didn't drink coffee since she was nursing.

When Melinda slid into her chair, Preston picked up his fork. They all began eating.

"This is a fine, fine cake," Preston said, after he'd carefully brought the first bite to his mouth, chewed it and swallowed.

Annie said, "Melinda and I baked it together."

"You did a fine job."

Melinda and Annie spoke in unison. "Thank you."

Preston was watching Melinda. She knew what was coming and steeled herself.

It came. "So. If you and my son don't have a child together…do you have a marriage?"

Annie shifted miserably in her chair. "Dad, you have to understand. I…I didn't know how to tell you that Brady was mine, and so Cole and Melinda were only trying to—"

Preston silenced her with a look. "Let one of *them* answer. It's *their* marriage we are discussin' here."

Melinda tried to get the words out. All she managed was a silly, strangled sound.

It was left to Cole to say it. "No, Dad. We're not really married."

Preston brought his coffee cup to his lips and drank without spilling a drop. He set the cup down. "Then you'd better either *get* married, or stop sharin' the master suite."

Annie couldn't stay out of it. "They're not. Honestly. Melinda sleeps in the nursery and—"

Cole glared at her. "Annie."

She hunched up her shoulders and stared down at her cake. "Sorry," she said in a tiny voice.

"So, then," Preston said. "Not every conclusion I jump to is the wrong one."

The silence that followed said it all.

Preston picked up his fork again and carefully cut himself another bite of his dessert. "Oh, yes," he said softly. "This certainly is one fine red velvet cake."

Chapter 17

After the cake and coffee, Preston thanked them all for the party.

"It's been...real enlightenin'," he said. "I am feeling just a bit tired now. But I'm sure by morning, I'll be ready to join you all at the table again." After sliding his napkin under the rim of his empty cake plate, he turned his chair around and wheeled himself back to his room.

Annie handed the baby to Jimmy and began clearing off. "Well. That didn't work out so bad at all now, did it?"

Nobody answered, though Brady did let out a happy little gurgle in his father's arms.

Melinda stood. "Annie, you and Jimmy go on. I'll clean things up."

Annie's eyes glowed. "Oh, would you?"

"Sure."

Jimmy rose to his feet a little awkwardly, because of the

baby. He and Annie stared at each other. Clearly the passionate embrace they'd shared earlier had not been nearly enough.

Annie shook herself and gave a bright smile to Melinda. "Listen. Why don't you just leave it? We can take care of it in the morning."

"Don't worry about it. You can leave the baby with me if you want to."

"No," Jimmy said, holding the small body closer. "We'll take him with us."

"Good enough."

Annie set down the plates she'd gathered. Jimmy shifted the baby to one arm—and put the other around his wife. They turned as one, headed for the front hall and the stairs that led to Annie's room.

Melinda picked up the plates Annie had set down. But before she could leave the table, Cole's hand closed over her wrist, warm, rough—and undeniable. She met his eyes.

He seemed to be having a hard time deciding what to say.

"What, Cole?"

He let go of her wrist. "I'll help you." He stood.

"No, really, it's—"

"I said, I'll help."

Together, they carried everything to the kitchen, where they loaded the dishwasher and put the remainder of the cake in the freezer so that the ice cream center wouldn't melt. Then Cole got the stepladder from the closet in the front hall and took down all the crepe paper Annie had put up. Within a half an hour, all was back in order again.

Cole turned to her. He said, "You're leaving, aren't you?"

All she could do was nod.

"When?"

"Tomorrow. In the morning, after breakfast."

He took her hand, turned it over, kissed the center of her

palm. The tender touch pierced her deep down inside. He laced his fingers with hers. "Is the door closed, then?"

She didn't have to ask what he meant. She thought of Preston, of how he wouldn't approve. "Your father—"

"This isn't my father's decision to make." He asked again, "Is the door closed?"

Slowly she shook her head. "No. It's not closed."

He wrapped her fingers over his arm. They turned for the door to the front hall and went up the stairs together, just as Annie and Jimmy had done.

At the top of the stairs, Melinda saw that Annie's door was shut. Her own door stood open. She could see Spunky in there, already curled in her spot in the center of the wedding ring quilt. Sergeant waited, stretched out, a few feet from Cole's door.

They went into Cole's room. He paused at the threshold to signal the dog, who rose and followed after them. Cole shut the door. The dog wandered over and dropped to a sprawl by the sofa.

Still holding hands, they walked to the bed and sat down side by side.

Cole let go of her hand and pulled off his boots. She slid off her shoes.

Then they just sat there, in the gathering darkness, shoulders touching, staring off toward the window that looked over the oaks in the front yard, as if they'd both lost the will and the energy to turn to each other. As if the heat and yearning that always burned so hot between them had all at once faded to embers and ash.

Outside, the bats had emerged from their daytime sleep. They wheeled and dived beyond the crests of the trees.

Cole said. "I know I shouldn't ask it. I know what you'll say. But if I don't, I'll always wonder if it might have made a difference."

Melinda closed her eyes—against the question, against her longing to answer yes.

"Will you marry me, Melinda?"

She forced her eyes to open, turned to him—and shook her head. "I'm...not good enough for you, Cole."

He looked confused. "Not good enough? What are you talking about?"

"You're...such a wonderful man. The way you care for your father, the work you do that means so much to the people around here. The way you came after Annie in L.A. and wouldn't leave until she finally came home with you. You... you're so fine. You can do better than someone like me."

"That's not true."

"Yes, it is."

His face had changed. The confusion was gone now. His eyes burned with a fervent light. "There is no one better than you. *You're* the one that got Annie home. And you brought my father out of his room. Pretty much everything that needed fixing around here, you took care of. If there's one of us who's too good for the other, that one isn't me."

His words warmed her—but not enough to change her no to a yes. "I told you from the first. I'm not...I don't even really know who I am. Why would you want to marry someone like me?"

"Because *I* know who you are. You don't see your own value. You look in the mirror and you see what others have taught you to see. Someone so beautiful, someone born to money, someone who never had to work a day in her life. You don't see what's really there. A good heart and a helping hand. A fine mind and a willing spirit. But I do, Melinda. I see what you really are. If you think I'm so *good,* maybe you ought to have a little faith in my judgment."

She cried, "Oh, Cole. It wouldn't work. You know it wouldn't."

"No, I don't. *You* know it wouldn't."

"And I am right."

He made a low sound, something that hung midway between a laugh and a groan. "Well, that's true. If you know it won't work and you don't *let* it work, then you will turn out to be right."

She spoke urgently, willing him to see it her way—the difficult way, but the realistic one. "We…we had an accident. And all this happened. But it's not our real lives."

His gaze didn't waver. "What *is* your real life, Melinda? A man you loved who turned out to be a whole lot less than you wanted him to be? A baby you would have loved with all your heart—if it had been born? A job you lost that didn't really mean that much to you in the first place?"

"Yes," she said forcefully. "All those things…they are my real life."

"No." He shook his head. "Those things are the past. Your real life is now—from this moment on."

"But I have to—"

"Think," he said. "Listen. Isn't it just possible that your real life could be here—in the middle of Texas, in this house with me and my troublesome father and my bossy little sister? Could you have, maybe, found your real life by accident?"

She put a hand against his lips, to try to get him to stop saying such hopeful, impossible things.

But he didn't stop. His mouth moved against her fingers. "Your real life is *your* choice. Don't you see that? Can't you figure that out? Your real life isn't something your parents made up for you. It's not all the bad things that happened to you, or the choices you made once that didn't work out. Your real life is right now. It's what *you* make it, what *you* want it to be."

She dropped her hand, turned away. "I…I know that. I do."

He took her shoulders, pulled her around to face him. "No.

No, you don't." His fingers dug in, hurting her a little. "You don't trust yourself. You don't trust your own heart. You think your heart has betrayed you—will betray you again." He looked at her hard.

Whatever he sought in her eyes, he didn't find. He let go of her abruptly and asked with a kind of dull fury, "There's no point in this, is there? I might as well beat my head against a wall."

"Oh, Cole—" She reached out.

He flinched away. "No."

"Cole, I—"

"Look. I shouldn't have asked."

She couldn't stop herself. She needed to touch him. She reached out once more.

He caught her wrist, held it between them. "I shouldn't have asked," he repeated. "And I won't be askin' again. I've got a heart, too, Melinda. And you've pretty much broken it."

"Oh, don't say that. I didn't mean to do that. I never wanted—"

"I know you didn't. Neither of us did. We never should have started this. You should have stayed away after that first night, once I kissed you and you turned me down. And me, I should have done a better job of resistin' my hunger for you. But you didn't. And I didn't. And now, well, I've asked you to marry me and you have said no. There's not much else to do but kick dirt on this campfire and move on down the trail."

He let go of her hand. She pulled it protectively against her heart as he said with great weariness. "It was a bad idea, my askin' you to come in here tonight. I think you better just pick up your shoes and go back to your own room now."

When she didn't move, he bent down, picked them up for her and held them out. "I'll be gone on rounds when you leave tomorrow. So I'll say it now. Thank you. For helpin' me get my baby sister back home, for getting my father to come out of his room. And goodbye, Melinda."

She wanted to cry out, to beg him to let her stay with him for this last night.

But she said nothing. What good would begging do? He didn't want her to stay.

She took the shoes from him and made herself stand.

He looked up at her, spoke gently. "You be careful on that long drive home."

Home? she wondered. Where was that?

He waited. For her to go.

She forced her feet to start walking, across the braided rug and the stretch of bare floor to the door between their rooms. She went through it.

When she got on the other side, she shut it quietly and dropped her shoes on the floor. Then she took off the rings that had belonged to Cole's mother. She set them on the bureau and climbed onto the bed. The gray cat started purring. Melinda closed her eyes and listened to the steady, soothing sound.

The next morning, Melinda was all packed before she went down to breakfast. She waited until the meal was done to tell Annie, Preston and Jimmy of her plans.

Preston said, "Does Cole know this?"

Melinda kept her shoulders very straight. "Yes. We…said goodbye last night."

Preston lowered his gray head, a movement that seemed to speak of acceptance. After a moment, he raised his eyes to meet hers again. "I had hoped you might stay with us."

"I'm sorry. I can't."

"You are welcome here. Anytime you might choose to return."

She thanked him and looked at Annie, but Annie said nothing, only pursed her mouth and glared.

Melinda stood, thinking that she would load up her car and then say a last goodbye to her friend. "I want to get going. I have a long drive ahead."

Annie stood, too. "You're not going anywhere. Not till you and me talk. Alone."

Melinda didn't like the sound of that. But what could she do? She turned for the stairs and Annie followed right after.

In Melinda's room, Annie shut the door and leaned against it, as if she could hold Melinda there by force. "What are you doing? This is all wrong. You can't just leave."

Melinda rubbed her eyes. They were achy and red from lack of sleep. "Annie. Come on. You don't need me here anymore."

"Of course I do. I'll always need you. And Cole—he needs you, too." Annie slumped against the door, her face crumpling. "Oh, don't leave, Melinda. Please don't leave. I know you love him. I know he loves you."

Melinda drew herself taller against the bone-deep exhaustion that kept trying to drag her down. "Annie, stop. I can't… take it, right now."

"But you belong here. With us."

"No. No, I just don't know where I belong."

"That's a lie," Annie cried. "You are lyin' to yourself. Breaking your own heart, and Cole's heart, too. Why? Why do a thing like that? Cole is not that man who hurt you, that man who didn't want his own child. Cole is good. Cole is—"

Melinda put both hands out, in a warding-off gesture. "Annie, please. You can't have everything your way all the time."

"Oh, why not? Why not as long as what I want is what's right and what is meant to be?"

"Annie, please. Just let it alone, will you? I did what you

needed. Now, I really have to go." She took her purse from the bed and slung it over her shoulder, then picked up the suitcases, one in either hand. "I left your mother's rings on the bureau there."

"They're *your* rings, Melinda. You know that they are. And you are the sister of my heart."

"Please. Just…give them to your father."

Tears streamed unheeded down Annie's smooth cheeks. "Oh, Melinda. Melinda, don't go. You gave me so much. I want…you to have the best. I want…you to have Cole. And for Cole to have you…"

Melinda couldn't bear to hear more. Swiftly she cleared the distance between herself and Annie, dropped the suitcases and grabbed her friend in one last, tight hug.

Annie sobbed and clung. Her tears wet Melinda's shirt. "Be well," Melinda whispered, stroking the silky brown hair. "Be happy. Kiss Brady for me."

"Oh, don't go. Don't go…"

Melinda took Annie by the arms and pushed her back, away from the door. Then she flung it open, grabbed the two suitcases and fled. Annie's sobs echoed behind her as she hurried across the landing and started down the stairs.

Jimmy Logan met her halfway. She froze, with a few feet between herself and Annie's young husband.

His dark eyes accused her. "I can hear my wife cryin'."

"She's okay. She just…doesn't want me to go."

"Maybe she's right. Annie's right a lot of the time."

"Not this time."

His mouth curved in a humorless smile. "You sound like me—and you're runnin', aren't you? You're runnin' away."

Behind her, Annie's sobs continued. She couldn't stand hearing them anymore. "Please step aside. I have to go now."

For a moment, she thought he wouldn't budge. But then he flattened himself against the railing. She swept past him.

He called to her back, "Runnin' never does work. It only goes in a circle—right back to where you started."

She didn't reply, didn't turn, just continued down the stairs and out the front door.

It must have been her exhaustion from the grim and sleepless night just past.

Because somehow, Melinda managed to take the wrong road. She thought she was doing fine until she came to a town called Mason—she distinctly recalled that she and Annie had driven through Mason on their way to Bluebonnet the week before. But then, evidently, she had turned right when she should have turned left. Or something like that. She drove about thirty miles in the wrong direction before she came to a town called Llano, got out her map—and discovered she'd been going east instead of north and west. She pulled out onto the road again and got herself turned around—she thought.

But forty minutes later, she was driving into Fredericksburg—which was distinctly south of Bluebonnet. She got out the map. Really, the route looked very simple.

So why in the world couldn't she get it right? She rubbed her eyes, folded up the map—and tried again.

This time she definitely went north, as she should have. She was certain. She'd been on that particular road four times, after all—two trips down and two trips back.

How could she get it wrong now?

The problem was, on the other two trips, she'd had to turn onto a smaller road at a certain point to get to Bluebonnet. And this time, when she got to that turn, well, she must have just instinctively taken it all over again.

Thus, approximately three hours after she'd left it, she ended up in Bluebonnet once more.

She rolled into town, staring blankly out her windshield, past the red phone booth and the post office. The same two old men who had been there the day before yesterday were sitting on the grocery store bench. The black dog lay, as before, near the steps down to the street.

Her foot seemed to step on the brake without any order at all from her fatigued, bewildered mind. She parked in the same place she had parked the other day. She got out, shut the door. The man she and Annie had spoken to before, Mr. Tolly, gave her a wave. She waved back.

And then she went around the front of the car, across the short space between the store and the empty building—and up the steps Annie had pulled her up before.

The sign was still there: Store For Rent. She stared at it, wondering what she was doing here.

The dirty windows seemed to beckon her. She didn't have the will or the incentive to deny them. She pressed her nose against the glass.

And right then her tired mind played the cruelest trick of all.

She saw neat shelves and gleaming display cases. Racks hung with practical, attractive clothing. Rows of handsome wood shelves filled with interesting items that a shopper might choose as a clever, special gift. In one corner, there was a counter, with a coffee machine behind it, as well as a soda fountain. A sign on the wall advertised varieties of ice cream and other treats.

Melinda gave a small cry. She backed away from the window, blinked her eyes, rubbed them. She looked in again.

And saw only dusty floor and empty, rather grimy-looking display cases.

She whirled from the window.

And realized she just *had* to make a phone call. She had to call Zach in Wyoming.

She marched back down the steps and straight to her car. But then, before she even yanked open the door she remembered that she hadn't seen her cell phone in weeks. She had lost it the day of the accident, never found it again—and never quite gotten around to getting it replaced.

She glanced across the street. The red phone booth with its floor of drying grass seemed to actually twinkle at her in the bright, hot sunlight. It was ridiculous, of course. That phone booth could not be twinkling. The paint was old and had lost its shine. And the glass in the top half of the thing wasn't that clean.

She waited for an old truck to rumble by slowly and then crossed to the other side of the street. The phone booth kept twinkling at her. The door was wide-open. She cautiously stuck her head inside.

It had a rotary dial phone, of all things. And she didn't see a place to stick her calling card in.

Change. She would need change—lots of it.

She whirled, hung back as two more vehicles drove by, kicking up dust, and then flew back to her car, got her purse and marched up the steps of the grocery store.

The black dog looked up at her and thumped his tail against the porch floor as she went by. Mr. Tolly and his friend grunted and waved.

Inside, the woman at the checkout counter took a ten and handed over a roll of quarters. "Long distance, huh?"

"Yes. Yes, long distance. Very long, actually. Years' worth of distance."

The woman's forehead crinkled. "You feelin' all right?"

"Oh. Yes. Just fine. I seem to be driving in circles, but I'll straighten out. Eventually."

The woman chuckled, somewhat nervously. "Well. Drive careful."

"I will."

Melinda carried her quarters outside, waved again at Mr. Tolly, smiled at the black dog and crossed the street to the phone booth. She tried to close the door, but it seemed to be stuck in the open position. That was all right, she decided. There was no one nearby to listen in. And it would probably be too hot anyway, all shut up in there.

Melinda got out her address book and found Zach's number. She picked up the phone. A dial tone buzzed in her ear.

So. The thing did work.

She peeled the wrapper back on her roll of quarters and put one in the slot. Dialing took forever. If she hadn't lost all her fingernails cleaning bathrooms at the Yuma house, she probably would have broken one.

Finally, when she got through the whole number, the line clicked and a voice told her how much money to put in. She realized she should have peeled all her quarters *before* she'd tried to dial. But she hadn't. So she scrunched up her shoulder to hold the handset against her ear and started tearing the spiral of paper wrapped so snugly around her change.

She got it about halfway. But then the peeling hand was also trying to hold the loose quarters. Oh, how in the world did people ever make phone calls when they had to use a phone like this?

She made a little, impatient noise, and tried to be careful as she tore the paper.

But she wasn't careful enough. The quarters went flying. They bounced against the side of the booth and thumped to the dry grass under her feet. With a frustrated cry, Melinda dropped to a crouch to retrieve them. The hard metal cord was too short. The phone yanked itself away from her—and bonked her on the side of the head for good measure.

That did it—getting hit with the phone.

That was the final indignity in a day full of wrong turns.

She just, well, she could not take it. She could not take it anymore.

Pointless, irritating tears had clogged up her throat. They rose higher, to her eyes—and they started spilling down.

Melinda sank to her haunches on the brittle grass, drew up her knees and leaned back against the booth wall. The phone dangled near her ear, the dial tone buzzing again.

Cut off. Cut off. Cut off before she even got through.

Was that the story of her life or what?

Sobs bubbled in her throat and came out, sounding ridiculous, making her think of Annie.

Annie, her dear friend. Annie, whom she'd left sobbing and begging her not to go.

Melinda clutched her knees. The sobs came harder. She didn't even try to stop them. She just sat there on the grassy floor of the red phone booth, tears rolling down her cheeks, the dial tone buzzing near her ear.

She didn't know what it was that made her look up. But she did. She hiccuped and swiped at her running nose with the back of her hand—and looked out at the street through tear-blurred eyes.

She saw the blue pickup glide past slowly. It pulled to a stop a few feet beyond the booth.

Chapter 18

Melinda just sat there, her heart pounding hard, her sobs frozen in her throat, listening to the pickup door open and shut, to the crunch of boots on gravel, coming her way.

The boots stopped right in front of the open booth door. She looked at them. They were Cole's boots. She looked up, over his denim-clad legs, his lean waist, his plaid Western shirt.

She looked into his eyes, which were shaded by his hat brim and she said, "Hi."

He smiled, a crooked sort of smile. And he said her name with tenderness.

She sucked in a shuddery, teary breath. "I…I can't seem to get out of Texas. So I tried to call my brother, but I didn't have my cell phone…"

Cole took off his hat and dropped to a crouch. He fiddled with the hat brim for a minute, then tossed the hat on the ground.

He reached out his hand. She put hers in it. Oh, it felt so good. So *real*. So much like the place where her hand was meant to be.

He stood, pulling her up with him.

And then she was in his arms, right there on Bluebonnet's main street. In front of the red phone booth, across from the grocery store, in plain view of Mr. Tolly, his friend and the black dog.

She breathed in the scent of him. Dust. Shaving soap. Cole. Home.

He whispered, "Maybe you just oughtta give up and stay here, since you're havin' so much trouble getting away."

She closed her eyes, hugged him closer. "Cole?" she asked against his shoulder.

"Yeah?"

"Shouldn't you be at work?"

He pulled back enough to look down at her. "I couldn't work. I gave up. I packed up my truck. I was headed for L.A."

She brushed at his hair a little, just to feel him, with the back of her fingers right above his left ear. "Not again. You poor man."

"I figured I was in for another two weeks in a motel room."

"But you said…you wouldn't ask me a second time."

"I lied. I've been doin' too much of that lately, I guess."

She sniffed, swiped at her nose. "I…had a vision. I think. Or maybe it was hallucination. I'm not sure. But I saw…what could be. I saw…what Annie tried to show me."

"And what's that?"

"What you tried to tell me. That my real life is here. That I might have found it by accident, but that doesn't make it wrong."

He pulled her close again. She felt his lips on her hair. "I love you. Marry me."

"Yes," she said. "I love you, too. I will choose my real life. And it will be with you."

Melinda called her brother that night. He said he and his family would come to her wedding in the Bluebonnet Christian Church.

And the Bravos did come, Zach and his family from Wyoming, Melinda's sister, her husband and children from Philadelphia—and Elaine and Austin, only somewhat under protest, all the way from their summer house in the Hamptons.

Annie was the matron of honor, Jimmy the best man—and Preston Yuma wheeled up to the front of the church before the bride walked down the aisle.

He quoted from the Song of Solomon.

> *"My beloved speaks and says to me:*
> *Arise, my love, my fair one.*
> *And come away;*
> *For lo, the winter is past.*
> *The rain is over and gone.*
> *The flowers appear on the earth.*
> *The time of the singing of birds is come..."*

* * * * *

FAMOUS FAMILIES

YES! Please send me the *Famous Families* collection featuring the Fortunes, the Bravos, the McCabes and the Cavanaughs. This collection will begin with 3 FREE BOOKS and 2 FREE GIFTS in my very first shipment— and more valuable free gifts will follow! My books will arrive in 8 monthly shipments until I have the entire 51-book *Famous Families* collection. I will receive 2-3 free books in each shipment and I will pay just $4.49 U.S./$5.39 CDN for each of the other 4 books in each shipment, plus $2.99 for shipping and handling.* If I decide to keep the entire collection, I'll only have paid for 32 books because 19 books are free. I understand that accepting the 3 free books and gifts places me under no obligation to buy anything. I can always return a shipment and cancel at any time. My free books and gifts are mine to keep no matter what I decide.

268 HCN 9971   468 HCN 9971

Name _____ (PLEASE PRINT)

Address _____ Apt. #

City _____ State/Prov. _____ Zip/Postal Code

Signature (if under 18, a parent or guardian must sign)

Mail to the **Reader Service:**
IN U.S.A.: P.O. Box 1867, Buffalo, NY 14240-1867
IN CANADA: P.O. Box 609, Fort Erie, Ontario L2A 5X3

* Terms and prices subject to change without notice. Prices do not include applicable taxes. Sales tax applicable in N.Y. Canadian residents will be charged applicable taxes. This offer is limited to one order per household. All orders subject to approval. Credit or debit balances in a customer's account(s) may be offset by any other outstanding balance owed by or to the customer. Please allow 4 to 6 weeks for delivery. Offer available while quantities last. Offer not available to Quebec residents.

Your Privacy- The Reader Service is committed to protecting your privacy. Our Privacy Policy is available online at www.ReaderService.com or upon request from the Reader Service.
We make a portion of our mailing list available to reputable third parties that offer products we believe may interest you. If you prefer that we not exchange your name with third parties, or if you wish to clarify or modify your communication preferences, please visit us at www.ReaderService.com/consumerschoice or write to us at Reader Service Preference Service, P.O. Box 9062, Buffalo, NY 14269. Include your complete name and address.

FFBPA11